W. J. Burley is a Cornishman born and bred, going back five generations. He started life as an engineer, and later went to Balliol to read zoology as a mature student. On leaving Oxford he went into teaching and, until his retirement, was senior biology master in a large mixed grammar school in Newquay. He created Inspector (now Chief Superintendent) Wycliffe in 1966 and has featured him in Cornish detective novels ever since.

Wycliffe

AND THE DUNES MYSTERY

W. J. Burley

CORGI BOOKS

WYCLIFFE AND THE DUNES MYSTERY

A CORGI BOOK : 0 552 14221 2

Originally published in Great Britain by
Victor Gollancz Ltd

PRINTING HISTORY
Gollancz edition published 1993
Corgi edition published 1994

Set in 10/11pt Monotype Plantin by Kestrel Data, Exeter

Corgi Books are published by Transworld Publishers Ltd,
61–63 Uxbridge Road, Ealing, London W5 5SA,
in Australia by Transworld Publishers (Australia) Pty Ltd,
15–25 Helles Avenue, Moorebank, NSW 2170,
and in New Zealand by Transworld Publishers (NZ) Ltd,
3 William Pickering Drive, Albany, Auckland.

Reproduced, printed and bound in Great Britain by
Cox & Wyman Ltd, Reading, Berks.

To Muriel

Prologue

The holiday chalet was perched on the fringe of the foredunes, nearer the sea than most of the others. Built on stilts for the view, as well as for protection against the invasive sand, it was reached by a long flight of wooden steps.

The weekend was GG's idea. 'Let's make it a *manic* weekend, something to remember.' Manic was her current in-word, which was odd in view of what was to happen. The arrangements had been delicate; parental concern had been allayed by ingeniously vague fabrications, and without knowing it GG's mother was contributing the use of her chalet. So early in the season there were few if any other people on the site.

There was a sense of occasion. During their five terms in the sixth form the three boys and three girls had somehow gelled into a group – almost an institution, regarded by the rest of the sixth with puzzled tolerance. Now it was almost over; in a matter of weeks A-level examinations would mark the end of their schooldays and they would be caught up in the last round of the scramble for college places or jobs.

They had just arrived at the chalet and were still lumbered with the stuff they had brought. At least the weather was holding – almost a May heatwave, and according to the pundits it would see them through the weekend.

'Let's take a photo.' Barbara, plump, fair and common-sensical, had already developed a maternal instinct for ordering and recording her chicks.

7

'Dump your bags and make a group by the steps . . . No, sit down, for God's sake! You look like a bus queue.'

Barbara had her camera on a tripod and it was fitted with a delayed action trip.

'You could look a bit more affectionate, GG; I dare say Julian could stand it. And push your hair back, I can't see you.'

GG had red hair to her shoulders and half the time her view of the world was mediated by a curtain of red strands.

'Tuck your feet in, Paul! You can cuddle up to Lisa but there's no need to look as though you're going to rape her.'

Paul was a long, lean, bespectacled youth with the solemnity of an owl.

'Julian! Try not to look like cold pudding – and Alan, make room for me, I'm setting it going . . . Ready? . . . Ten seconds!'

And so the photograph was taken which, fifteen years later, would affect all their lives.

That evening, her arms resting on the veranda rail, Lisa looked out across the bay and watched the sun go down behind St Ives. The sky was cloudless and the sea shone. As the last remnant of the disc vanished, the whole coastline was transformed into a dark and strangely fashioned cut-out.

In the room behind her the radio pumped out pop with a heavy beat. Lisa turned her head to look through the open window. GG was playing the fool, her red hair swinging about, hiding her face. She contorted her body, wriggling her hips, sticking out her breasts and bottom and making supposedly lascivious gestures with her hands and arms.

Julian, squatting Buddha-like on the sofa, watched her with more tolerance than interest.

The two were alone in the room. Barbara, in the

8

kitchen, had volunteered for the short straw taking charge of the evening fry-up; Alan and Paul were in town shopping for a few cans of beer and a couple of bottles of wine.

In the afternoon they had played games on the deserted beach. Alan and Julian had wet suits and boards; Paul and the girls fooled about in the surf, but the water was cold. Afterwards there was a fair amount of boisterous sex play. Now they would drink a little and eat a lot and eventually it would be time for bed.

Which made Lisa uneasy; there were three cubicles, each with a double bed and room for little else. Lisa was not a virgin but she was troubled at the prospect of a whole night spent with that bony body in the intimacy of a double bed. Yet it would be assumed that she and Paul . . .

Lisa sighed and wondered if she was normal.

The sky over the dunes had turned from deep blue to green and in the distance there was a vague mist, a first intimation of approaching dusk. She was mildly surprised to see a lone figure, a man, trudging across the sands from the Gwithian direction. He was young, with a mass of lank black hair; he carried a rucksack and wore an all-weather outfit of jacket and trousers which seemed slightly absurd in a heatwave. He stopped short of the chalet and looked up at her; he was very pale.

'Hullo! I don't suppose there's a chance of a glass of water? I'm parched.' A pleasant voice and an easy manner but for some reason Lisa did not care for the look of him. His deep-set eyes? Or the puckered little mouth?

'You'd better come up.'

He climbed the steps. 'Kind of you . . . I'm Cochran. I'm supposed to be walking the coast path . . .'

'I'm Lisa.'

He followed her into the living room.

'Meet Gillian, known to all as GG. And this is Julian . . . Cochran has come for a glass of water.'

She left the three of them together and joined Barbara

who was frying onions in the kitchen. 'We've got a visitor; he wants a drink.'

'Is he expecting to stay for the meal?'

'God! I hope not.'

'How old is he?'

'Twenty, give or take. He's a rambler of some sort. Student type. I suppose he's all right but he looks a bit odd to me. Anyway, all he asked for was a glass of water.'

'Up to you. There's enough if he does stay. Hang on, I'll take him his water.'

When Barbara entered the living room, Cochran was sharing the sofa with GG while Julian lounged in the wicker chair.

Cochran was saying, 'Only a short stint today – from St Agnes, but hard going.' He took the glass of water and drank it off. 'Thanks, that was wonderful.'

Barbara said, 'You're on your own?'

'I started out with a friend but I ditched him. You know how it is.'

Barbara was thoughtful. 'I think I must have seen your friend earlier on, fair and on the plump side. He was looking for somebody who sounded like you.'

He grinned up at her. 'Really? that was a good miss, then.'

GG laughed and drew attention back to herself. 'Cochran, that's a rather unusual name.'

'You can say that again! My mother's maiden name, wished on me by my father. At school they called me "the Cock".'

Alan and Paul returned with the drinks and were introduced. Alan, a rugby type, was naturally gregarious, while Paul had little to say.

GG said, 'Well, Barbie, can you stretch it to include Cochran?'

Barbara and Lisa exchanged looks. If the newcomer protested he was not heard.

Barbara said, 'All right. If you lot fix the table it will be ready in ten minutes.'

GG had the last word. 'What about getting us a real drink, Alan, while we do the table?'

After the meal they talked, and Cochran did tricks with coins and glasses, with playing cards and with a ring on a string.

'A chap I got to know in hospital was a professional and he taught me.'

'You've been in hospital?'

A shrug. 'A sort of hospital – a place where they're supposed to iron out one's mental kinks.'

Julian was thoughtful. 'Is your name Wilder?'

The little mouth twitched into a grin. 'You've rumbled me? "Son of MP on Theft Charges." The hospital was a cosy alternative to jail.'

Lisa thought: he wanted us to know. It's all part of the act.

'Now the witch-doctors have let me out, Papa thought it would be good for me to, as he put it, "Face some physical challenge". In the old days it would have meant the colonies, now walking the coastal path is more practicable. Of course, I had a minder but I shook him off.'

At some time after ten he looked out of the window. 'God, it's dark! I must push on; I've got to find somewhere to stay in Hayle.'

GG said, 'You can't go now. At least we can make up some sort of bed on the floor – or there's the sofa.'

It was settled.

Julian produced a cigarette pack. 'Smoke?'

Cochran fished in his pocket and came out with a slim plastic box. 'I roll my own. Like to try one, anybody?'

Julian said, 'Hash?'

'Not any old rubbish, the very best resin. I get it from—'

Julian finished for him. 'A chap you knew in hospital.'

Chapter One

Monday, 11 May 1992

On almost every morning since his retirement Jerry Cox had taken his dog for a run and a forage in the sand dunes. It had become a ritual, and when onshore gales whipped the sand off the foredunes into blinding, stinging clouds and forced them to stay indoors, they felt cheated and their whole day was spoiled. They had experienced three days of it, with westerly winds gusting above fifty knots, battering the coast, raising tremendous surf in the shallow bay, driving sand and salt before it.

Now it was over; the surf still tumbled and there were white horses out to sea, but the sun shone, the sky was an intense blue and the wind was as if it had never been. It was warm, the air was balmy, it was spring.

Smudge, an English setter, showed such impatience as was consistent with dignity and they wasted no time among the landward dunes. Stabilized by vegetation, they had been spoiled by a rash of huts and chalets built for the holiday trade and unoccupied at this time of year. The gale had changed little here; just a sprinkling of newly blown sand over the fescue grass, and little heaps of the stuff piled against the sun-bleached and sand-blasted planks of fences and walls.

Man and dog made for the sea, for the marram-grass hillocks and foredunes rising from the beach. There were new slacks and blow-outs; one dune had been sliced through, exposing a face of darker sand and a veritable delta of marram-grass roots which penetrated many yards into the mound. Jerry plodded, and picked his way between the slopes rather than pursue a punishing roller-coaster course up and down the dunes. Now and then, through a fortuitous sequence of gaps, he glimpsed the white surf and the turbulent sea beyond. Smudge lolloped ahead, diverted sometimes by a fresh scent, but anxious for that romp on the fringe of the surf which would crown their morning.

Suddenly, out of sight, Smudge started to bark – and kept it up, which was unusual. Jerry called him to heel but there was no response and the barking continued. Jerry followed the sound and came upon the dog in a shallow, recently formed blow-out. At first sight Smudge seemed to be barking at the sand itself but bending down, Jerry saw the abraded face of a watch protruding slightly from the sand, and the vague form of a hand, still buried. Gingerly, and with distaste, he brushed the sand away and exposed a leather watch-strap attached to a shrivelled and mummified wrist.

Jerry said, 'No beach for us today, Smudge.'

The time was half past eight.

At nine-fifteen Sergeant Coombes concluded, 'I reckon this one belongs to CID.'

His newly fledged constable said, 'You think it's a man, Sarge?'

'It's a man's watch. I'm not too good at sexing withered wrists.'

'And you think he was murdered?'

'Well, somebody buried him and this isn't the place I'd choose as a last resting place for a dear departed.'

The dry sand was fluid and even cautious movements on the slope set it flowing in rivulets and cascades. Coombes growled, 'We'd better get the hell out of here or Scenes of Crime will be shouting about flat-footed wooden-tops.'

It was eleven before the area was cordoned off and the full coven assembled. Policemen in shirt-sleeves played at being archaeologists, cautiously removing the sand from around the body. The aim was to expose it for examination *in situ* and to discover anything in the

14

immediate neighbourhood which could have been associated with the dead man.

A police surgeon and a Scenes-of-Crime officer attended and Detective Inspector Gross was in charge. Three or four opportunist herring gulls kept watch from neighbouring mounds in the hope that there might be something in it for them. DI Gross, new to his rank and to the division, brooded on the prospect of sand and sky and reflected that it was just his luck to be landed with a long-dead stiff in the middle of a desert.

The man had been buried on his left side and a sheet of some sort seemed to have been put under him. Presumably it was of nylon or a similar fabric for it appeared almost unaffected by burial and the lapse of time. The body had probably been naked when buried and the degree of putrefaction varied greatly. It was almost complete in the trunk, where the skeleton was largely exposed, but minimal in the extremities where mummification had occurred and the skin, though shrivelled, was almost intact. The head hair itself, straight and dark, was scarcely affected though it had parted company with the blackened skull from which all traces of skin had disappeared. The lips, too, had vanished, exposing apparently perfect but gumless teeth.

DI Gross surveyed the body with all the professional detachment he could muster. Dr Hocking, the police surgeon, an irritable little fellow with red hair and freckles, was complaining, 'I'm not taking the responsibility for shifting him. Franks should be here.' Franks was the pathologist.

Gross was deferential. 'Can't you tell me anything, Doctor?'

The little man frowned. 'He's dead, but perhaps you can see that for yourself. It's obvious that his skull is fractured but if you ask me whether the injury was inflicted before or after death, your guess is as good as mine. As to when it all happened, God only knows. This is blown sand – a tricky medium for burial; one to be avoided if you want a pathologist to tell your friends exactly what happened when they dig you up again.'

The doctor added as an afterthought, 'And I'm not even a pathologist.'

The Scenes-of-Crime officer was taking pictures when one of the policemen, still shifting sand, said, 'There's something here.'

The man had uncovered a small area of blue-grey canvas-like material. 'Looks like a rucksack, sir.'

'All right, dig around but don't shift it.'

It was a rucksack and it had been buried close to the body. The material had stood up well and the bag bulged with whatever it contained.

Gross had already noted the untarnished gold watch and was thinking that this chap could have been no loner, unmissed and unmourned. He would certainly have appeared on somebody's missing persons list, perhaps locally. Gross would check before the big boys moved in and it would help if he had some idea of how long since. He tried again. 'Can't you give me any idea, Doctor, of how long he might have been here?'

'I've told you – not my job. Certainly many many months, quite possibly years. You'll have to get Franks in. Maybe he'll treat you to a lecture on mummification as against the formation of adipocere – I'm not going to try. Anyway, he'll need to be on the table before anybody can begin to give an opinion.' The doctor looked about him at the omnipresent sand before adding, 'Even then, coming out of this stuff, it will be no more than a guess.'

Detective Chief Superintendent Wycliffe was trying to decide how long it would be before he could decently go to lunch. For almost three weeks there had been nothing to take him away from the office and he had kept office hours. For the first few days it had been a novelty, now he was bored. He sat in his executive chair, swivelled gently from side to side and tapped his teeth with a ball-point. With supreme distaste he regarded the fat pink file on his desk: *Proposals for a Revision of the Command Structure with a View to a More Efficient Use of Resources.* A note clipped to the file read: 'For suggestions and detailed comment. EAP.' Which last, in translation, meant 'Early attention please'.

'Bloody hell!'

Wycliffe rarely swore but, for some reason, this seemed a special occasion.

He looked around his office, air-conditioned, double-glazed and sound-proofed, and wondered by what strange, and presumably auspicious twists of fate he had got there. Many years ago, when he was nineteen and naïve, he had joined the police: his ambition then, to become a CID sergeant. Now he was a chief super. Some climb the ladder, others take the lift, and he supposed that he must have been one of the others. The thought did not please him and, when he had nothing more pressing to think about, his plush office troubled him.

Once or twice he had tried to share such misgivings with his wife, but her reaction had been brusque. 'Don't be absurd, Charles! You worked damned hard for what you have, surely you should find the self-confidence to enjoy it.' Perhaps she was right. Women usually are.

He opened the pink file and decided that he needed a scratch pad on which to draft the predictable puerilities required of him. He looked in the top drawer of his desk and ten minutes later he was still absorbed in the complex and largely speculative history of some of the things he found there. Among the dried-up ball-points, pencils and paper clips, there was a cotton reel, a broken comb, a couple of foreign stamps torn off an envelope, several newspaper clippings and a boiled sweet still in its wrapping . . .

Even Diane, his personal assistant, pretended ignorance of the contents of 'his desk'.

She came in now, on cue. 'What's this, then? A spot of archaeology?'

'You wanted me, Diane?' Tight-lipped.

'Mr Kersey would like a word.'

'Ask him to come in.'

He swept the random assortment of objects off his desk-top, back into the open drawer, closed it, and so ensured their preservation for another season.

DI Kersey arrived, carrying a rolled-up map. Kersey was lanky, loose, and big-boned, with deeply lined features, and the look of a man who has slept in his clothes. Differences of temperament and disparity of rank had never hindered their close relationship.

Kersey unrolled his map and spread it on the desk-top. 'St Ives Bay area, sir. Gross, the new boy down there, has inherited a corpse buried in a sandhill.' He pointed to a pencilled cross. 'That's his map reference. It's in the dunes running along the east side of the bay, not far from a bunch of holiday lets. The body was found early this morning by a dog-walker, partly uncovered by the recent gales.'

Wycliffe studied the map. 'Any clue as to who he was, what he died of, or how long he's been there?'

Kersey grinned. 'I fancy old Hocking has been giving our new boy the run-around; he won't commit himself to much more than the fact of death. But it seems obvious that the body was deliberately buried, and there's a skull fracture, though no certainty that he collected it before death. They found a rucksack near the body and it looks as though he was on some sort of walking holiday . . . Gross thinks he was an upper-crust type.'

'What gives him that idea?'

'Well, he was wearing a Rolex watch and it seems that the rucksack is a quality job. Anyway, it's a job for Franks and probably for us.'

Wycliffe did not argue. 'I'll get Franks on the line and we'll go down and take a look. Send Fox on ahead with a DC.' Fox was the squad's Scenes-of-Crime officer.

Wycliffe telephoned Franks and was in luck; the

pathologist was not only in his office but anxious to be out of it. So much so that he made an effort to be helpful. 'I'll pick you up.'

'Thanks, but no!' Franks drove a Porsche and Wycliffe professed to believe that even to sit in the thing when parked was a threat to his life expectancy.

He telephoned his wife. 'I have to go down west – St Ives Bay – No, in the dunes . . . I may not be back this evening so I'll take the emergency bag . . . Yes, I'll ring . . . And you, love.'

A spell with his deputy, a word with the chief, and not long afterwards, in his own car with Kersey driving, he was crossing the Tamar. The rail bridge, Brunel's swan-song, spanned the river just a stone's throw away. The sun shone on the broad waters below, on a host of small craft, and on a couple of pensioned-off warships looking sorry for themselves.

Wycliffe's spirits were rising, though the fact made him feel like an undertaker. He consoled himself with the Cornish wreckers' prayer: 'Lord God we pray thee, not that wrecks may happen but if wrecks there must be, that thou wilt guide them to these shores for the succour and support of thy needy servants.'

They were on the Liskeard by-pass before either of them spoke, then Wycliffe said, 'I wonder if that chap could have been there for fifteen years?'

'Would it mean anything if he had?'

'It might. Remember Cochran Wilder?'

Kersey was impressed. 'I do; he disappeared, walking the coastal path or something . . . Was that fifteen years ago?'

'It was – I checked, and he was last seen near Gwithian. We must watch our step on this one; there was enough trouble about him the first time round.'

'But we weren't involved.'

'Not directly, it was handled by the divisional people because everybody except the boy's father assumed that he'd committed suicide – drowned himself.'

'Now it looks as though the father could have been right. And he's a minister now.'

'Yes, but before we start worrying about him, let's make sure it is in fact Wilder.'

The disappearance of Cochran Wilder, son of a tub-thumping backbencher, in May 1977, had been a nine-day wonder. Inshore lifeboats, RAF rescue helicopters and coastguards had scoured the sea, the beaches and the cliffs with no result. At a lean time for more highly spiced morsels, the tabloids had dramatized the thing and even dug up parallels with the disappearance of Augustus John's son, forty years earlier.

An hour later they were on the outskirts of the little town and port of Hayle. Wycliffe had a map. 'Turn off next right across a bridge, then left, through a village called Phillack with a church and a pub. We should be almost there.'

They were. The village seemed to be little more than a single street, a row of neat cottages, each with its own tiny garden, facing south across the valley to Hayle itself. They passed the church and then the pub.

Wycliffe said, 'See the sign over that pub? The Bucket of Blood.'

It was their introduction to a certain zaniness, one of the attractions of Hayle. At the far end of the village a uniformed copper stood at a point where a strip of tarmac led off into the dunes through a scattering of chalets.

Wycliffe's car was recognized. The constable advised, 'You can drive along there for a hundred yards or so, sir. You'll see the other cars parked. From then on it's walking.'

The tarmac petered out in a small, sandy arena where the Scenes-of-Crime van, with other police vehicles, was lined up beside the Porsche.

Kersey said, 'Franks has beaten us to it.'

'So much the better.'

Despite Wycliffe's years in the south-west, the dunes were still something of a novelty. As they left the chalets

behind and entered the real dunes he was touched by a
sense of unreality and isolation. Great mounds of sand,
crowned with spiky marram grass, hemmed them in, and
the muffled sound of unseen surf seemed to come from
all directions.

'Here we are.'

A white tape stretched between two posts defined the
exclusion zone, beyond which the police were at work.
There were human spectators now, dog-walkers in place
of herring gulls; several, of both sexes, occupied vantage
points on neighbouring dunes, trying to look as though
they were there for the view.

Gross came to meet them. Wycliffe had last seen Gross
at the promotion board when he was made up to DI. One
of Wycliffe's colleagues on the board had said: 'He may
be a good copper but he looks like a bloody rabbit.'

It was not only the poor man's intrusive incisors but
also his pinched cheeks and conspicuous ears.

'Dr Franks is here, sir, so is DS Fox. DC Curnow is
taking a statement from the man who found the body; he
lives in Phillack, the village you came through on the way
here.'

Franks squatted on a sandbank grinning like a plump
gnome. 'What kept you? I've taken the liberty of sending
for the van. There's nothing I can do here, and probably
not much when I get him back. They've found his
clothing bundled into a plastic bag near the rucksack and
I reckon they're going to be more help to you than I am.'

Wycliffe stood over the body. 'I suppose he was
left-handed . . . The watch, it's on his right wrist.'

Franks stood beside him. 'So it is; I hadn't noticed.
One small step. Anyway, I don't imagine identification
will be a problem, what with his teeth, his clothing and
the clobber in his rucksack.'

'Have you anything at all to tell me?'

'Not a lot. He's been here a long time – years rather
than months, is my guess. It's obvious that he was
deliberately buried, and the sheet that's still under him

suggests he was carried here. Add that to a severely depressed fracture affecting the vertex of the skull and you'll have to look at unlawful killing as a strong possibility.'

Franks was looking about him at the mountains of sand. 'My parents brought me here for a holiday once, when I was a kid, and I used to slide down those dunes with a bit of driftwood under my backside imagining I was doing the Cresta Run. I wouldn't mind trying it now.'

'Fascinating! Is that all?'

Franks sighed. 'You're too intense, Charles. Where does it get you? Anyway, his teeth make it certain that he was a young man. He was about five-nine in height and probably of medium build, that would give him around a hundred and fifty to a hundred and sixty pounds or seventy kilos in new money.'

'A tidy weight to lug through the dunes. Not really a job for a man on his own.'

'I shouldn't think so, but that's your problem.'

'All right, leaving that aside, would you say that the location of the injury at the vertex suggests a blow rather than a fall?'

Franks nodded. 'Yes; fall-injuries are almost always to the sides or back of the head. As I said, at the least, you've got an unlawful killing on your hands, Charles. But turning to more immediate things, did you get any lunch?'

'No.'

'Neither did I. Where's that bloody van?'

Fox, Wycliffe's Scenes-of-Crime officer, was hovering. He was tall and so lean that he looked taller than he was; a walking, talking matchstick man with a large nose and a sad expression.

'There's not much for me here, sir, until they move the body. Divisional SOCO covered the ground. Do I have to bag the rucksack as it is or can I unpack it in my van?'

'All right, go ahead but leave the clothing for the lab.' The Scenes-of-Crime van was equipped for a certain amount of on-site work. 'Let me know immediately you find any evidence of identification. And Fox, make sure the sheet he was wrapped in is dealt with separately, urgent and special attention. It may be our main link between the body and the actual scene of the crime.'

Kersey was standing on one leg emptying sand from his other shoe. 'I've been talking to one of Gross's chaps. He says there's a handy place going begging if you decide to set up an Incident Room in the town. It's a little building belonging to the council and, until recently, it was used as a meeting house by some odd-ball religious sect. It's on the main street with plenty of parking.'

'I'll get Shaw to take a look at it.' Shaw was Wycliffe's administrative officer, quartermaster and general dogs-body. 'Meanwhile, you'd better get them to bring in a van, otherwise you'll have no home or habitation. I shall go back this evening; whether or not I come down tomorrow will depend on what we find out. For the moment I'll leave you here with Curnow.'

Three men from the mortuary service arrived with a stretcher and a plastic contrivance in which to man-handle the body back to their van. Franks supervised the removal and Wycliffe arranged for an officer to attend the autopsy.

Franks promised, 'I'll be in touch some time to-morrow.'

Men were still turning over the sand and sifting through it but there was little more that could be done on the site. Wycliffe, thoughtful, walked back to the cars and to the Scenes-of-Crime van and ran into the vanguard of the media – two local reporters.

'What we have is the body of a young man which was buried in the dunes, and uncovered by the recent gale. It's clear that the body has been there a long time but we do not know who he was, or how he came to be there. There will, of course, be a post mortem and that may tell us something of the cause of death. That is all I have for you.'

'Can we take photographs at the scene?'

'There's nothing to stop you.'

In the Scenes-of-Crime van, Fox was in his element, surrounded by artefacts in tagged polythene bags of different sizes. 'Most of the stuff in his rucksack is remarkably well-preserved and it's more or less what you'd expect, sir: change of underclothes and socks, toilet gear, a pair of house shoes, a couple of sci-fi paperbacks and a guide book to the coastal path . . . I get the impression he must have been a bit of a dandy.'

Wycliffe had learned patience in dealing with Fox. 'What's this?' He pointed to a garish picture postcard which had not yet been bagged and tagged. It was badly stained but otherwise undamaged.

'You can make out the writing; it seems to be from his sister, sir, written from Cyprus.'

Wycliffe drew a deep breath. '*Whose* sister?'

Fox turned the postcard over. 'It's addressed to Cochran Wilder at a nursing home in Kent.'

The text was brief: 'I'm here with Jem. Having a wonderful time but (believe it or not) too hot!! Delighted they're opening the cage. Don't let Dad get you down. We shall be home before you are. See you soon. Your one and only sister, Podge.'

The postmark was dated 19 April 1977.

Wycliffe said, 'Ah!' because he could think of nothing else to say that would not unnecessarily upset Fox.

The identification was enough to proceed upon.

Back in his car Wycliffe telephoned the chief. Oldroyd was not appreciative. 'God, Charles, trust you to spoil a nice day! Papa Wilder always said his boy had been murdered. And, if you're right, he'll be on my neck before I can say, "Yes, Minister". What is he now, by the way?'

'Minister of State for something or other, I can't remember what.'

'Yes, well, last time when he made such a noise he was only a backbench MP. Then he yelped at me like a bad-tempered Pekinese. Silly little man! . . .' A pause. 'All the same, if his son really was murdered . . . Everybody thought the lad had drowned himself – I mean, there was a history of instability . . . Papa Wilder spends a lot of his free time with a daughter who lives in St Germans. Of course, he won't be there now with parliament in session, but the daughter will. It might be an idea for you to talk to her. The personal touch . . . Let me think . . . My wife is on some committee with her . . . Yes, her married name is Bissett – Molly Bissett, that's right! Her husband's in the navy and away a lot . . . It's on your way home, Charles, so why not look in on her, break the news and spend tonight in your own bed?'

There was no point in argument; in any case it would be a chance to meet one of the family and to get something more on the boy's disappearance than the predigested gobbledegook on file.

He found a St Germans' Bissett in the directory and telephoned. A woman with a mellow attractive voice answered, 'Molly Bissett.'

He introduced himself. 'I would like to come and see you at about six if I may . . . It's about your brother . . .'

She was silent for a moment or two, then, 'He's been found?'

'Yes, I think so.'

Another pause, then very quietly, 'The body in the sand dunes?'

He was taken by surprise. 'Yes. I'm very sorry.'

'It was on the radio just an hour ago and it set me wondering whether it could possibly be . . . But it was such a long time ago . . .'

'Your father hasn't been told.'

'No, it will be best if you leave that to me. Thank you for telephoning; I will expect you. I live at the west end

25

of the village, near the almshouses. The house is called Franklin's.'

Kersey came to the car. 'Are you off, sir?'

'Yes, but I'd like a word . . .'

Kersey got into the passenger seat and Wycliffe brought him up to date. 'I think we can assume that the body is Cochran Wilder's, so we are dealing with an incident that happened fifteen years ago. The body was naked, it was deliberately buried, and there was a skull fracture caused apparently by a blow, so there is a strong presumption of murder or manslaughter. At the moment we've only looked at the contents of his rucksack but we've got his clothes and the contents of his pockets to come. The file on his disappearance will provide background and we still have the family. But we've got to find out what we can here, on the ground.'

'It's what we're to do here on the ground that bothers me, sir. You've got to admit there's not a lot going for us. It will be like stirring yesterday's cold pudding.'

'Yes, well, all I can suggest is that you get the locals involved. We want to know what the situation was at the time Wilder arrived. Who owned the chalets in the immediate vicinity? Which, if any, were occupied, and by whom? Sow the seed, Doug, and get the gossip started.

'Of course, it's just possible that he was dead on arrival – brought here by car as a convenient place to dispose of the body, though humping it through these dunes wouldn't be my idea of convenience.

'I know it's all pretty thin, Doug, but we've got to start somewhere. You and Curnow are on your own but when you need help, say so. What do you think?'

Kersey eased his length out of the car. 'I think it would have been better for everybody if he'd stayed buried.'

Lisa stood by the window of her living room looking across the bay to Godrevy, to Gwithian, to the sand dunes and to the wooden bungalows and chalets which dotted the sands near the Hayle estuary. As so often before she told herself that at such a distance she could not pick out a particular bungalow, one with a veranda and a flight of steps leading up to it. And when her eyes belied her she experienced a sudden emptiness inside and turned away. It was a disquieting but compulsive game which she played with herself when depressed.

Behind her the radio babbled, 'Radio Cornwall News at five o'clock.'

She kept the radio on most of the time; it was company and a reminder that life went on outside the little house in Carbis Bay in which she spent her days alone. Lisa was married to Martin Bell, a schoolteacher, and under pressure from him, she had given up her job as a nurse.

Abruptly, meaning crystallized out of the cascade of words from the radio. 'The body of a man was recovered this morning from sand dunes near the Hayle estuary. Exposed by the recent gale, the body was discovered by a local man exercising his dog. The police are unable to say how the man died, or when and in what circumstances his body came to be buried in the sand. Further information is expected from the post mortem.'

Lisa switched off the radio and stood over it. She felt faint, and steadied herself against the table. She would have liked to telephone somebody – one of the others, but it was after five and Martin would be home soon. She heard the sound of a car and made a determined effort to control herself. She went back to the window. Martin was pulling into the driveway. He got out, carrying his briefcase bulging with exercise books to be corrected. She met him at the door.

'Had a rough day?'

'Is there another kind?'

Martin would notice nothing; he could be relied upon for that. He put down his briefcase, glanced at himself in the hall mirror and patted his hair. 'I don't suppose it's started?'

'It has, actually.' Brittle.

He turned to face her. 'Thank God for that! I know

you want a child, Lisa, but I don't think I could stand you being pregnant just now.'

Dr Alan Hart was writing out a prescription for his last patient of the afternoon. At thirty-three Alan had given up rugby and taken up golf. For him medicine had been a pushover; a good memory, a strictly limited imagination, and a cheerful acceptance of mortality had proved the ideal recipe for success as a GP. In order to marry Barbara he had become a Catholic, but that only bothered him in so far as she could be difficult. He was settling into a groove; on the whole a very pleasant one, and memories only troubled him when Barbara suffered one of her occasional and irrational bouts of depression, always rooted in the same cause.

His patient was a chatty, arthritic old man. 'So they've dug some poor bloke out of the sand on the towans. Bin there for years they reckon.'

Alan looked up, suddenly tense, 'What's that?'

'Uncovered by the gale. Jerry Cox over to Phillack found 'n – or 'is dog did. I 'eard it in the pub this dinnertime. The p'lice bin out there. Some do there was an' they're still at it.'

Alan hustled the old man out with his prescription and returned to sit at his desk. Should he phone Barbara? Or go home at once? She was certain to hear and in the fourth month of pregnancy with their second child, Barbara was emotional.

'God, this is all she needs!'

He was on the point of leaving when he changed his mind and picked up the telephone. 'Oh, Joyce, will you get me Stanton and Drew, the estate agents in Hayle, please.'

The ringing tone, and a girl's voice, bored, said, 'Stanton and Drew.'

'This is Dr Alan Hart. I would like to speak to Mr Paul Drew.'

Silence, then a man's voice, slow and pedantic, 'Paul

Drew speaking. I know why you are calling, Alan, but I would rather not discuss the matter. In fact, the less discussion of any sort the better. I mean that very seriously and I'm sure you will see the wisdom of it . . . And, Alan, if you do have to contact me again – and I hope that won't be necessary – please ring me here and I will come to see you. I don't want Alice to be distressed by any hint of . . . um . . . difficulty.'

Alan replaced his phone. 'Bloody fool!'

Paul, lean, lanky, short-sighted and solemn, had not changed, but now he was an estate agent and he had acquired a matching wife.

Gillian Grey's up-market health shop in St Ives attracted a discerning clientele and the most discerning free-spenders among them received GG's personal attention. Hairdressers had maintained the tint if not the texture and lustre of her hair, but beauticians had failed to disguise the hardening and sharpening of her features.

In her little office behind the shop she had listened to the five o'clock local news with one ear while the other was on the shop and what her two assistants were doing there.

She was not sure how to react. She supposed that it was bound to happen at some time. But was there anything at all to connect her and the others with this fifteen-year-old corpse? The answer was a decided No! But she was uneasy. She reached for the telephone and dialled a number. She waited while the ringing tone repeated itself many times.

'The bastard is probably asleep, or in bed with his tart.'

A deep, lazy voice said, 'Studio Limbo; Julian speaking.'

'It's GG.'

'Sorry, no vacancy at the moment, love.'

GG reached out and shut the door into the shop. 'I know, I've seen her. You want to watch it, Julian; importing pets without the benefit of quarantine.'

'The same old GG, always concerned for the welfare of others. You'll wear yourself out, darling.'

'Never mind that, have you heard the news?'

'I only listen to good news and they never have any.'

GG lowered her voice. 'This is serious! The gale uncovered something in the dunes across the water.'

'So what? You'd be surprised at what I've found in those dunes. Don't worry about it. Concentrate on your hypochondriacs, GG, they pay a damn sight better than my pictures.'

St Germans village is tucked into the south-east corner of Cornwall on the borders of the Eliot estate. Unspoiled, with its almshouses and its cottages of local stone, it is a picture-book village; yet it has a remote and sombre air, as though isolated in time as well as space. It was dusk when Wycliffe arrived and there was not a soul to be seen.

Franklin's was set well back from the road with a gravelled drive and laurel hedges, a four-square house with a squat hipped roof and overhanging eaves. The lady herself answered his ring. She was on the short side, inclined to plumpness, dark, with smooth clear skin, and features set in a mould of good humour. She wore a snugly fitting cherry-coloured jumper with black trousers.

'Do come in.'

The drawing room was large, shabby and comfortable, with a random assortment of furniture that had seen better days. A black and white border collie, sprawled on the hearthrug, regarded him with a lazy eye. There was an electric fire burning on the hearth, and an open book on the floor by the chair in which Molly now sat herself.

The preliminaries over, it was she who got down to business. 'You were able to identify my brother?'

He handed her the postcard she had written fifteen years ago, now in its polythene envelope.

She was clearly moved. 'How very strange! After all

30

those years . . .' There was an interval before she asked, 'How did he die?'

He delayed answering with another question. 'Your brother was left-handed?'

She looked puzzled. 'Yes, he was. Why?'

'He wore a Rolex watch on his right wrist.'

She smiled. 'Of course! It was a present from father on his twenty-first birthday.'

Wycliffe decided she was not the sort to appreciate protective camouflage. 'We don't know how he died. His skull was fractured but whether that was the cause of death remains to be seen.'

'You will know after the post mortem?'

'I hope so.'

She was frowning. 'He was actually buried in the sand?'

'Yes.'

After some hesitation she asked, 'Fully clothed?'

'No, the body was naked.'

'Doesn't all this make it certain that he was murdered?'

'It makes it very unlikely that he took his own life.'

She reached for a cigarette pack from the arm of her chair. 'I still have this wretched habit. My husband tries to scare me out of it, but he's in the navy and away most of the time. Will you join me?'

He refused. She lit her cigarette and inhaled deeply. 'Father will be relieved.'

'Relieved?'

'Why do you think he was so aggressive when the idea of suicide was suggested? He was afraid that it was true and that he had driven his son to take his own life.' She smiled with tolerance. 'Father is a typical politician – when you're not sure of your ground, then you attack.'

Wycliffe said nothing and she went on, 'They never hit it off. Cocky – we always called him that though father disapproved – Cocky was to be the son who would take over the business. At that time father owned Westcountry Plastics. They have a factory just outside Plymouth . . .

Anyway, Cocky didn't measure up; he was rebellious, and often silly. There was fault on both sides. Our mother had died when Cocky was only nine so that when the crunch came he had no-one to turn to.' Her eyes were glistening.

On a side table there were photographs in silver frames. Molly was there, in her wedding dress with her newly acquired naval-officer husband, but the others recorded incidents in the public life of Wilder senior. He was portrayed planting a tree, cutting a tape, or, glass in hand, chatting with the Prime Minister . . .

Molly said, 'This is father's house, it's where he and mother settled when they were married. And, of course, it was Cochran's home.'

The curtains were undrawn and the window looked out on total darkness; no sound came from within the house or from without. The dog shifted uneasily, lifted its head and looked up at Wycliffe before going back to sleep. Did this woman spend most of her time in this house alone with her dog?

She seemed to read his thoughts. 'I'm a do-gooder, Mr Wycliffe, coffee mornings, committees, jumble sales, eating for charity . . . You know the sort; always busy doing rather futile things.' She looked at him with a sly smile. 'Pathetic, isn't it?

'Anyway, getting back to Cochran, I don't know who if anybody is to blame or whether it was some genetic thing, but in his late teens he went off the rails completely. He started to steal, pointlessly, things he couldn't possibly want; and he developed a sexual kink, forcing his attention on girls in cafés, shops and cinemas, even in the street. I distrust labels, especially when they are dished out by psychiatrists, but they said that he was manic-depressive. Of course, as you must know, he ended up in the court.'

She looked at her cigarette which was only half-smoked, and crushed it out in an ashtray. 'Fortunately, the magistrates showed a bit of sense and, after a psychiatric report, he was bound over on condition that he received treatment in an approved psychiatric hospital, and he spent just over a year there.'

'And then?'

'Shortly after he came out father had the bright idea of sending him off on this walking holiday.'

'He went with someone?'

'Oh, yes; with the Creep. That's what I call him; his real name is Leslie Mace and at the time he was working in father's office as a trainee accountant – I couldn't stand him but father thought the world of him. Of course Cocky gave him the slip and I don't blame him for that.'

'What happened to Mace?'

'He went back to his work in the office but when father sold up to go into full-time politics we lost touch. I don't know whether or not he's still there.'

'Where did your brother live after coming out of hospital?'

'Here with me. It was only for a couple of weeks.'

'How did he seem?'

She hesitated. 'He was quiet, amenable – too amenable.' She shook her head. 'I don't know. I couldn't feel at ease with him. To be honest, I don't think the so-called treatment did him much good.'

'Was he on any sort of medication?'

'I remember they gave him a lithium preparation which was supposed to help stabilize him – stave off attacks – but he said it made him feel sick.'

Wycliffe explained about the contents of the rucksack and that the young man's clothing would be available shortly.

She asked, with concern, 'Will someone have to identify the body?'

'I don't think so, merely those of his possessions which have been recovered.'

'I shall telephone father. I tried earlier but I couldn't get hold of him.'

Wycliffe stood up. 'I'll keep in touch and I'm very grateful for your help and understanding.'

She walked with him to the gate. It was very dark; lights were on in many of the windows in the village, the only sign of life. It was also silent, not even a breath of wind to stir the leaves on the trees. She stood by the gate and watched him drive away.

He felt depressed. Even after more than thirty years in the police he still found it hard to accept that happy families are a rare breed. It was strange the extent to which his upbringing and the stories he'd read as a child still conspired to colour his outlook on life, his judgements and his expectations.

Fifteen minutes later he passed through St Juliot and was approaching the Watch House. He could see the estuary gleaming in the darkness, the twinkling navigation lights and a vague outline of the opposite bank against the sky. He turned into his own drive and stopped by the garage. As he got out of the car Helen came towards him. 'I'd almost given you up.'

When he came downstairs after a quick shower there was a plate of sandwiches and a glass of Barsac, misted over, on the little table by his armchair.

It was good to be home.

Chapter Two

Wycliffe made the mistake of looking at himself in the bathroom mirror; really looking. It was an occasion of self-examination quite different from his daily inspection to decide whether or not he had shaved properly. In consequence he went downstairs preoccupied and unsettled.

Helen asked, 'Will you be going down west again today?'

'I've no idea.'

'Perhaps you'll let me know if you're not coming back this evening.' Tight-lipped.

He realized that this was going to be one of those mornings when tension seems to condense like mist out of clear air. He poured himself some coffee. 'I'll phone you.'

'Good!'

"The discovery, yesterday, of a body in the sand dunes near Hayle, is being linked with the disappearance, fifteen years ago, of Cochran Wilder, only son of Royston Wilder, Minister of State in the Department of Social Reconstruction. The police have so far refused to comment on—'

With an irritable jab Wycliffe throttled the radio, and buttered a piece of toast.

Helen said, 'You haven't forgotten that your daughter is arriving this evening?'

When Helen talked about 'your daughter' storm cones were being hoisted; it was high time to give domestic issues an airing. Their daughter, Ruth, was personal

35

assistant to a money man, one of the younger generation of that faceless breed of currency manipulators, and for some years she had been living with him. Now a sudden, unexplained and unaccompanied visit was causing concern.

'You think they're splitting up?' Although he would never have admitted it, Wycliffe was hopeful. He did not care for his wily unconsecrated son-in-law.

'I thought she might be pregnant.'

'After all this time?'

'Why not?'

Wycliffe decided that silence was his best option. He could hardly say that he hoped Ruth had more sense.

He left soon afterwards, and fifteen minutes later he had joined the queue for the ferry. It was raining, a continuous drizzle out of a leaden sky. He switched off the engine, glared at the back of the car in front, and brooded on life and the way he was living it. Did others feel that they had lost sight of themselves in playing roles which seemed to have been thrust upon them?

Sometimes, in such a mood, he wondered what had happened to the real Charlie Wycliffe, the genuine original. Did he still exist? What had he been like . . . ? He couldn't remember . . . Perhaps it didn't matter . . . Perhaps, after all, he was no great loss.

A tooting driver reminded him of the obligations of his present persona.

Time to move on.

His space in the car park was labelled 'Det. Ch. Supt.', and the man on the desk greeted him with instant recognition and a respectful 'sir'.

In his office, Diane was sorting the mail. She said, 'Oh, Records say you'll want the file on the Wilder disappearance and they've sent it up.'

Other people seemed to know who he was – or thought they did, so perhaps that was all that mattered. He consoled himself with the thought that there would probably have been no reserved parking for that original

Charlie Wycliffe, and it was unlikely that anybody would have called him 'sir'.

'You deal with the mail, Diane, and let me know if there is anything . . .'

Diane had worked with him for more years than he cared to remember. She had come as a girl in her twenties, obviously fair, and apparently fragile, but from the start she had run the office with ruthless efficiency and with her austere indifference to males she soon became known as the Ice Maiden. Now she was a legend in her own time.

Alone, Wycliffe opened the Wilder file at random and found himself looking down at a photograph of the young man. He gave small credence to the theories of Lombroso and his successors which relate criminal tendencies to physical types, but here, he felt sure, was the face of a maladjusted youth, more likely than not to find himself at odds with society. Lank, straight black hair framed a long narrow face, a receding forehead, deeply set eyes, a rather pinched nose and a twisted little mouth.

Wycliffe skimmed through the file. On leaving school Wilder had been entered for a course in business studies at the polytechnic and from early on he had distinguished himself by throwing lavish open-house parties, buying quantities of expensive clothes which he mostly gave away, and sleeping around. At first, his father had footed the bills under strong protest, but when the screw was finally tightened Wilder turned to shop-lifting, forging cheques and forcing himself on the girls he could no longer attract; so ending up in court.

Somebody had slipped into the file a press cutting from one of the tabloids:

Royston Wilder's Son Missing

Cochran Wilder, only son of crime-bashing MP Royston Wilder, is missing on a walking holiday in Cornwall. He was last seen on Saturday evening, on the North Cornwall coastal path between Gwithian and Hayle . . . Cochran, known as 'the Cock' to his friends, was recently discharged from a psychiatric hospital where he had been detained under a court order following convictions on a number of charges including theft and indecent assault . . .

The file was bulky; psychologists and psychiatrists were thick on the ground with the occasional probation officer thrown in. There were pages of jargon sprinkled with phrases which rolled off the tongue, and there was much hedging of bets.

'The subject, despite his youth, appears to be suffering from an affective disorder strongly suggestive of a manic-depressive psychosis . . .'

A much later pundit had written, 'In the early stages the manic phase was dominant and the situation might properly have been diagnosed as unipolar, but during hospitalization depressive episodes increased in frequency and duration, so that towards the end of hospitalization a fairly classic pattern of bipolarity was established. In these circumstances the decision to discharge the subject was, perhaps, unfortunate . . .'

In other words, the gentleman was saying that young Wilder had been let loose with a recipe for suicide in his pocket. And that seemed to have set the tone for the whole police inquiry which, from the start, was heavily biased in favour of suicide.

The telephone rang. It was Franks. 'Had a good night, Charles? – I didn't. Business is looking up all of a sudden and it was early morning before I got round to your chap. Anyway it's pretty certain that he died from brain damage resulting from a depressed fracture of the skull. In fact the table in the area of the vertex is pretty thin – not exactly egg-shell, but it wouldn't have taken much of a blow to cause the injury.'

'So it was a blow.'

'I think so; obviously, as I've said, I couldn't swear to it. Incidentally, there were fragments of some sandy substance in the wound.'

'You surprise me, especially as he was buried in the stuff.'

'*Not* sea sand, Charles! These look like fragments of concrete. I can have it checked if you like.'

'Of course I like. What are you telling me? That he was hit on the head with a concrete block?'

Franks was mild. 'I suppose there are other concrete objects more amenable to use as a weapon.'

'Anything else?'

'Not a great deal. I found no other signs of injury or disease but that isn't saying much; decomposition of the soft tissues in the trunk was complete. There was a certain amount of mummification but it was confined to the extremities.'

As Wycliffe replaced the telephone there was a tap at the door and DS Lucy Lane came in.

Lucy Lane had been involved with Wycliffe and Kersey in all the major cases of the past six years and Wycliffe had come to rely upon her no-nonsense logic which nicely opposed his own tendency to woolliness and Kersey's inclination to flog dead horses.

She was carrying a 'lab box'. 'The contents of Wilder's pockets, sir, all logged and photographed; the clothing is still under examination. Apparently it's been very well-preserved by the plastic bag in which it was found.'

'Any news of the sheet or whatever it was in which he was wrapped?'

'Only that it was a nylon bed sheet; it's not clear whether they will be able to tell us any more.'

Wycliffe said, 'I can't stand nylon bed sheets.'

Lucy removed several items from her box and laid them on the desk along with a bundle of photographs. Each item was enclosed in a separate polythene bag and carried a label. 'Take a look at this, sir.' She pushed across one of the bags for Wycliffe to examine.

Through the polythene he was looking at a necklace. It consisted of a chain made up of elaborate filigreed links and a pendant in the form of a very feline cat.

Lucy Lane said, 'It's pretty, and it must have cost a bit.' She referred to a list. 'The whole thing is in hallmarked silver and the cat's eyes are seed pearls. The back of the pendant is engraved with a monogram of the letters L.M. and a date: 1 May 1977. Somebody's birthday, I suppose.'

'And this was found in his pocket?'

'In his left trouser pocket, sir. A bit odd, don't you think? I suppose it could have been his but even if he was gay it seems unlikely.'

Wycliffe pointed to the case file. 'There's no suggestion here that he was gay, rather the contrary; in any case his initials were C.W. and he was born in November.'

Lucy grinned. 'So it doesn't add up.'

Wycliffe was looking at the file. 'That date – 1 May 1977, is less than a week before Wilder disappeared.'

'Perhaps it was a present for his girlfriend which he never got round to giving her.'

'And he carried it around, loose in his trouser pocket. Sounds a bit improbable, don't you think? Anyway, what else have you got?'

Lucy picked up a bag containing a blue plastic box. 'This was in the right-hand pocket of his jacket. It contains about fifteen grams of cannabis resin, a packet of cigarette papers, a little rolling-machine and five "joints". The box has compartments as though it was made for the purpose.'

Wycliffe said, 'No trendy young man should be without one.'

Lucy Lane went on, 'There's nothing remarkable in the other bags – nothing more than one would expect to find in his pockets – a wallet with a few pounds and a credit card, some loose change, a packet of ordinary cigarettes and a lighter . . .'

Wycliffe fiddled with the bag containing the little

plastic box. 'I've been thinking about the young man who was supposed to look after him – Leslie Macc. According to the report they spent their last night together at a boarding house in St Agnes. The landlady testified that they were arguing shortly after they arrived, and next morning at breakfast they scarcely spoke.'

'And what was Mace's version?'

'Mace said the argument had been about the walk, how far they would go and where they would spend their nights. That day, their last together, they had a late snack-lunch at the pub in Gwithian and when they were about to leave at around two, Wilder picked up his rucksack and said, "I'm going to the loo; see you outside in five minutes." That, according to Mace, was the last he saw of him. He says he spent most of the rest of the day searching the area along the coastal path between Gwithian and Hayle before reporting by telephone to the boy's father. He says Wilder didn't seem particularly worried, confident that his son would soon come back of his own accord.

'Mace was told to stay around the area for another day, seeing what he could pick up, but he was on no account to stir up local interest or go to the police.'

Lucy Lane pouted. 'So there's no record of anybody having seen him after two o'clock?'

Wyclife flipped the pages of the report. 'Yes, there is. A chap called Bunny – John Bunny – out walking his dog, says he saw a young man answering Wilder's description and wearing a backpack trudging along in the direction of Hayle at about eight in the evening. That was on the coastpath about two miles east of the estuary.'

'I suppose that means he would have arrived in the neighbourhood where his body was found during the next half-hour or so. It also looks as though Mace was telling the truth.'

'Yes, and the boy's father thought Mace did his job to the best of his ability. It seems that Wilder senior had a high opinion of Mace, but I had a different view from the sister when I saw her last night. She called him a creep.'

'What did you say his name was – his first name?'

'Leslie – Leslie Mace; why?'

'I don't suppose there can be anything in it, but his initials are the same as those on the pendant – L.M.'

Wycliffe was thoughtful. 'We need to know more about Mace, whatever he's like.'

The telephone rang and Lucy answered. 'A woman by the name of Bissett wants to talk to you, sir.'

'Tell them to put her through. It's the boy's sister.'

'Molly Bissett, Mr Wycliffe . . .' Her manner was relaxed, as though she had known him for years. 'I expect you'll be hearing from father, if you haven't already. He's very relieved, as I told you he would be, though he may not sound like it to you. I hope he's not too unbearable. Now, I wanted to tell you that I had a call from Leslie Mace this morning asking if the body found in the dunes was Cochran's. Of course, he was his same oily self. I suppose I'm unfair, what he said was quite kind, but it's his manner, the way he talks.'

'He's still at the plastics factory?'

'Oh, yes, and he wants me to keep in touch. He telephoned from the works where he's quite a big-shot; secretary-accountant or something.'

Wycliffe thanked her, then asked her about the pendant found in her brother's pocket.

'I'm quite sure it's nothing to do with the family and I doubt if he had it when he was here with me.' She paused. 'To be honest, I remember going through his things on the quiet. I know it was underhand but there was ten years' difference in our ages and I felt responsible.'

'Perhaps you found the little plastic box?'

'I did.'

'Did you know what it was?'

'Yes, and I must admit I was relieved. If he had been experimenting with hard drugs I wouldn't have been

42

surprised; as a matter of fact, that's what I was looking for.'

He thanked her again, with sincerity. He liked the woman; a motherly sort with plenty of not-so-common sense. Odd that she seemed to have no kids of her own.

Wycliffe had rarely felt more helpless at the start of an investigation. He pushed the file away. 'We've got to be clear about what we are trying to do, Lucy. Franks thinks he died from the blow to the head which was probably inflicted with something made of concrete; there are concrete fragments in the wound. It could have been a fall but the fact that the injury was to the vertex and that such an elaborate attempt was made to conceal the death makes it unlikely. On the other hand, it seems the boy had a thin patch in his skull, so murder is also a doubtful starter and manslaughter more of a probability. But however he died, he didn't bury himself. A possible scenario is that the argument between him and Mace was serious and he cleared out of the Gwithian pub because he felt threatened. Mace claimed he spent most of that day searching for him without success but suppose Mace was lying, suppose he found Wilder and the argument came to a fight?'

'And there was a lump of concrete handy, and Wilder happened to be naked at the time? I suppose one could construct a scenario along those lines.' Lucy was disinclined to flights of fancy. 'Anyway, I take it, sir, that I start with Mace.'

'No, I'll attend to Mace; you concentrate on the necklace. Try to persuade the two local TV stations to put it on their early evening news and if you can get it in tomorrow's paper as well, so much the better. At the same time you might get an opinion from a jeweller about its possible provenance . . . And leave me a set of the photographs.'

'And the link with the case?'

'Found among the effects of the deceased.'

*   *   *

Wycliffe did not have to go in search of Mace. When Diane brought in his coffee she said, 'There's a man called Mace – Leslie Mace – downstairs, asking to see you in connection with the Wilder affair.'

'Tell them to send him up.'

'Another cup?'

'No, hold him till I've had mine.'

Diane gave him five minutes then came in, removed the tray, and almost immediately afterwards ushered in Mace.

Leslie Mace was fleshy with thinning fair hair and a large smooth face with smallish features crowded together so that the rest looked strangely naked. Wycliffe had the impression that beneath the grey suit and pinstriped shirt his whole body would be pale, and smooth and hairless. He was quick to smile, though not with his wary blue eyes, and his responses were abrupt and bird-like. From the visitor's chair his darting glances took in the whole room then his attention focused on the case file which Wycliffe had in front of him. The label on the cover was conspicuous: Missing Persons. Cochran S. Wilder. 7.5.77.

'I hesitated about coming to you, Chief Superintendent, but it seemed best to go to the top . . . It's good of you to see me; you must be a very busy man.'

Wycliffe was polite but cool. 'Have you come to obtain information, Mr Mace, or to give it?'

A brief hesitation. 'I came in case I might be helpful.'

'Good! There are one or two questions I want to ask you.' He passed over the photograph of the necklace. 'Do you know anything about the original of this?'

Mace looked at the photograph in surprise. 'No, I've never seen anything like it that I can remember.'

'It was found on the body.'

The little eyes widened and he shook his head. 'I don't know where he got it.'

'You can make no suggestion?'

There was a pause. 'I suppose you know that he . . .'

A vague gesture. 'I mean, you must know that he had been in trouble with the police for taking things . . .'

'You think he might have stolen this?'

Mace became uneasy. 'How can I say? He was supposed to have been cured.'

Wycliffe changed the subject. 'In your statement you said that the argument you had with him during that last evening at St Agnes was about planning your walk – the ground you would cover in a day, where you would stay – that sort of thing. Was that really the case?'

Mace looked down at his girlish hands with their short, tapering fingers. 'No, but if I had said what it was really about, Cochran's father would have been angry at having it made public.' There was a pause before he resumed. 'You see, he wanted to go off on his own – he didn't want me with him, he said he didn't need a keeper, but his father had insisted.'

'So?'

'He offered me money to leave him to his own devices but to report to his father as if I were still with him. When I refused he seemed to accept the position, but in the morning he was sullen and I could scarcely get a word out of him. Then, as I told the police at the time, when we arrived at the Gwithian pub he gave me the slip.' Mace looked pained. 'There was nothing I could do to prevent him going if he really wanted to, but he didn't even tell me.'

'And you spent the rest of the day looking for him without success?'

'Yes; of course it was a hopeless business, I had no real idea where to look; he could have gone anywhere.'

'Was it made clear to you by Mr Wilder senior exactly what was expected of you?'

A moment or two for thought. 'Not in so many words but I knew that he wanted me to be a friend to Cochran and to try to keep him out of trouble.'

'Were you his friend?'

A pause. 'I wanted to be, but to him I was simply his father's paid spy.'

'What kinds of trouble were you supposed to look out for?'

Mace looked down at his hands. 'Women, I suppose, and pilfering.'

'Drugs?'

A quick upward glance, apprehensive. 'He wasn't on drugs as far as I know.'

'He was smoking pot; didn't you know about that?'

He spread his hands. 'I suppose I did, but I didn't take it very seriously.'

'You know the spot where the body was found?'

Mace frowned. 'Well, I know it was in the sandhills not far from the chalets just north of Hayle.'

'You must have passed somewhere near there when you were looking for him. Did you keep to the beach or were you in sight of the chalets?'

'I was in sight of some of the chalets. I spoke to a girl from one of them.'

'Which one?'

Mace took his time. 'It was one nearer the sea than most, with steps leading up to it. The girl was halfway up the steps. I asked her if she had seen anything of Cochran – I mean, I described him. She said she hadn't seen anybody except her own friends.'

'So this chalet was definitely occupied?'

'It must have been; there was pop music coming from inside.'

'Can you remember anything about the girl?'

The moon-face furrowed in concentration. 'It's so long ago. She was a bit abrupt but girls never spend much time talking to me. She was blonde and on the plump side, and I remember she was wearing a blue T-shirt and trousers.'

'How old, would you say?'

'Eighteen? About that.'

'You have a good recall, Mr Mace.'

46

A quick smile of pleasure, like the tail-wagging of a petted dog. 'People tell me that.

'The following morning I went back to the chalet in case they had seen anything since, but it was shut up.'

'You went back the following morning – at what time?'

A furrowed brow, then, 'I stayed the night in Hayle and I started looking for him again around nine – it must have been about ten when I got to the chalet.'

Wycliffe thanked him and he left. When he was gone Wycliffe telephoned Kersey and put him in the picture.

Kersey was beginning to like Hayle, which was strange; few people are attracted to the little town at first acquaintance. Sprawled along the margins of a muddy estuary with sand dunes to the north and east and the honey-pot of St Ives over the river to the west, Hayle is for most people a place on the way to a chalet or caravan park, or to the great stretch of sand on the east side of the bay. But Kersey had found attractions which were easily overlooked: the Copperhouse Arms, a pub where neither the bar nor the beer had been plasticized by a brewery; a café where the locals gathered to eat bacon and egg at all times of day; a multiplicity of little shops instead of chain stores – and friendly natives.

The incident van was parked on waste ground between Copperhouse Pool – a tidal waterway, and the long, congested street which links the elements of the town together – originally two towns, the one called Foundry, because that was where the principal foundry was, and the other, Copperhouse, because of the copper-smelting there. The van was next to the little building they hoped to use.

Kersey had Sergeant Coombes with him, the first policeman on the scene after the discovery of the body, and they were studying a sketch plan showing the disposition of the chalets in the immediate neighbourhood of the burial.

Coombes was smoking a pipe, Kersey a cigarette, filling the air of the little cubicle with a menacing blue-grey haze. Outside it was raining and the windows of the van were steamed over.

Coombes pointed with a thick forefinger. 'You see, sir, there are just three chalets within a hundred yards or so of where the body was buried. The rest are well inland where the dunes are more stable.'

Kersey said, 'It's those three that interest me. Does one of them have a flight of steps leading up to it?'

Coombes nodded. 'The one called Sunset Cott.'

'That's the one, then. We know that one was occupied during the weekend when Wilder went missing. What we want to know now, is who owned it and who was in it at the time.'

Coombes, watching his words, always wary of CID types, however human they appeared, referred to his notebook. 'Actually, I've made a few inquiries about those three chalets and they all belonged to the Grey family. At that time the Greys ran a small engineering firm in Camborne, but they lived in St Ives and Mrs Grey acquired the chalets as an investment, letting them out to visitors in the summer months.'

Kersey drew curlicues with his ball-point in the margin of the plan. 'These Greys, are they still around? Do they still own the chalets?'

'I doubt it. Grey retired, sold out, and moved up north four or five years back, but their daughter is still in St Ives and she runs a health shop.' Coombes removed the pipe from his mouth and contemplated the bowl. 'My wife is a bit of a health freak, she intends living to be ninety and she's a regular customer. All I can say is the extra years don't come cheap; that shop must be a gold mine.'

Kersey said, 'It might be worthwhile looking in on the Grey girl.'

'She's no girl – wrong side of thirty, anyway.'

'Married?'

'No, but from what I hear she doesn't go short of a man in her bed.'

A couple of roundabouts and three miles or so later Kersey arrived at the outskirts of St Ives. The rain had stopped, the skies had cleared and he was looking down through pine trees at a sea of Mediterranean blue. He parked behind the Sloop Inn and set off in search of the health shop. Ambling around St Ives in the sunshine out of season is a pleasant occupation in itself and Kersey was in no hurry. The tide was out and the harbour was an expanse of yellow sand where boats careened themselves if they were not propped on stilts. On the Wharf, men in peaked caps, hands in pockets, strolled up and down, or stood in groups of two or three, arms resting on the guard rail.

Kersey found the health shop in a narrow street which bordered the sea but was totally cut off from it by houses and shops. It was larger than the others, its glass and paintwork gleamed and the inscription on the fascia had been carried out in a flowing script: St Ives Bay Health and Homoeopathic Centre.

Inside, the premises had something of the appearance of a Chinese medicine shop upgraded to Bond Street. After the more or less familiar honeys, diabetic preserves, juices and cereals, Kersey was lost before shelves stocked with pickled, dried, bottled and packeted foods and supplements of which he had never heard.

One of the two white-coated assistants serving, saw her customer out and turned to Kersey. 'Can I help you, sir?'

'I want to talk to Miss Grey.'

'She's with a client.'

A door behind the counter had a notice over it: 'Homoeopathic consultations by appointment'.

'I'll wait.'

Kersey studied the shelves and wondered at what he might be missing. Was he getting his ration of calcium, potassium, magnesium and iron? Could he do with a little lecithin or a soupçon of selenium? Then there were the vitamins, more of them than he remembered as a boy doing biology at school. And his favourite, vitamin E, had moved up in the world; in his day its sole recommendation had been a facility for enhancing the fertility of rats, now it seemed to have acquired a definite though ill-defined respectability. He was growing interested, when the door behind the counter opened and a plump matron with a mauve-tinted hair-do came out. She cooed and was being cooed over by a younger, white-coated woman with startlingly red hair. 'The same time next week, then. Thank you, Mrs Hartley. Goodbye!'

The redhead interrogated one of the girls with a look, then turned her attention to Kersey. 'Can I help you, Mr . . . ?'

'Detective Inspector Kersey . . . Miss Grey? . . . I would appreciate a word in private.'

A quick look. Apprehensive? Why should she be? She didn't look the sort to be intimidated by a mere policeman. Perhaps he was mistaken.

'You'd better come into my office.'

The room on the other side of the door was flooded with light from a window overlooking the bay. Only a footpath and a rail separated the house from the rocks and the sea. The room itself had the severe functionality of a doctor's consulting room.

Kersey was amiable. 'A pleasant room.'

'I like it.' She pointed to the client's chair across the desk from her own.

'Perhaps you have an idea why I'm here?'

'No. I'm waiting for you to tell me.'

Her manner was abrupt, down to business, but she was also sizing him up as a man. Kersey recognized the type; whatever her preoccupations, sex was never far from her thoughts.

'I expect you've heard of the discovery of a body in the dunes across the bay?'

'I heard about it.'

'Please understand that this is a purely routine inquiry. Fifteen years ago, in early May 1977, when the young man disappeared, your family owned the three chalets nearest the spot where the body was found.'

'So?'

'Is it likely that any of them could have been occupied at that time?'

With a practised movement she swept back the hair which was beginning to hide her face. 'In early May? I shouldn't think so. It's not the kind of holiday people take early in the season but I can't say that it never happened.'

'At the time, Wilder's disappearance made quite a stir and that might have helped to fix things in your memory.'

A sudden smile which softened her features. 'My dear man, I was eighteen in 1977, with other, more interesting things to think about.'

'We have evidence that the chalet called Sunset Cott was occupied during the weekend that Wilder disappeared.'

'Really? I told you I didn't know; it just sounded unlikely.'

'And your parents? Is it likely they might have some recollection?'

She thought before answering. 'It's possible. Mother kept a record of her lettings, but whether she's still got it I don't know. You can ask her if you like; they're living in Shropshire now and I'll give you their phone number.'

Kersey was puzzled. His mind told him that the woman was being as helpful as he had any right to expect but he had an uneasy feeling that in some important respects he was being taken for a ride. Perhaps it was because her attitude did not square with her hard face and harder eyes.

She was looking at him with a speculative, slightly amused expression. 'I'm afraid I haven't been much help.'

'Your mother might be. In any case at this stage we're searching for a black cat in a dark room.' Kersey stood up.

She said, 'Are you married?'

'Two daughters at university.' Kersey was proud of his daughters and he let it show.

'Really? You don't look like one who's been snared and tamed.' She got up from her chair. 'I'll see you out.'

Kersey found himself out in the narrow street, wondering.

Almost opposite the health shop a lane led up steeply to join the main street and on the corner there was a shop, straight out of Dickens, with small window panes and woodwork which looked as though it had long ago been treated with paint stripper, then forgotten. The lettering on the fascia was just decipherable, The Modelmakers. In the window there was a model of a three-masted sailing ship which had obviously been there gathering dust for years, and a notice in bold script: 'No dogs, children or food inside the shop. Casual visitors not welcome'. Kersey was aware of being watched by someone whose head came just above the screen at the back of the window.

Back in the caravan there was a call from Wycliffe and the two exchanged notes. Wycliffe said, 'So we know that one of the chalets nearest to where the body was found, the one called Sunset Cott, with steps leading up to it, was occupied at the time Wilder disappeared. We know too that the chalet belonged to this Grey family which you've dug up.'

'Yes, and there's an off-chance that Mamma Grey may have kept the records of her lettings. It's a long shot but worth trying.'

'Even if it comes off there's nothing but proximity to suggest that whoever was there had any connection with Wilder, but I agree we must follow it up.'

'Anything on the necklace, sir?'

'Lucy has fixed to have it on TV this evening and in

some of tomorrow's papers. Anyway, how are you getting on down there?'

Kersey laughed. 'I like it; it's odd. But, for some reason I feel that whatever Hayle once had, it was all over before I got here. By the way, Shaw has fixed up for us to have the place next door. He expects to have it equipped with all systems go by Thursday morning.'

Wycliffe made a point of being home early because Ruth was due. He found them in the garden, in the evening sunshine, admiring Helen's 'Darjeeling' magnolia, flowering for the first time since its planting a dozen years before.

Helen said, 'Isn't that rich pink wonderful with the light coming through the petals? I wasn't expecting it to flower for another year or two . . . And it's got the fragrance!'

Ruth was pale and, he thought, thinner. She said little but she hugged him and placed her cheek against his. Helen looked on and lifted her shoulders, telling him, mutely, that she was none the wiser.

'I hope you can put up with me for a while, Dad.'

'It's your home, love, whenever you want it. You know that.'

'Yes; and it's a good place to be.'

They drank sherry in the kitchen where Helen had indulged herself in a small television. The Wilder case made the national news, and so did the necklace.

'Police in Cornwall are treating the death of Cochran Wilder, son of Minister of State Royston Wilder, as a case of unlawful killing.

'Cochran Wilder disappeared fifteen years ago while on a walking holiday in Cornwall and yesterday his decomposed remains were discovered in a sand dune near the little port of Hayle. The police are anxious to trace the owner of a necklace found with the body.'

The lab photograph appeared on the screen and the newsreader continued, 'The silver pendant, in the form of a cat, is inscribed on the back with the initials L.M. and—'

Ruth said, 'Are you involved in this one, Dad?'

A wry grin. 'This afternoon the minister, on the telephone, explained to me how deeply I am involved.' Wycliffe sighed, 'I can sympathize with him as a father but the man is a bombastic cretin.'

Helen said, 'Your glass needs topping up, Charles.'

Lisa was laying the table for the evening meal. Martin in an easy chair, a pile of exercise books on the floor beside him, was marking on his lap and muttering to himself at intervals. The early evening news was on the television.

Place mats, knives, forks, spoons, salt and pepper pots, sweet chutney for Martin . . . Through the window she could see the sea, a flat plain, quite still, and above it a single greyish-white cloud hanging, suspended in space. A surrealist painting. In a nightmarish fashion every movement she made seemed to bring nearer that moment when the newsreader would say . . . What would he say?

That morning there had been a photograph of Cochran Wilder in the newspaper, as he was at the time of his disappearance. Over the years she had retained only a vague idea of what he looked like. In her thoughts and nightmare dreams she saw a featureless face framed in dark hair with blood soaking through it and running in rivulets over the whiteness of his skin. But in the newspaper photograph she saw again the young man who had hailed her as she stood on the veranda of the chalet, arms resting on the rail, watching the sunset. She had disliked him on sight but he had asked for a glass of water.

She shivered. 'Do you really want the television on, Martin? You're not watching.'

Martin looked up from his marking. 'I can hear it, can't I? It's the only chance I have to catch up with the news.'

Lisa did not know what it was that she feared but she felt sure there would be something to further torment her jangled nerves. Even so, when it came, she could not restrain a little cry of shocked surprise.

'The body of a young man discovered on Monday in the sand dunes on the north Cornish coast has now been identified as that of Cochran Wilder, 21-year-old son of the minister. Cochran disappeared fifteen years ago while on a walking holiday in Cornwall. In connection with his death the police are anxious to trace the owner of a necklace found with the body.'

And there on the screen was her necklace which she had not seen for fifteen years.

The newsreader's voice, suave and indifferent, continued. 'The silver pendant, in the form of a cat, is inscribed on the back with the initials L.M. and a date, the first of May 1977 . . .'

Martin said, 'What's the matter? You look as though you were going to faint or something.'

She tried to pass it off and said, foolishly, 'I'm being silly. May the first is my birthday.'

'So what?' Martin looked blank, shrugged, and returned to his marking.

It was a quarter to nine; Alan was late, detained by an emergency house call. Daniel was in bed asleep, and there was a casserole in the oven keeping warm. Barbara could have watched television while waiting for Alan but the early evening news had been more than enough. Her first impulse when she saw the necklace had been to telephone Lisa, but Martin would have been there . . . She thought that it must be worse for Lisa; at least Alan was involved and there was no need for secrecy between them.

She had made a big thing of giving Daniel his supper, reading him his story and putting him to bed; now she was forced back on herself. She went upstairs and rummaged in the bottom drawer of the big chest on the landing. From under a mass of discarded underclothes and woollies she came up with an envelope from which she removed a photograph, and took it downstairs. Now, perched on the kitchen stool, her elbows on the worktop, she gazed at it as though she had not seen it before.

Three boys and three girls, all in their late teens, sprawled on the grass and smiled, grinned, smirked or grimaced at the camera according to their natures and their moods. She did not need the photograph to recall their faces but it was the one material link with her Pandora's box of memories.

She was there, with Alan's arm around her shoulders; a school romance which blossomed. Lisa was there. At eighteen, Lisa had shoulder-length blonde hair which accentuated her rather long face. Her lips were thin and her smile for the camera was hesitant and non-committal. Of course she was wearing her necklace. Paul Drew, lanky and serious, was pressed clumsily against her, his hand on her thigh. Luckily for Lisa, that had come to nothing, though whether she had fared any better with her schoolmaster was another matter.

That left Gillian Grey, a freckled redhead, known to everyone as GG, and Julian Angove, short, stocky, and powerful, the maverick of the party.

She heard the engine of Alan's little runabout being punished on the steep hill from the town and listened as he turned into their drive, slammed the car door and let himself into the house.

'Barbara!'

'In the kitchen.'

He stood by her, put his arm around her and kissed her hair. 'Are you all right?'

'There's a casserole in the oven, keeping warm.'

'Where's Daniel?'

'In bed asleep.'

Gently he turned her face toward him and then he saw the photograph on the bench in front of her.

'I thought we agreed to destroy that years ago.'

'I know, but I couldn't bring myself to. Don't be annoyed, Alan, please!'

'But why torture yourself like this, darling?'

She shuddered. 'Whenever I think of it, I can hear that awful breathing.'

They were silent for a moment or two while he continued to hold her then, abruptly, her manner seemed to change and she became aggressive. She broke away from him and pointed to Lisa in the photograph. 'You see! She's wearing that bloody necklace . . . With jeans and a T-shirt! She'd have worn it in bed if it wasn't uncomfortable.'

'And she lost it. But does that matter now?' He was treading gingerly, trying to say what was soothing and conversational.

'The police think it matters. You haven't heard; they found it with the body and they had it on TV this evening, asking people to identify it . . . When somebody does . . .' She spoke calmly again, resigned.

'But who will? Certainly none of us, nobody in the photograph. She hadn't had it more than a few days and who else would remember after fifteen years?'

She looked up. 'Somebody will . . . Somebody will.' There was certainty and resignation in her voice which troubled him. Then, 'Don't try to coddle me, Alan! I'm not a child and I've known all along that one day this would catch up with us.' She turned away and said, more quietly, 'We should never have had children; we had no right . . . Whenever I look at that snapshot – and I do sometimes – I say to myself, "That was before . . . And there's no going back."'

Chapter Three

When Wycliffe arrived in the office, Diane greeted him. 'You look a bit down this morning.'

'Anything in the mail?'

Always the same question, though the answer was laid out on his desk, opened, and arranged in classified heaps.

She pointed to the little heaps of correspondence. 'Nothing on the case.'

Wycliffe's desk calendar showed Wednesday 13 May. At least it wasn't Friday. Two days since the discovery of the body, about fifteen hours since the necklace appeared on television, and fifteen years since young Wilder's body was buried in the dunes. As a rule, if an inquiry was going to be short it was usually on the third day that things began to happen, but this one had a history. All the same, he would have expected some reaction to the necklace, if only from the nutters, but so far there was nothing.

Because of Wilder's pressure tactics Wycliffe was afraid of being forced into one of those public relations exercises in which scores of officers are committed to a lucky-dip routine, asking vague questions of unlikely people, chasing shadows; taking megabytes out of the computer software, and adding to the waste-paper mountain. Occasionally such routines pay off though usually as much would have been achieved by a few officers working in full knowledge of the case. But there are no media points in that.

The local daily was neatly folded beside his mail and

he glanced at the front page. Beneath a photograph of the necklace there was a two-column spread:

The Body in the Sand Dunes
A Suspicious Death

The body of a young man discovered in the dunes near Hayle on Monday has now been officially identified as that of Cochran Wilder, only son of Government Minister Royston Wilder. The young man went missing while on a walking holiday almost exactly fifteen years ago. Post mortem evidence suggests that he was attacked and that he died as a result of injuries received.

The police are unwilling to comment on their investigations at this stage but it is understood that in addition to their efforts to trace the owner of the necklace found with the body and shown in our photograph, they are interested in a chalet near where the body was found and thought to have been occupied at the time of the tragedy . . .

Wycliffe was puzzled. As far as he knew only two contacts could have given rise to speculation about the chalet: his interview with Mace and Kersey's with the Grey woman at the health shop. Odd. It was a small thing but leaks always troubled him; they meant watching your rear.

Lucy Lane arrived.

'Anything on the necklace, Lucy?'

'Nothing to write home about, sir. The silver carries the London hallmark and the date letter for 1859. Old Minors down at Gellet's says he's never seen anything quite like it before; he thinks it's a family piece almost certainly made to order and he says it would fetch a good price at auction.'

The house telephone rang. 'The chief would like to see

you in his office when convenient, Mr Wycliffe.' It was the chief's protective dragon, known disrespectfully as 'Queenie', but Queenie had a soft spot for Wycliffe and she added, *sotto voce*, 'I think the Minister has got him ruffled.'

Wycliffe went along the corridor and through the padded door. Queenie, with more secrets tucked away beneath her silvery hair than most, revelled in her intercessionary role. She whispered, 'He's waiting for you. Go straight in.'

Chief Constable Bertram Oldroyd was a good policeman who had built up a sound administration, leading from the front, but never interfering with a subordinate who was doing his job. He had always vigorously resisted any attempt at manipulation from Whitehall or from anywhere else, and as he neared retirement his sensitivity in such matters had increased.

'Come in and shut the door, Charles. Sit down.' It was obvious to anybody who knew him that the chief was still simmering. 'I've just been talking to Wilder. I gather that he telephoned you yesterday afternoon and that he was dissatisifed with your response.'

'Yes, I think that sums it up.'

'Well, I told him that I am fully satisfied with the way in which this investigation is being conducted and that if he's got a complaint, he should make it to the Police Authority or to the Home Office. I can sympathize with the man, but he's not going to flex his political muscle in my direction.'

Oldroyd sat back in his chair, feeling better.

Wycliffe said nothing because there was nothing that needed saying and, after a pause, the chief went on, 'Incidentally, he's arranging the funeral for Saturday morning at St Germans. I take it that raises no problems with the case?'

'No, sir. The coroner has opened the inquest and adjourned for further police investigation, but he is issuing a disposal certificate.'

'Good! Now, Charles, fill me in.'

In Hayle, Kersey finally succeeded in getting GG's mother at the end of a telephone. 'Yes, I've kept the record of my lettings but how do they concern you?' A worthy mother for the redhead, knowing precisely how many pence make a pound.

Kersey explained.

'All right. It sounds round about to me but I suppose you know your own business. Leave me your number, I shall have to ring you back.'

Obviously she would telephone her daughter. Whatever she did, it took her fifteen minutes.

'No, Inspector, none of my three chalets was let during the week which included the seventh of May 1977 or for another fortnight after that.'

'We are interested mainly in Sunset Cott, the one with a flight of steps leading up to a veranda. A witness says he saw a girl entering the chalet on the day in question and that there was music coming from inside.'

Madame was unimpressed. 'I can't help what your witness says he saw. I suppose it could have been a relative of the woman who kept the chalets clean and looked after the linen. I can only tell you what I know.'

'Yes, I understand that. So there was a woman who had a key to the chalets and looked after them?'

'I didn't do it myself.'

'Is this woman still around?'

'I suppose so; I've really no idea.'

'Perhaps you will let me have her name, and her address at the time?'

'I can't imagine what she could tell you that I can't.'

'We have to double check wherever possible.'

'Very well, her name is Maggie Reynolds – as to her address, I've got it here somewhere . . . Yes, here it is – Three Russell's Ope – that's just off Foundry Square.'

'Just one more question, Mrs Grey. Did you provide nylon bed sheets in your lets?'

She was more amused than disturbed by his question. 'We all did – those of us who supplied linen at all. They're easy to wash.'

Kersey walked to Foundry Square through drizzling rain and found Russell's Ope. It was a row of white-walled cottages fronting on the blank ramparts of a deserted foundry complex left over from the days of Hayle's greatness. Once, the vast cylinders for mine pumping engines were cast here, and it was from this foundry that the Dutch commissioned the largest pumping engine in the world, to empty their Haarlem Lake. Now it had about the same relevance to modern industry as a flint-knapper's yard.

The door of number three stood open to the living room and Kersey could see inside a heavily built man with machine-clipped white hair, sitting by an open fire. He had a tabby cat on his lap and a newspaper lay crumpled on the floor at his side.

Kersey tapped on the door.

'What do you want?' Guttural and demanding.

'Mr Reynolds?'

'That's me.'

Kersey advanced into the room and the old man turned towards him, his face round, bronzed and smooth as an apple. A real son of the soil matured in the broccoli fields. Kersey prepared to cope with rural naïvety.

'Detective Inspector Kersey.'

'What can I do for you, Mister?'

'I want to talk to your wife – Mrs Maggie Reynolds, I believe.'

'You can't talk to Maggie, she ain't here. You'll have to make do with me.'

'I'm afraid it's important that I speak to your wife, Mr Reynolds. Is there somewhere I can get in touch with her?'

'You could try the cemetery.'

Son of the soil snatches metaphorical mat from under

clever detective. Kersey had worked in the country long enough to have known better. 'I'm sorry.'

'Not half as sorry as I am, Mister. Maggie was a good wife.'

Kersey grinned. 'Let's start again.'

The old man's eyes sparkled. 'You've come about "the body in the dunes", that's what they call it in the newspaper, but where does my Maggie come in?' He shifted more comfortably in his chair and brought his great hands together, disturbing the cat but preparing to enjoy himself.

'I'm told that your wife looked after three chalets on the towans for a Mrs Grey.'

'She looked after several for different people who let – kept 'em clean and did the washing.'

'Mrs Grey tells me that none of her three was occupied at the time young Wilder disappeared but—'

'I reckon she wouldn' have much idea one way or t'other.'

'She says she kept a record, and she must have had some way of checking her bookings.'

The old man looked enigmatic. 'Bookings is one thing; they as weren't booked is another.'

Kersey had learned his lesson. 'You know something I don't.'

A deep-seated chuckle. 'It was like this, Mister, in the off season that chalet with the steps leading up to it was a sort of doss for family and friends. There was a son and a daughter – the redhead – her that's now got the shop in St Ives. It was her mainly.'

'She used to bring her boyfriends there?'

'It started when she was still a schoolgirl, and soon it was most any boy or man she happened to pick up with. Proper little tart she was – still is, from what I hear.' A long drawn-out sigh. 'Sometimes I think what I missed.'

'You're a wicked old man.'

A gust of laughter. 'P'raps I never had the chance to be a wicked young one.'

'Did Mrs Grey know about what was going on?'

The old man shrugged. 'Hard to say. Maggie thought so. By all accounts she weren't all that different herself.'

'These unofficial visitors to the chalet, I don't suppose you have any names?'

A shake of the head. 'They was mostly just names to me when Maggie talked about 'em; 'twas a case of in one ear and out t'other. But there was one who lasted longer than most, a fella called Penrose, a lawyer over to St Ives. But he was late on – too late to be any use to you.' The old man yawned. 'That's all I can tell you, Mister.'

Kersey thanked him and got up to go. At the door he paused, 'Shall I shut this?'

'What for? I ain't afraid of burglars.'

It was lunchtime. When did the old man eat? And what? Through the drizzle Kersey made for the pub. He was not proud of his morning's work. All he'd learned was that one of the chalets had been occupied at weekends in the off season. No dates and only one name, a lawyer who had come on the scene too late to be relevant. There was certainly nothing to connect the chalet with the death of young Wilder. On the other hand, his niggling, totally unfounded suspicion of the redhead in the health shop had somehow been rekindled. She had answered his questions and seemed willing, if not anxious, to help, but his policeman's antennae had received contradictory signals. Now she had cropped up again.

There were tasty looking pasties being served at the bar but after a suicide breakfast (the full menu with sausage and fried bread), his conscience, and thoughts of his wife, persuaded him to a sandwich and a half of bitter.

He was supposed to be listening to gossip but in the pub interest in the body in the dunes seemed to have flagged and the all-absorbing topic was the state of fishing in the port, in particular the sanding-up of the bar.

'I don't fancy it above an hour either side of high water and not then if there's any sort of a blow.'

Another skipper put down his glass and wiped his lips.

'Dredging's no answer either. What we need is the sluice and until they do something about East Quay there's not much hope o' that . . .'

Kersey was out of it, so he ate his sandwich, drank his beer, and left.

Back at the van he telephoned headquarters and reported to Wycliffe who sounded weary and mildly irritable. 'All you can do is keep at it. Tackle the Grey woman again . . . Of course there may be no connection but that's the name of the game; we soldier on and keep our fingers crossed. By the way, in this morning's paper they refer to police interest in a chalet that was occupied at the time of Wilder's disappearance. Have you said anything?'

'No, and I'm quite sure Coombes wouldn't.'

'That's what I thought. I wonder who's feeding them.'

'Anything fresh at your end, sir?'

'No, it's the same story. Lucy's team hasn't come up with much. She's been through the statements taken when Wilder disappeared, picked names out of the hat, and chased up as many as possible in case something was missed. Wilder seems to have been a Walter Mitty type with an unpleasant twist; he tried to live out his fantasies. I suppose his illness was to blame. He wasn't popular in the hospital; at one stage he was involved in a punch-up but it doesn't lead anywhere. And there's the cannabis angle, another blind alley – no ring or anything of that sort, just an opportunist user in a small way.'

Wycliffe sighed. 'It's a waste of time, Doug. If Franks is right the boy died from being hit over the head with a concrete object of some sort. Even if he was, that hardly amounts to a premeditated crime, but a spur of the moment thing. And it happened fifteen years ago.'

'What about Mace?'

'He seems a harmless type. Naturally we've done some checking and the most we could find was that his name cropped up in connection with some porn videos.'

Kersey was not the only one finding it difficult to

sustain genuine enthusiasm for a fifteen-year-old corpse. Unprofessional, of course, but some policemen are only human.

It was depressing, and by six o'clock Wycliffe was home.

With two women in the house he found the atmosphere subtly different. He was fed and watered, even cosseted, but the centre of gravity had shifted, and the household no longer revolved about him. He was not grumbling, a more peripheral role could have its advantages.

And in bed that night Helen confided Ruth's secret.

'She told me this afternoon while we were working in the garden. She and David are separated; they've been living apart for the past three months. It was all quite amicable; the flat is hers and there was a settlement. In fact he's been generous in the circumstances. Of course, the settlement includes her severance pay; she could hardly continue to work as his PA.'

'What circumstances are you talking about?'

'Well, it was Ruth who wanted it; he was anxious that they should marry and have children.'

'But Ruth didn't want that?'

'No.'

Wycliffe stopped himself just in time from sounding pleased. Instead he said, 'Why ever not?'

'I think you'd better ask her that. Anyway, she's come home because she feels she needs time to take stock.'

Thursday morning, 14 May

Wycliffe was an early riser and he was surprised to find Ruth already in the kitchen with the coffee made. Over their first cup, she asked, 'Mum told you?'

'Yes.'

'I'll put on the toast.' She busied herself cutting bread (sliced bread had never crossed the Wycliffe threshold). 'What do you think?'

66

'It's your life, love.'

'But you're not disappointed?'

'No, I'm not.'

She ran a hand through her hair in a gesture so like her mother's when concerned, that Wycliffe was moved. 'I've always known you didn't care for him, Dad, but although he's a hard man in business, in private life nobody could be kinder or more considerate.'

'Well, then?'

'I know. You're asking me why in that case I don't do what he wants.' She was putting slices of bread into the toaster. 'It sounds silly. I want him but I don't want his children . . .' She broke off. 'No, that's not true! What I mean is that I don't want my children brought up to believe in money as the answer to almost everything, I don't want them over-indulged. If I have children I want them to grow up wanting things they can't have – until they've learned to value what they've got.'

After a longish pause she looked up. 'Would you go along with that?'

'You don't need to ask . . . But don't leave it too late, Ruthie. You need somebody.'

After a disturbed night, spells of sleeplessness alternating with uneasy dreams, Lisa toyed with her shredded wheat and watched Martin butter a piece of toast and cut it into five equal fingers. She watched him pick up one of the fingers, bite it precisely in half, and return the remainder to his plate while he chewed and swallowed the other. She watched, as she had done hundreds of times before, and marvelled that she had never until now wanted to scream. The performance over, Martin drained his coffee cup, patted his lips and moustache with a paper tissue, looked at his watch and said, 'I must be going.'

It was a ritual as immutable as the Mass.

Lisa followed him into the hall where he picked up his

bulging bag. 'I shall be late this evening. There's a full staff meeting.'

He stooped to examine his reflection in the hall mirror and seemed satisfied with what he saw. He had shaved cleanly, his hair showed no sign of thinning or of grey streaks and his broad moustache was neatly trimmed. The black hair accentuated his natural pallor and gave him, he thought, a certain distinction.

But Lisa noticed for the first time a tiny patch of baldness on the crown of his head and experienced a tremor of uncharitable satisfaction, immediately followed by guilt.

Martin had his hand on the snap lock of the front door when the flap of the letterbox rattled and a small shower of mail dropped into the wire cage.

'Better see if there is anything . . .' He sorted through the envelopes in his large bony hands. 'Electricity bill . . . A catalogue for you . . . This is for you too – looks like a letter from your aunt . . . Bank statement . . . What's this . . . ? It's addressed to you.'

He held out a plain postcard. The address was type-written, and on the other side somebody had drawn a little map of what appeared to be a stretch of coast with a heavily indented estuary. 'What is it?'

'I've no idea.' Her voice trembled but he was too preoccupied to notice.

'I'll see you tonight, then.'

The door slammed and Lisa returned to the kitchen, the mail in her hand. She selected the postcard and dropped the rest on the table. The supposed map had no labels, no contours and no scale, but Lisa was in no doubt about what it was intended to convey. She stood, looking down at the card, feeling slightly sick, and it was some time before she could think clearly about how she would react. Do nothing? That was not in her nature. But what? She slipped the card into the pocket of her dressing gown and went upstairs.

*   *   *

Wycliffe arrived at the office still thinking of Ruth.

Diane said, 'You're looking more cheerful this morning. Does that mean progress?'

'Progress in what?'

'The case, of course.'

'Why bring that up? Anything in the mail?'

'Only routine stuff apart from one anonymous. I haven't opened it but it's not from one of our regulars.'

The address was typewritten, evidently on an old machine, and in the envelope there was something about the size and stiffness of a postcard. The postmark was simply 'Cornwall', the Post Office having done away with local marks in case they might be useful to somebody. He used the approved technique for opening suspicious packages and drew out a plain postcard with a section cut from a snapshot stuck to one side.

It was a photograph of a blonde girl in her late teens, seated on grass with her legs tucked in. She was smiling, a hesitant smile, a pretty girl in the inevitable T-shirt and jeans.

Wycliffe put on his spectacles which he still regarded as an expedient of last resort and saw that she was wearing a necklace which looked like the one found with the body. He thought he could make out the form of the cat and the filigree whorls of which the necklace itself was made. He was sufficiently convinced to experience a tremor of satisfaction. Apart from the grass, which looked like the fine fescue found on fixed dunes, just behind the girl's head he could make out what appeared to be a flight of wooden steps. It was enough.

Lucy Lane came in and he passed her the card. 'Keep your fingers off, but what do you make of it?'

'It certainly looks like our necklace.' Lucy was thoughtful. 'She must have been about eighteen then which would put her in her early thirties now.'

'What about the photograph itself?'

Lucy took her time. 'It's obviously been cut from a snap probably of a group. There was somebody sitting very close to her on her right, and there was somebody in front of her; I can see the top of a head.'

Wycliffe said, 'Take it upstairs and see what they make of it . . . Tell them to enhance and enlarge it to the best advantage. Say, a dozen prints to start with.'

Was this the breakthrough? If the photograph was genuine, and there was no reason to doubt it, there should be no great difficulty in identifying the girl . . . But what then? There was no proof of any direct link between her and Wilder. It was quite possible that she had lost her necklace, or had it stolen. Of course there were other, more encouraging, possibilities, but Wycliffe was the sort to see a glass half-empty rather than half-full. Either way, the photograph must be followed up and it was going to be his excuse for getting back into the field.

He telephoned Kersey. 'What's the weather like down there?'

'Drizzle.'

'Well, I'm coming down; I've got a photograph for you to look at.'

It was almost an hour before the prints were ready but still only half past ten. On the house phone he spoke to his deputy, John Scales, 'I want you to keep my chair warm for me, John . . .'

As on every other morning, Paul Drew parked his car and walked the hundred yards or so to the estate agency in which he was a partner. More than six-foot tall, he carried himself like a guardsman and proceeded with measured stride, head held high, looking neither to the right nor to the left. His sombre grey suit was creaseless and his briefcase had the sheen of well-polished leather.

As it happened, the police caravan was parked on waste ground immediately opposite his office, so that whenever he entered or left he was made uncomfortable by the feeling that he was being watched. It was absurd, he could see no-one, yet at times he could persuade himself that the police had chosen that spot solely because of him.

The office, formerly a shop, had a large window almost wholly taken up by a board displaying the usual photographs and details of properties for sale. Once inside, hidden by that display board, he felt better. He and the girl assistant shared the outer office while Stanton, the senior partner, had a room to himself.

'Your mail's on your desk.'

The girl was Stanton's niece and her treatment of him was casual. It was her job to open all the business mail and to sort it between the partners according to which of them was dealing with a particular transaction.

'There's one marked personal; I've put that separate.'

He often received personal mail at the office and he wondered vaguely why she had made the point. He sat at his desk, adjusted the position of his chair, telephone, and in-tray, and turned his attention to the mail.

The personal item was a plain postcard. On the communication side there was a sketch map and the words, poorly typewritten, 'I'll be in touch again soon.'

He felt faint. The girl looked across at him. 'What's the matter? You look awful.'

'I had a bad night – something I ate.' For a couple of minutes he went through the motions of reading and sorting his mail, then, 'I've got an appointment in St Ives; I shall be back in about an hour.'

At the door she called after him, 'Aren't you taking your briefcase?'

He went back to collect it.

'Don't you want a tape?' She handed him one of the little pocket recorders which had taken the place of notebooks.

The bloody girl was doing it on purpose and by the time he was on his way again he was so flustered that he all but tripped over the step. And still he could not keep his eyes away from the police van where a plain clothes man lounged indolently in the doorway, apparently watching him.

He forced himself to walk at his normal pace to where he had parked his car and as he walked he told himself repeatedly, 'Mustn't panic! Mustn't panic!' He made a short-lived effort to review and analyse rationally the significance of what had happened so far: the discovery of the body, the finding of that wretched necklace, and now, the arrival of the postcard which he carried in his wallet. In his car he sat motionless at the wheel while his mind insisted on reliving that nightmare time when, holding grimly onto his corner of the sheet, he staggered through the dunes, ghostly in the darkness, sometimes sinking up to his knees in the sand . . .

He arrived at the health shop with scarcely any memory of how he had got there, expecting to see GG at once, but she was with a client. He stood awkwardly in the shop not knowing what to do with himself. As it happened there were no customers and the two assistants watched him, exchanging amused glances.

Eventually the consultation was over and GG, with honeyed words, ushered her client into the street and turned to him. One look, and she said, 'You'd better come into my office.'

When he was seated in the client's chair she went on, 'What you need is a good cup of tea.' She called to one of the girls.

Fifteen minutes later, when Drew had left, GG picked up the telephone and dialled a number.

'Penrose, Solicitors? . . . Mr Penrose, please . . . Arnold? . . . I've had Paul here in a state . . . He's cracking up . . .'

Lisa and Martin had not shared a bedroom for three or four years though he made occasional visits to hers. She had the smaller of the two front rooms and there was a view over the bay from the window. The single divan, its duvet half on the floor, clothes littered about, a colourful twin-track cassette recorder sharing a shelf with a gaggle of paperbacks – all conspired to suggest the refuge of a teenager rather than the bedroom of a woman of thirty-three.

Lisa unlocked an old-fashioned writing case and, from among the tinted envelopes which she never used, brought out a photograph of a group of young people.

She was there, at eighteen, with Paul Drew. He was sitting uncomfortably close and his hand was on her thigh. Even now she could recall the grip of his bony fingers – possessive, not a caress. Now an estate agent, Paul had acquired a wife who might easily be mistaken for his sister.

Alan Hart had his arm around Barbara Morris and they both looked absurdly pleased with themselves. Now they were a married couple, expecting their second child, and Alan was one of the town's doctors. That left Gillian Grey – GG, and Julian Angove. The two were sitting close but there was no embrace; already they were old hands. In the following years neither had married. GG had her health shop and Julian had a queer little studio on the Wharf where he painted pot-boilers for tourists in summer, and survived the winter by courtesy of Social Security.

Lisa had made up her mind to approach one of the five, but which? Although remarkably they were all still living in the same neighbourhood – those who had gone away had come back again – they did not socialize; in fact, they seemed to avoid one another. For reasons which she preferred to leave undefined she decided on Julian, the painter. At first she thought that she might telephone, but she decided against that; she would call without warning.

She dressed rather carefully for the street, tightly fitting turquoise trousers of some stretch material, a Liberty top and a tailored jacket. But it was drizzling with rain and she had to wear a mac and carry an umbrella.

She arrived on the Wharf shortly after half past ten. Julian's studio was wedged between a shop and a café and its one-room width rose to three storeys, like a slice cut from a slab cake. In the tiny shop window, displayed on an easel, a colourful picture of the harbour looked like an illustration from a child's story-book. The door was locked, though stuck to the glass was a notice which read 'Open at ten'. There was a bell-push and Lisa pushed. She heard a distant ring and waited but nothing happened. Through the glass door she could see mail lying on the mat and beyond, a dim passage-like vista; the walls were lined with framed pictures and at the far end there was a barred window.

Having made up her mind Lisa was not to be put off; she put her finger on the button and kept it there until she heard movement. Shortly afterwards, she saw Julian himself coming towards her between the rows of his pictures. He wore a dressing gown, his feet were bare, he was unshaven and his mop of dark hair framed his plump features like a corona.

He fiddled with the lock and opened the door. 'God! It's you.' He stood aside to let her in and locked the door behind her. 'What time is it?'

'A quarter to eleven.'

He looked about him, his lips moist and slack. 'I was in bed. I take it you haven't come to buy a picture, so you'd better come upstairs.'

'Aren't you going to take your mail?'

He looked at her oddly, but he stooped and collected the three or four envelopes from the mat. As far as she could see there was no card. The painter grumbled, 'Bloody bills, that's all I ever get.' He looked at her again, increasingly puzzled as he recovered his faculties. 'What brought this on? . . . Anyway, come on up. Leave your mac and umbrella here.'

At the end of the shop, by the barred window, there was an easel with a half-finished painting and, in an alcove, stairs led up to the next floor.

'After you . . .'

At the top of the stairs she found herself in a narrow

74

living room, starkly furnished, with a window over-looking the quay. More stairs led to the top storey.

'Sit you down.'

He sat beside her on a long, hard bench which must have come from a railway waiting room, and looked her over. 'I see you around sometimes. You're wearing well. From the rear you look just as you did as a schoolgirl. I fancied you then – good legs and a nice little bum. You're wasted on that constipated schoolmaster but you always went for that sort. I remember you had a thing with Paul Drew and you ended up by marrying the type specimen of the breed.'

It was strange that Lisa, a trained nurse, accustomed to slapping down randy convalescents, felt no inclination to do the same with the painter. Julian sighed, and his dressing gown parted exposing his chest and a tangled mat of hair. Lisa reminded herself of what she had come for and handed him the photograph from her bag.

He studied it intently. 'What's this in aid of?' . . . Then, under his breath, 'God, we were a smug-looking bunch!'

Lisa gave him the postcard. He looked at the sketch map, turned the card over and saw the stamp. 'So it came like this; no envelope. Somebody being a bit nasty.'

'You haven't had one?'

'No.'

There was a movement on the stairs from the room above and they both looked up. A girl was standing halfway down; she was plump, very dark, in her early twenties, and she was naked.

Julian said, 'For God's sake, Elena, put something on; we've got a visitor. Then you can make some coffee and open the shop.' He added, to Lisa, 'She's a nice kid, but not very bright.' He was still holding the card. 'Have you asked any of the others?'

'No, I was wondering what to do.'

'Nothing. Forget it! Somebody's conscience is pricking and they're trying to take it out on you.'

The telephone rang and he answered it. It was on a little table at the top of the stairs.

'Yes, it's me . . . A card? I don't know what you're talking about. Nobody ever writes to me . . . Others? What others?' A longer interval than before. Then, 'You can come over if you like but I don't see what I can do . . .'

He dropped the telephone and returned to the seat. 'That was GG; I fancy she's wetting her see-throughs. She's had one of your cards and I gather Paul Drew's been there looking for a shoulder to cry on.' He grinned. 'I feel left out.'

Lisa said, 'It's no laughing matter, Julian.' But she was beginning to feel relaxed, the very last thing she had expected.

Chapter Four

Thursday (continued)

The day was soft with misty rain and intervals of watery sunshine. The roads were quiet and Wycliffe made, for him, good time, so that by shortly after twelve he was in Hayle where he found Kersey installed in the newly established Incident Room. It was next to where the van was parked, an odd little building and, like a great many others in Hayle, it had experienced successive incarnations, first as a bank, then as a post office, followed by a library, a social club and, lately, a meeting place for the *Heralds of the Second Coming*.

There was a large room, almost a hall, for the *hoi polloi*, and a little one to serve as an office for whoever was in charge; also a minute kitchen and rather grim toilets. Shaw had worked his usual minor miracle in persuading central stores to disgorge the necessary equipment, and the utility services to revitalize their connections; all with a minimum of red tape.

The two sat at a table in the little room beneath a lurid print of Armageddon under which some wag had scrawled with a felt pen 'Coming Shortly'.

Kersey studied one of the prints Wycliffe had brought with him. The lab had done a good job; contrast had been enhanced and the enlargement made the most of what detail there was. Kersey said at once, 'God! She's wearing the necklace; and those steps must mean that it's the Greys' chalet.' Then, after an interval, 'Somebody's playing silly buggers.'

'In what way?'

'Trying to pull strings. Whoever sent this, knows the

girl. Why not give us a name? Why cut away the rest of the picture and take her out of context?'

Wycliffe said, 'I thought we'd try this out on the Grey woman. Will you see her, or shall I?'

Kersey grinned. 'Time you got to know the cast, sir, don't you think?' He was still studying the photograph and finally he muttered, 'There's a smell about this.'

Wycliffe agreed though he would not confess it. 'Is there anywhere we can get some lunch?'

They lunched off pasties in Kersey's pub. Old Reynolds was there, well-established behind a pint and a pasty in what was obviously his corner. He looked across at Kersey, raised his glass, and gave him a knowing wink.

Afterwards Wycliffe drove to St Ives and parked in the yard by the police station, which reminded him of another time and another case.* He had a soft spot for St Ives; a little town which had grown out of mining, fishing and Methodism into an integrated community. Now mining was dead and the other two were on shaky legs, but tourism had come to the rescue. The community had taken a battering, but physical aspects of the old town survived, the narrow streets and tiny, stone-built houses; and the street names remained: Bethesda Place, Fish Street, Cat Street, Salubrious Place, Teetotal Street, Virgin Street . . . He was in search of Bethel Street, leading to Skidden Hill.

He found it, and the health shop; it would have been difficult not to find the health shop, the other shops in the street were modest and restrained by comparison. Indeed the one on the opposite corner – called The Modelmakers – looked derelict.

As it happened, the redheaded woman was in the shop. He introduced himself and she looked him up and down with a searching stare which would have detected a single undone button or a refractory gravy stain. 'You'd better come into my office.'

*Wycliffe and the Scapegoat

He was momentarily distracted by the backdrop of sky and sea; the sun was struggling through a mass of dove-grey cloud in an explosion of light. He recovered himself, produced his photograph and laid it on the desk in front of her.

She did not look at it immediately. Perhaps to indicate that this was not a professional interview, perhaps for other reasons, she slipped out of her white coat and hung it in a metal cupboard. Underneath she wore a green silk blouse and a severely tailored skirt. Only when she eventually sat down did she pay any attention to the photograph.

'What do you expect me to say?'

'Whether you recognize the girl, the necklace, or both.'

A pursing of lips. 'I've seen photographs of a similar necklace in the newspapers and on TV recently.'

Wycliffe sat back in his chair. 'Miss Grey, perhaps it was as a result of the publicity given to the necklace that we received this, and unless we succeed in some other way I've no doubt that by publishing this photograph we shall identify the girl.' After a pause he went on, 'Then it could be embarrassing for those who knew her and did not volunteer the information.'

GG played with an expensive looking ball-point. 'Is that a warning? Perhaps a threat?'

'Neither, it is a statement of fact. As far as we know this girl – woman as she must be now – has done nothing wrong, but we need to identify her because the necklace she is wearing in the photograph was found in association with the body of Cochran Wilder.'

She was weakening but not quite ready to give in. 'How does that concern me?'

'Because we know that you and your friends were in the habit of using one of your mother's chalets, the chalet called Sunset Cott, which is nearest to the spot where the body was found. And, in case you were there during the critical weekend, it is natural that we should come to you for any information you may be able to give before the inquiry widens.'

Gobbledegook; but delivered slowly and with significant pauses, it sounded almost menacing. She thought it over, put down the ball-point and straightened the sleeves of her blouse.

'Very well! We agreed that if it went this far we should talk. The truth is—'

Wycliffe interrupted her with intent. 'If I thought you were about to incriminate yourself it would be necessary to warn you.'

A forced laugh. 'Set your mind at rest, Superintendent, there's no risk of that. As I was saying, the truth is that we were at the chalet – a small group of us – during the weekend that Wilder disappeared. We were sixth-formers, within a week or two of our A-level examinations, having a final fling.'

She was watching him through half-closed lids. 'Our parents had been given varying versions of how their offspring intended to spend that weekend, but they wouldn't have approved of the truth – a mixed party of six in a chalet with three double beds.' She treated him to a broad smile. 'I'm not sure what the reactions of parents would be today, but this was fifteen years ago.'

The V-neck of her blouse displayed an area of freckled skin, plague of redheads.

'Did you see anything of Cochran Wilder during your stay at the chalet?'

'I did not; neither as far as I know did any of the others.'

'Presumably you did not admit to being in the chalet at the time because of your parents' attitudes, but what has stopped you coming forward since the discovery of the body?'

She spread her hands. 'We had nothing useful to say. And would you want the indiscretions of your youth put up for public discussion without good reason? We all six of us still live in this neighbourhood; Alan Hart is a doctor, married to Barbara – one of the girls. Paul Drew is an estate agent with a dragon for a wife; Lisa, another of the girls, the one with the necklace, is married to a stuffed-shirt schoolmaster . . . That kind of publicity would do none of them any good, or me. Then there's Julian Angove, the painter.'

Wycliffe noticed that she had slipped in the names, ahead of his questions. She sounded reasonable and she was obviously regaining her confidence which had been temporarily shaken.

'Do you have a copy of the photograph from which this was taken?'

She hesitated. 'No, I think it was a snap taken by Barbara. I must have had a copy but I lost it.'

'Just one other question, Miss Grey. How do you account for a necklace belonging to one of your party being found in the possession of the dead man?'

A slight shrug. 'Do I have to account for it? Surely, that's for Lisa – it was her necklace. But I do know that she lost the thing and made one hell of a fuss about it. Lisa comes from what used to be called a 'good family' and the necklace was a family hand-me-down, an heirloom if you like, given to her on her eighteenth birthday only a few days earlier. She was tedious about it; you would have thought it was part of the crown jewels. And then she went and lost the damn thing in the sandhills. But you'd better talk to her.'

It could all be genuine but Wycliffe had the impression of a very good performance. 'I must ask you for a statement setting out what you have told me, Miss Grey. Of course none of it will be made public unless it proves essential to our inquiry.' Wycliffe was at his starchiest. 'I shall also need a list of the five names you mentioned, the five people who were with you during that weekend.'

'You can have them now.' She reached for a scratch pad and began to write very rapidly. She looked up. 'By the way, unless you want a couple of marital crises on your conscience I suggest that you should be diplomatic in your approach to Lisa Bell – that's her married name – and to Paul Drew.'

She handed him a sheet torn from her pad. 'There you are!'

Perhaps she expected him to get up and go, but he sat on and she began to fidget.

'A lawyer called Penrose – do you know him?'

She immediately settled in her chair. 'You've been listening to gossip, Superintendent.'

'So you do know him?'

'Arnold is my cousin, Mr Wycliffe – his mother is my mother's sister . . . Right? And we've been good friends since we were at school.'

Wycliffe glanced at the list she had given him. 'He wasn't one of the chalet party.'

'No, Arnold went to boarding school but we saw a good deal of each other in the holidays.' She made a sudden gesture of impatience. 'Let's get this out into the open! I enjoy the company of a man, and not always the same one, so I've never married. I'm made that way – promiscuous if you like. I've never tried very hard to cover up the fact. Arnold and I have had an intermittent relationship extending over many years.'

'Presumably he feels the same as you do.'

Her lips pursed. 'Arnold is married with three children.' She broke off. 'Why this interest?'

'Your names were linked in connection with the chalet.'

She smiled. 'Yes, we used to go there at one time.'

Wycliffe stood up. 'Well, thank you for your patience.' He had his hand on the knob of the office door when he paused. 'You live above here?'

'I do. I have a very nice flat. Do you want to see it?'

'Not at the moment, thank you.'

Then he was out in the street, wondering how much he had really learned from the redhead. He crossed the road and found himself staring at the window of the derelict shop. In the window was a model sailing ship, beautifully made, but dusty and neglected, like the shop.

'No dogs, children, or food inside . . .'

A movement in the shop drew his attention. An apparently disembodied head had appeared above the screen at the back of the window. It was the head of an elderly man with sparse grey hair, thin features and a goatee beard. He looked like a desiccated Chinese mandarin. A hand and an arm joined the head, signalling peremptorily that he should come in.

When he reached the door it was open and the man, a wispy little creature wearing sagging trousers and a waistcoat over his shirt, waited for him. 'Come in and let me shut the door!'

The shop was also a workshop. Just inside the door, on shelves, there were models of small sailing craft of every description. Some were complete, finished in their colours and fully rigged, others had been abandoned in various stages of construction.

'Come through.'

The workshop was spacious with a window opening on to a wilderness which had once been a garden.

'Stand in the light where I can see you.'

For some reason Wycliffe obeyed the man and submitted to an inspection. To keep in countenance he said, 'You are Mr . . . ?'

'Badger – Henry Badger. Don't bother to tell me, I know who you are.'

They were standing by a workbench equipped with a great range of small tools in racks, and the centre of the room was taken up by a table on which a large, complex model was under construction. It was not a boat, but a building, of the sort that is on display in the architectural gallery of the Royal Academy and, like everything else there, it was covered in dust and had obviously not been worked on for months, perhaps years.

'That doesn't look like a boat.' Wycliffe, being ponderously jovial.

83

The old man grinned. 'No, I'd call it more of a toyshop. It's the new computer centre for IPF.'

'You take commissions for that sort of thing?'

'It helps to fill the rice bowl. They want to build it on the edge of the New Forest and my model is intended to con the planners into believing that a mega chicken coop can look like a stately home.' He chuckled. 'Plenty of toy trees, that's the secret of architectural models. Of course they never plant 'em when the place is built.'

He looked Wycliffe in the eye as he spoke as though challenging him to mention the accumulated dust but Wycliffe held his peace.

Against one wall there were several shelves stacked with books; books with faded and cracked spines. Wycliffe could never resist other people's bookshelves and he was running his eye over the collection. Books on sailing ships, their history and construction, took up a lot of space but there were also works on history, archaeology and anthropology, and a great many biographies.

Badger said, 'You're interested in books? You read a lot?'

'A fair amount.'

'Biography?'

'I read biography.'

'Not the kitsch stuff from media nonentities, but the lives of real people. Is that right?'

'I suppose so – yes.'

'To find out how they managed it.'

Wycliffe was becoming irritated. 'To find out how who managed what?'

'Living – how other people manage it. Isn't that why you read 'em? I only had to look at you crossing the road to realize you're like me, a man not too sure of himself, always looking over your shoulder, in need of a prop. God knows what made you a policeman! Have you read Holroyd's biography of Augustus John? There's a man for you! I reckon if I'd read something like that when I was a youngster it would have changed my life. You must have the guts to go after what you want and to hell with the consequences.'

Wycliffe had had enough. 'I understood that you wanted to talk to me.'

'I *am* talking to you. Anyway, here's what I have to say: I can't help noticing that your people are taking an interest in the Grey woman. Presumably it's about the finding of young Wilder's body in the dunes. I can't help you with that, but there's something I want you to know. I want you to know that my life may be in danger.' He held up a cautionary finger. 'I don't say that it is, but in case I'm found dead in my shop or my bed one of these days I want you to know that things may not be as simple as they seem to be.' He added after a pause, 'Just that!'

Wycliffe was disturbed; the pale grey eyes were gazing up at him with great earnestness. 'But you must tell me what you are afraid of—'

'I'm not afraid of anything, certainly not of dying. After all, life itself is a terminal illness. Time and chance, Mr Wycliffe. But I don't fancy dying as a cover-up for others.'

'What causes you to feel threatened?'

'That's my business. I'm not asking you to do anything about it; in fact I shall resent any attempt you make to pry into my affairs. All I'm asking is that *if* anything happens to me I shan't be shuffled off to the crematorium with no questions asked.'

'But—'

'There are no buts, sir! You've listened to what I had to say and you'll get no more from me on that subject.'

Wycliffe tried a different tack. 'You live over your shop?'

The old man grinned. 'Some people would say I live in it.'

'You look after yourself?'

'A woman comes in mornings. She does my shopping, cleans the place a bit – not much, as you see. Mostly she fills my freezer with prepared stuff and all I have to do is heat it up.' Another grin. 'I rarely go out by day. I'm a night bird, Mr Wycliffe.'

He was like a mischievous overgrown elf.

'Do you have friends – friends who visit you?'

The old man snapped, 'What's that to do with you?' But he relented. 'There's one chap who comes here, a young fella, Angove – a painter, he calls himself, sells pot-boilers to the tourists. Can't paint, no idea, but he's a bloody fine cartoonist. Won't take it seriously. Damn fool could make a fortune. I'll show you one day if you're still around and I'm in the mood.'

Wycliffe thought that he had seen enough and heard as much as he was likely to. At the door, the old man said, 'Your Grey woman . . . she's mixed up with a lawyer called Penrose.'

'So?'

'Just that Penrose is a shady customer . . . Now you're going to warn me about making that kind of statement, but don't bother. I can look after myself. Just remember what I've said – all of it, mind!'

As he closed the rickety door behind him Wycliffe felt like Alice after her disorientating interview with the contentious caterpillar.

Kersey lit a cigarette. 'Do you believe the Grey woman?'

'No, but they've obviously agreed a story.'

'With a tame lawyer to make sure their lies are plausible.'

'It could be.'

Kersey was reflective. 'I've never known six people hold together on the truth, let alone on a lie. So it's a question of one at a time. Is that what you think, sir?'

'Probably.' Wycliffe looked over GG's list. 'There's one name here which I'm pretty certain was mentioned by Badger as a friend of his – a painter called Angove.'

Kersey reached for the phone book and fluttered the pages. 'Here we are: Angove, Julian, Studio Limbo, The Wharf, St Ives.'

'Sounds promising.'

Kersey referred to the list. 'Paul Drew, Estate Agent – there's an estate agent across the road, Stanton and Drew. I've seen them going in and out. There's a grey-haired type in his sixties, short and sprightly; a girl with a lot of leg who shows most of it; and a six-footer-plus who looks a bit like an owl worked off a battery.'

'How old?'

'Early thirties.'

'Could be our man. Better have a word. According to the Grey woman he's got a dragon for a wife so go warily until we know more than we do now.'

Kersey said, 'How about Old Father Time in the Modelmakers? Do we take him seriously?'

Wycliffe laughed. 'Badger – Henry Badger; somehow it suits him. I must admit that he left me with a very odd impression; there's something about him that makes you feel uncomfortable. Coombes, the local sergeant, seems a dependable sort and he knows his patch. Get him in for a chat and at the same time see what he can tell us about the Grey woman's lawyer friend.'

'Will you be here, sir?'

'No, I'm going to have a look around.'

'Will you be staying overnight?'

'Yes. What's your place like?'

'Comfortable. The food's OK, the beer's drinkable and they've got room; or they did have last night.'

The telephone rang and Wycliffe answered. 'Mrs Bissett on the line, sir.'

The search-button of his memory was engaged for an instant, then he had it: St Germans. 'Put her through.'

Molly Bissett sounded relaxed, and friendly as ever. 'I hope father hasn't prejudiced you too strongly against us Wilders. I want you to do me a favour.'

'If I can.'

'Cocky's funeral is on Saturday morning at eleven. It will be a very quiet affair, just the family – such as it is, and a few close friends. The point is that father will be here all the weekend and I wondered if you would drop in some time. I think you might do him a bit of good. At the moment he's not quite sure what's happening to him and in those circumstances he's always difficult.'

Wycliffe said, 'Of course I will. Would early Saturday evening suit? Say about six?'

'Six o'clock will be fine. And thanks!'

After Wycliffe had left for St Ives, Kersey crossed the road to the estate agent's office. It was raining again: Scotch mist; Cornish drizzle. The leggy girl had a desk to the left of the door and the man had his to the right. Kersey, who despite appearances was house trained, wiped his feet.

'Can I help you, sir?' From the girl, very pert.

Kersey ignored her and turned to the man who had reacted unmistakably to his arrival. 'Mr Drew? Mr Paul Drew?'

Drew pretended to be involved in sorting through some papers and he looked up, unconvincingly surprised. 'Yes?'

Kersey, with his back to the girl, showed his warrant card. 'A routine matter, Mr Drew.'

'What is it?' In a whisper. All colour had drained from the man's face.

'A few minutes chat across the road will probably straighten it out . . . More convenient than here, don't you think?'

'Yes . . . Yes, I'll come over.' And he added in a louder voice, in an attempt to sound normal, 'I shall be glad to help if I can.'

Kersey left, with a derisory smirk at the girl who was all eyes and ears. Back in the Incident Room he waited in the outside office, and just three minutes went by before he saw Drew come out, darting glances about him like a nervous rabbit, and cross the road.

Kersey said to the duty officer, 'Wheel him into the other room, I'll see him there.'

'Mr Drew, sir.'

Drew, apprehensive, took in the features of the little room as though it might prove to be a cell. 'I'm not sure what—'

'Come in and sit down, Mr Drew . . . Cigarette?'

'I don't smoke.' He took off his heavily rimmed spectacles and began to polish them. His eyes looked naked and he blinked rapidly.

Kersey looked at a paper in front of him. 'I've got a little list, Mr Drew, and your name is on it.'

'A list?'

'A list of youngsters who spent a naughty weekend in a beach chalet fifteen years ago. Six of them – three boys and three girls.' Kersey leered.

Drew replaced his spectacles. 'I know what you are talking about but I assure you—'

'That weekend included the Saturday when Cochran Wilder disappeared, and your chalet is close to the spot where his body was recently found—'

'I must insist that—'

Kersey went on, relentless. 'As I was saying, where his body was recently found. The body was naked and it had been deliberately buried in the sand. His clothes and other possessions were buried with him. He seems to have died from a cracked skull due to a blow, not a fall.'

Drew was clasping and unclasping his long bony fingers. 'I assure you, Inspector, that I saw – that *we* saw nothing of Wilder.'

Kersey nodded. 'I know that's what you and your friends have agreed to say.' He shrugged. 'It could even be true, but you must admit it doesn't seem very likely. You are saying that all this went on within a hundred yards of you and none of you saw or heard a thing? What were you doing? Don't tell me! I've got a photo to show you.'

'A photo?'

Kersey passed over the enlargement of the fragment showing the girl with her necklace. 'Recognize her?'

'No . . . well, yes. It's Lisa.' He added in a confiding burst, 'She's married now, to a schoolteacher called Bell.'

'Good! We're coming on. Have you got a copy of the original snap from which this was taken, Mr Drew?'

A momentary hesitation then, 'Yes.'

'We would like to see it. No hurry, just drop it in some time – like later today.' He pushed over his list of names. 'Are these the people who were in that photo?'

Drew took the paper and studied it. 'Yes.'

'Nobody else? Not Cochran Wilder, for example?'

'I've told you he wasn't there. I've told you we *didn't see him*!'

'All right, Mr Drew; no need to get worked up.'

For some time Kersey said nothing; he sat, smoking and watching the other man as though waiting for him to make the next move. Finally Drew reached into his inside pocket and brought out a wallet. From a pocket in the wallet fitted with a zip he produced a photograph about postcard size. It was slightly bent but otherwise undamaged. He passed it to Kersey. 'There you are, you can see for yourself.'

Kersey studied the photograph; it was obvious that the fragment sent to the police had been cut from an identical print. 'Good! We're really making progress, Mr Drew, but there's one thing that still puzzles me: in the photograph Lisa is wearing her necklace, the one that was found with Wilder's body; how did he get hold of it if none of you ever saw him?'

Drew sighed. 'She lost it.'

'Where?'

'How do I know? In the dunes, I suppose. And Wilder must have picked it up.'

Kersey sighed. 'Wilder's last day on earth seems to have been pretty busy.' Abruptly he held up the enlarged fragment showing the girl with her necklace. 'Do you know how we got this? It came to us out of the blue, dropped into our laps, just a bit cut from a print like yours, and we enlarged it. We've no idea who sent it.

Somebody trying to be nasty. Do you get anonymous bits and pieces sent to you like that, Mr Drew, to jog your memory? Mementoes of times past?'

'No.' The word was barely audible.

'All right. Now, we'll just make sure I can put the right names to these faces. No doubt about which is you – you haven't changed all that much in fifteen years . . . And there's Lisa, and the Grey girl, the future Dr Hart . . . Yes, I think I've got them all.' Kersey looked up, 'Well, Mr Drew, thank you for coming over . . .'

'You mean I can go?' Slightly dazed.

'Why not? You haven't done anything that need worry us, have you?'

Kersey saw him off at the outer door. 'They tell me Wilder must have weighed between eleven and twelve stone – not a heavyweight, but quite enough to go carting around the dunes at night, don't you think?'

Given a free choice of somewhere to stay, Kersey was more likely to end up in a pub than a hotel and this time was no exception, but the dining room was at the back of the house, away from the bar, and opened on to a little courtyard garden where a tortoise chewed away at lettuce leaves watched by a bored ginger cat. There were only four tables and they had the place to themselves. But Wycliffe was moody and Kersey was mildly anxious.

'Will this do you, sir? I know it's a bit basic. We get the same food as the family. Last night it was a lamb stew, tonight it's beef steak and kidney pie. The landlady is a good cook.'

The landlady herself served them with two portions of the pie on heated plates and a large dish of mixed vegetables to share. Her voice was rich and creamy, with a lilt. 'Now eat it all up! It's a lovely bit of steak and I didn't buy it to feed to the dog. Whatever you want to drink they'll bring from the bar.'

They helped themselves to vegetables and Kersey brought him up to date on the Drew interview.

Wycliffe listened and studied the photograph. In the end he said, 'As you thought, there's something wrong in all this, Doug. Whoever sent us that bit cut from the snapshot had access to a print like this, and they also had a grudge against the girl with the necklace, and probably against the others in the group as well.'

'So?'

'I wish I knew. Now you tell me you think Drew has been getting similar reminders – in other words that he's open to blackmail.'

'Yes, I do. I tried out the idea at random and the shot went home. No doubt about that. Drew is running scared; if he isn't actually being blackmailed, he thinks he's threatened. I suppose that could apply to the others as well.'

Wycliffe laid down his fork. 'But it doesn't make sense. Assume that this group of youngsters really was criminally involved in Wilder's death and that somebody has a spot of blackmail in mind – they would all be pretty vulnerable. But why bring us into it? A blackmailer would be as anxious as his victims to keep us out.'

Kersey nodded. 'There's something in that. Could it be that there's a third party in the know? . . . You're not eating . . . Try some of these carrots. They're good . . .'

But Wycliffe was not deflected. 'Now that there is some movement we need more people on the ground. We need statements from all six in the group and we need to know more about them, their backgrounds and their relationships. Some of this is tailormade for Lucy Lane but we shall need a couple of DCs as well. I'll fix that for the morning . . . By the way, have you had that chat with the local sergeant yet? – What's his name? – Coombes?'

'Not yet.'

'Then get him into the Incident Room first thing and we'll talk to him together.'

Kersey was secretly amused by the sudden invigoration of his chief. 'Anything else?'

'Yes, find out the present owner of that chalet. Now we know that it is where the six of them stayed and we have some grounds for suspecting that the crime might have taken place there, it's reasonable to give the place a going over.'

'Fox?'

Wycliffe hesitated. 'In the first instance, but if he finds anything we'd better bring in Forensic.'

'You think they'll find anything after fifteen years?'

Wycliffe was edgy. 'If not we'd better bring in the archaeologists; they seem able to tell us what Iron Age man had for breakfast. But whether they find anything or not, if this ever comes to court, how shall we look if we ignore the probable scene of the crime?'

They finished their meal almost in silence and Wycliffe crossed to the Incident Room to do some telephoning before setting out on his evening jaunt; that ritual which was part of being away from home.

There were few people about and cars were parked along the kerb. With more than an hour of daylight left he wanted to take his own look at the area where the body was found and at the chalet with the steps. A single flying visit had done little to give him the sense of place to which he attached so much importance.

He drove along Commercial Road, deciding that Hayle was a one-off, with a quirky appeal – an opinion confirmed almost at once by two shop signs: a DIY store called the Jolly Bodger and Jungle Herbert's Reptiles and Amphibians. Add those to a pub called the Bucket of Blood!

He made his way around the Pool by the Black Bridge (built from copper-smelting slag) and up Phillack Hill to the village.

The rain had gone but a mist had closed in to eddy and swirl over the valley so that one moment he saw the town on the other side, and the next he didn't. But Phillack Church, its pub, and its cottages were serene in evening sunshine. As he drove, Wycliffe carried in his thoughts and in his pocket, the print which Paul Drew had given to Kersey.

He found the clearing where he had parked on his first visit and soon he was among the chalets. On that other visit he had not singled out any particular chalet; now his only interest was in the one with a veranda and a flight of steps. When he found it, he was struck by its comparative isolation and by the fact that it was the nearest to where the body was found. Built of lapped planks, it was raised on brick piers, and a flight of twelve steps – he counted them – led up to the veranda.

He looked at his photograph. There they were, the six young people who, fifteen years ago, had somehow been in at the start of the Wilder case. And there in the background were the brick piers supporting the chalet, and the first few steps.

An ordinary group of youngsters in their late teens, they might have come from a sixth form anywhere and there was nothing to suggest that within the next few hours they would become involved in a sordid crime.

With the help of Kersey's briefing he could now put names to all the faces: the Grey girl, of course, and next to her, Julian, now a painter and friend of the Badger. The painter looked at the camera with a tolerant grin; probably the joker in the pack . . . And there was Lisa with her necklace, and next to her, the solemn-faced, bespectacled, Paul Drew . . . The plump fair girl wearing a blue T-shirt was Barbara, sitting next to Alan Hart, her future husband.

In the late afternoon or early evening of that Saturday Mace would arrive in search of Wilder. He would speak to Barbara – from his description it could only have been her.

'She was on the way up the steps . . . I spoke to her and asked her if she had seen anything of Cochran . . .'

'So this chalet was definitely occupied?'

'It must have been; there was pop music coming from inside.'

Wycliffe climbed the steps to the veranda. It ran the whole length of the little building and from it he could look into the living room and one of the bedrooms. With his arms resting on the rail he took in the view and experienced one of those moments when he regretted having given up his pipe. The mist was confined to the estuary, leaving the sea a vast silvery plain, and the sky above St Ives was barred with clouds, touched with gold by the sun which had already set.

Could he construct a scenario for the events of fifteen years ago?

Wilder, on his imposed coast walk, having shaken off his minder, arrives in the late evening and strikes up an acquaintance with the group. Not much older than they, but more experienced and worldly wise, he impresses them. He's good company. They offer him a bed on the floor for the night . . .

But then comes the gap – more a yawning gulf, for some hours later (if the indications were to be credited) these same young people are carrying Wilder's dead and naked body, wrapped in a sheet, through the dunes and away from the chalet. In the bare sand of the foredunes they will dig a grave, and in that grave they will bury the young man's body along with his clothes and his rucksack.

And, presumably, on Monday morning they were back at school, facing the run-up to their A-levels.

Was that by any stretch of the imagination credible? Group behaviour amongst young people is always less predictable and often more violent than is the case with individuals. 'The group so easily becomes the gang.' The policeman talking. But then he tried to recall his own children as adolescents; the twins, Ruth and David. They were contemporaries of the youngsters in the chalet. The thought set him wondering . . . In retrospect the twins seemed to have led a more or less placid existence, a cycle of school, homework, television, a Saturday-night disco, a weekend with friends . . . But what had he or Helen really known about them? They had been as enigmatic as they were apparently amenable. Had the parents of these youngsters seen them differently?

He could not have said how long he remained there, arms resting on the veranda rail, staring at nothing, but quite suddenly he was aware of St Ives as a mound of twinkling lights against a darkening sky.

Time he got back. Something, perhaps his copper-on-the-beat training, made him try the door of the chalet before he left and, at a slight push, it opened into the seemingly impenetrable darkness of the living room.

Damn! How often had he told himself that he should carry a pocket torch?

But even in the light there was he could see the raw wood where the flimsy door had been forced. It wouldn't have taken much; a screwdriver, even a stout knife, could have done it.

He felt for a wall switch, found and flicked it, but nothing happened. Who would leave the power on in an empty chalet? But his eyes were beginning to accommodate to the darkness and he could distinguish the sofa, the table and a couple of chairs which happened to be near the window. As a pipe smoker he had once carried matches and a lighter; not now.

It was possible that this was no more than a random break-in; equally possible that the break-in was connected with his case; and here he was blundering about in the darkness. Common sense told him to return to his car and call out the troops; have the place made secure, then let Fox loose in the morning. But he could now see the door into what was presumably the kitchen, and it was open. Curiosity killed the cat.

Two or three steps, and he was standing inside the doorway; he could see the outline of the kitchen window, a sink with a gleaming tap, and there was a glass panel, presumably in the back door. That was as far as he got; he was aware of a swift movement close at hand, followed at once by a blow to the back of his head. He tottered forward, coming down heavily on his hands and knees. He did not lose consciousness but he was dazed. He heard something clatter to the floor, running footsteps, then someone almost slithering down the steps outside, followed by silence.

He picked himself up, his head was sore and throbbing and he felt queasy. He had been wearing his hat, otherwise he wouldn't now be on his feet, feeling sorry for himself. It was a minute or two before he began cursing himself for a fool.

He made for the front door and stood, supporting himself on the veranda rail. St Ives looked the same as it had done a minute or two earlier, twinkling away, remote and indifferent. He practised deep breathing and it helped; at least the nausea was passing off; but his head hurt and he felt fragile. After a while he went down the steps, clinging to the handrail.

By the time he reached his car and clumped into the driving seat the worst seemed to be over. On the car phone he spoke to the St Ives' nick. An hour or two later and the smaller stations would have shut up shop for the night, and he would have been telling his tale to a desk sergeant at Division, to be stored away and embroidered, a good in-house story for the boys.

The thought was salutary. For the moment, he would tell no-one of the attack. He would report the break-in and arrange for the place to be under observation until it was made secure. He decided that he was well enough to drive back to the pub; and he did, with such circumspection that he was unlikely to attract the attention of any marauding patrol crew hoping for a driving drunk to break the monotony.

Kersey was in the bar. 'Are you all right? You look awful. What you need is a stiff whisky.'

'What I need is bed.'

He made his usual good-night call to Helen from a little booth off the bar and contrived to sound almost normal.

'How's Ruth?'

'No different from when you saw her this morning.' Helen seemed amused.

'David hasn't phoned?'

'No. We had a letter on Tuesday.'

'Yes, of course . . .'

He went to bed with a couple of diazepams, kept for emergencies, and after a prolonged struggle to find a comfortable position where his head didn't hurt, he slept.

Barbara came into the lounge where Alan was watching television. She looked tired – near the end of her tether. He thought: this bloody business is getting her down. He patted the settee beside him. 'Do come and sit down, love.'

'I can't, Daniel has woken up. Will you go up to him?'

He was halfway up the stairs when the telephone rang. There was one in the hall, so he took it there. 'Dr Hart speaking.'

It was Paul Drew, very excited. 'I'm in a phone box; I must see you, Alan. I haven't been home; I can't face Alice . . .'

'Have you been drinking?'

'No, but I can't go through the night without talking to somebody. I've been questioned . . . They know . . . They're just playing with us and I've done something terrible . . . You've got to help me.'

'Be at the surgery in ten minutes . . . All right?'

'I've been to the bloody surgery and it's all locked up.'

'Just be there! And for God's sake, calm down!'

Barbara had come into the hall. 'Trouble?'

'A patient. Sounds drunk to me but I'd better take a look at him.'

He was gone for the better part of two hours and Barbara was anxious.

'What happened?'

'The man is a bloody nuisance.'

98

'Who was it?'

'Just a patient; you wouldn't know him.'

Henry Badger was finishing his evening meal; a fish pie from the freezer which he had heated in the oven. With it he had drunk a couple of glasses of moselle, his regular tipple, and read a few pages of Fiona MacCarthy's biography of Eric Gill, sculptor and craftsman; another man who fascinated him. Such books had become his addictive tranquillizer, his literary Valium. He read and reread them as the devout read their sacred texts. But this evening the prescription had failed him; he remained uneasy, deeply troubled within himself.

Sometimes he wondered if he was going queer in the head. He would do things on the spur of the moment, silly things, for no apparent reason. Talking to that policeman was only the latest example; he had called him in off the street and said certain things . . . At such times he experienced an overwhelming need to be noticed; he would strive to be interesting, to say things that sounded dramatic, though they were rarely more than half-truths if not total fabrications. It could be dangerous.

But more worrying still, as time went on he seemed less able to distinguish between actual events and the fictions of his mind, between his dreams and his waking experience. He felt that he was getting out of step with life around him, becoming a stranger to normality. Had he reached that stage which the mealy-mouthed call confused?

He told himself that he was old and that he was alone. There was no cure for old age but finding company would have presented no problem. The truth was that generally he preferred to be alone but, as with everything else, there was a price to be paid.

The percolator had completed its vulgar repertoire; he poured himself a cup of strong black coffee and took it into his workshop and stood over the half-finished model. Not only was there dust, but a spider had spun its web between two of the skeletal struts. The web was perfect; a structure which in design, execution and sheer beauty should shame every architect and structural engineer. He reached out a hand to brush it away, then shook his head and let it be. He sipped his coffee and muttered to himself, 'They must've built the bloody thing by now.'

With no clear intention, he returned to the kitchen and climbed the stairs to the next floor. On the landing he switched on the light, a dim bulb coated with grime. Three doors stood open, one to his bedroom and an unmade double bed, another to a sitting room which had only been used during the brief period of his marriage, and the third to his bathroom and WC. There was an all-pervasive sour smell which he had lived with for so long that he was unaware of it.

Another flight of even narrower stairs led up from the landing to an attic; the door of the attic was immediately at the top of the stairs so that he had to stand on the top step to open it. The woman who looked after him was never allowed upstairs.

He entered the attic room and switched on the lights, two bulbs high in the rafters. The room, with its sloping roof, dwarf walls and dormer window, was large. Through the grimy panes of the window, Godrevy lighthouse flashed its warning out to sea, and away to his left half the town glittered under the night sky. There was a desk and chair by the window and a wooden filing cabinet stood against one wall, with a cupboard next to it. Much of the rest of the wall space was taken up by bookshelves and framed drawings.

Badger spent some time choosing a book from the hundreds on the shelves and having made his choice he carried it to the desk. Next, he unlocked the cupboard with a key from his pocket. The shelves were stacked solid with old magazines but in the bottom of the cupboard there were several bottles. Badger took one of them and cradled it in his hands for a moment or two before placing it on the desk by the book. The whole procedure had the appearance of a well-rehearsed ritual. An electric radiator placed near the desk was switched on, and he brought out a brandy goblet from one of the desk drawers.

Minutes went by before he was settled. He rolled the goblet between his hands; then came the first sip. He read a few words; another sip; a few more words, and a sense of calm began to take possession of his mind as the warmth spread through his body.

Chapter Five

Friday, 15 May

In the morning Wycliffe had a dull ache at the back of his skull and a nasty bump to show for it. Over breakfast he gave Kersey an unvarnished account of his performance in the chalet. 'I was a fool. The man had broken in at the front and was in the kitchen when I blundered in. He couldn't get out that way without making a row because the back door was locked; he was trapped and I walked right into it.'

Kersey said, 'You still look pretty groggy. Surely you should see a doctor?'

'I intend to. I'm going to phone Dr Alan Hart and ask for an appointment.'

'That should be interesting. And the case aspect?'

'The local chaps will have informed the present owner of the chalet. We must get Fox out there and see what sort of tale he has to tell.'

'You saw nothing of the guy who attacked you? Got no impression at all?'

Wycliffe felt as moronic as the average witness appears to be. 'No, I did not!' With finality. 'But I'll tell you this, Doug, I don't like being hit on the head and I want to know where each of our precious six was last evening between nine and ten.'

'Could it have been a woman?'

This set Wycliffe wondering again. 'I don't think so . . . No! The footsteps were those of a man. So let's say we need to know where the three men were – at least, where they claim to have been.' And a moment later he added, 'You can leave Hart to me. But apart from all that, this fellow, whoever he was, must have walked or driven there, and the road to the towans at this time of year isn't exactly the M25. He or his car must have been seen. Get somebody on to it.'

After a meagre breakfast but with more coffee than was good for him, he telephoned the doctor.

'Dr Hart?'

'Speaking.'

Wycliffe introduced himself. 'I have acquired a nasty bump on the head and I shall be most grateful for your opinion.'

Did that sound as ambiguous as was intended? At any rate Hart took a while to digest it, then, 'I could see you at nine o'clock. My surgery is just off Island Square.' Click. Not exactly a warm reception.

Wycliffe drove into St Ives and found the surgery without difficulty, a stone-built cottage which had been gutted inside and extended at the back. He was not kept waiting. The receptionist said, 'Dr Hart will see you now.'

The surgery did not look out on to anything, and the window was fitted with hammered glass panes. Hart left his chair to stand over his patient. He was tall and fairly heavily built, but his hands were long and slender, the fingers eminently tactile. They investigated the back of Wycliffe's skull.

'Ah, yes. As you say, a nasty bump. How did you manage to hit yourself there?'

'I didn't. Somebody did it for me.'

'Really?' No obvious interest. The fingers continued to explore his skull and neck.

Wycliffe said, 'I think you must know the place where it happened, Doctor, a chalet, called Sunset Cott, on the towans.'

'No sign of an extradural haemorrhage . . . Headache?'

'Yes, but it's going off. Last evening, quite by chance, I discovered that the place had been broken into. Foolishly, I tried to investigate in the dark and I was attacked.'

'We had better take a look at your pupils. Open your eyes wide and look at the light . . . An almost normal pupillary reflex. Did you get a look at this chap who attacked you?'

'Unfortunately, no.'

'Pity! Strictly speaking I should tell you to have the day in bed but I suspect that would be a waste of my breath. It won't hurt to take an aspirin or two if the headache troubles you, but no alcohol, at least until tomorrow.'

'Where were you say, after nine o'clock yesterday evening, Doctor?'

Hart had returned to his chair and he greeted the question with an uncertain smile. 'I am becoming confused as to which of us is exercising his professional skills in this consultation, Mr Wycliffe. However, until well after ten o'clock I was here, dealing with some of the paperwork we have to cope with these days. After that I was at home. Now, I'm afraid I have calls to make before my regular surgery . . . If you will be good enough to fill in the form my receptionist will give you—'

'Thank you, Doctor.' But Wycliffe did not move. 'As you know, I am investigating the death of Cochran Wilder. We have established that at the time of his disappearance you, and five of your fellow sixth-formers, were occupying the chalet close to where his body was found.'

'So?' Hart's face was expressionless.

Wycliffe ignored the question. 'You will also know that a necklace belonging to one of the girls in the party was found with the body and that is a link which requires explanation.'

Hart would have interrupted again but Wycliffe pressed on. 'In the circumstances I shall need formal statements from the six people involved concerning the events of that weekend.'

For some reason Hart was mollified. 'I see. Well, provided there is confidentiality, I am prepared to go along with that though I'm afraid I have nothing to tell you that you do not already know.'

'At least there will be a record. I will arrange it for some time this afternoon at the local police station. One of my officers will contact you.'

The doctor shuffled the papers on his desk, his manner more diffident. 'There is just one thing. As you probably know, my wife was one of the girls in that party. At present she is pregnant and inclined to be emotional and I cannot consent to her being interviewed.'

Wycliffe nodded. 'I don't think we need insist at this stage.'

Hart was getting up from his chair. 'Now, Mr Wycliffe, I really must ask you . . .'

Wycliffe still did not move. 'I won't keep you long but there is just one other matter; I would like your opinion on a medical question which has some bearing on my case.'

Hart sat down again. 'Yes?' His manner was discouraging.

'I see from the psychiatric reports of the time that, although he was so young, Wilder was diagnosed as a manic-depressive.'

'Indeed?'

'I've read somewhere that during a manic episode when the subject may seem to be expansive and convivial, the life and soul of the party in fact, a trifling frustration may provoke a disproportionate response; aggression, and even violence. Would you say that is broadly true?'

The grey eyes were wary. 'I am not a psychiatrist, Mr Wycliffe.'

'No, but I'm sure that your experience must have brought you into touch with such cases.'

A pause, then, 'Very well. What you say is, I believe, characteristic of the disorder in certain of its forms.'

When Wycliffe had gone Hart continued sitting at his desk and for the first time since the discovery of Wilder's body he experienced real fear, an emptiness inside, and with it a feeling of helplessness, almost of resignation. Drew, idiot though he was, had been right. They knew. The policeman had been sure of his ground and at the right moment, a moment of his choosing . . . That cretin had played into their hands by breaking into the bloody chalet!

He dialled Drew's office. 'I'm sorry, Mr Drew is not in today . . . He's unwell . . . If you would like to leave a message, or speak to our senior partner, Mr Stanton . . .' Hart replaced his phone and sat for a while staring at it before trying again. This time he looked up and dialled Drew's home number. 'Mrs Drew? . . . I wonder if your husband is available? This is Dr Hart speaking.'

A slightly cracked voice, resolutely refined. 'I'm sorry, Doctor, but he is not at home. Could I take a message?'

Hart hesitated, wary of creating domestic strife, but there were more important things at stake. 'I'm anxious to get in touch with him and they told me at his office that he was unwell.'

There was silence at the other end for a while, then, 'I told them that. I didn't know what else to say.'

'*Is* he ill?'

She answered, aggression beginning to surface, 'I don't know whether he's ill or not, Doctor. I don't even know where he is. I'm ashamed to admit it, but that's the truth!' The veneer was cracking. 'He came in yesterday evening, late, looking and behaving very oddly. I've never seen him like it before . . . Never! It was intolerable! . . . I know that you are one of his friends so I suppose I can talk to you. He said that he was going straight to bed but half an hour later I heard the car moving out of the drive, and he was gone . . . He must have crept downstairs like a . . . like a *thief*! And I haven't seen him since. I can't believe—'

Hart cut her short. 'Did he take anything with him? Clothes? Money?'

She snapped, 'I don't *know* what he's taken. I haven't looked!'

'I think we should talk, Mrs Drew; I may be able to help. If I called at the house within the next hour?'

After sitting and staring at nothing for a while, Hart dialled another number. 'Is that you, Julian? . . . This is Alan Hart. I'm coming round . . .'

The painter said, 'To what do I owe this distinction?'

Hart snapped, 'Don't play the bloody fool! You know what this is about and it's serious.'

When Wycliffe arrived at the Incident Room, Kersey and Coombes were standing looking up at the print of Armageddon, and as he joined them Coombes was saying, 'The second coming. The ones who put this up were a queer lot, but I suppose it's nice to have something to look forward to.'

Kersey reported, 'Coombes has got one of his chaps out at the chalet, sir, and Fox is due with Lucy and a couple of DCs at about eleven.'

'How about the owner of the chalet?'

'No problem there. The woman who owns it has recently lost her husband and she's got other things to think about. She says we can do what we like provided we make good any damage.'

Wycliffe's head still ached but he concentrated his wits and tried to recall the questions he wanted to put to Coombes. 'This chap Badger, at the Modelmakers in St Ives – do you know him?'

Coombes grinned. 'Who doesn't? He and his shop are part of the scenery.'

'He doesn't seem anxious for custom.'

'Certainly not over the counter. I don't know how things are now but at one time he used to sell most of his ship models through an agent in London, and he also made models of buildings for architects. I've heard that he was an architect himself once.'

It was a fine morning and the sun was striking through the window. Coombes ran a finger round inside his collar. 'But whatever he does or doesn't do I don't think the bailiffs will be troubling him. It was before my time here but while he was still a youngish man he married a widow, and not too long afterwards she died leaving him a nice bit of property and money to go with it. As far as I know he's never been much of a spender.'

'A local man?'

'The Badgers were local. He had two sisters; one married Penrose, the lawyer – the present one's father. She lives with her son and his family here in town. The other sister is the one who owned the chalets – Mrs Grey, mother of the health shop woman. She moved up north when they sold up in Camborne.'

'So Badger is uncle to Arnold Penrose and to the Grey woman in the health shop?'

Kersey took his cue from Wycliffe. 'Any idea what relations are like between uncle and nephew?'

Coombes looked blank. 'All right as far as I know. I've never heard anything different. Of course the old boy must be a bit of a problem. He's come near to being in trouble with us from time to time.'

'What for?'

Coombes spread his hands. 'Being a bloody nuisance about sums it up, sir. He gets ideas into his head – takes against people and harasses them, sends them threatening letters accusing them of taking bits of his land or of tipping rubbish on it. Once or twice he's written what you might call poison-pen letters to councillors about alleged backstair deals in planning . . . So far Penrose has managed to keep his uncle out of court but it can't have been easy.'

Wycliffe said, 'Badger told me he feels his life might be in danger. Does that surprise you?'

The sergeant hesitated. 'I'm not surprised that he said it.'

'But you think it's all in his imagination. On the other

hand, if he turns up with his throat cut tomorrow morning we mustn't blame you.'

'You put that very well, sir.'

Wycliffe tried again. 'Badger made sure I knew that Penrose was, as he put it, "mixed up" with the Grey woman and he went out of his way to warn me that Penrose was a shady customer. Any comment on that?'

Coombes grinned broadly. 'You're putting me on the spot, sir. It's all more or less in keeping with what we know of the old boy. Penrose inherited a good practice from his father and he seems a good lawyer. Of course there's gossip about him and his cousin – the redhead in the health shop; and I reckon he must have his problems with his posh house, expensive wife and three kids, but I suppose mother pays her way, and probably a bit more.'

Wycliffe said, 'You evidently know your patch. Just one more thing; I want to get some contemporary background on the chalet party, the six when they were teenagers. Any idea what school they would have gone to?'

'Sure to have been John Harvey's, sir. It used to be a grammar school, now it's a comprehensive.'

'Good. That's it then. I want your chaps to keep an eye on the Modelmakers in a general way, and let me know of anything that comes up in connection with the six who seem to be concerned in all this.'

The telephone rang and Wycliffe picked it up. 'Mr Arnold Penrose would like to speak to you, sir.'

Wycliffe said, 'Talk of the devil. Put him through.'

'Mr Wycliffe? . . . Arnold Penrose, Penrose and Son, Solicitors . . . I wondered if I might call at your office for a word – some time this morning . . .'

Wycliffe said, 'I shall be in St Ives later on; it would be more convenient for me to call on you . . . Shall we say about midday?' He put down the phone. 'Penrose seems bothered. Worried about his girlfriend?'

* * *

At shortly before eleven, Lucy Lane arrived with two DCs – the over-weight Potter, and Iris Thorn, a recent transfer from Traffic. Thorn was black, tall and slender, with a calm bearing and a serene expression. A smile seemed to play constantly around her lips, but her colleagues had already discovered that she was not always amused.

On Wycliffe's instructions Lucy Lane had brought with her the necklace, still in its polythene bag, but now officially logged.

Fox, in the Scenes-of-Crime van with Collis, his apparently willing serf, had gone directly to the chalet.

In the little office Wycliffe and Kersey brought Lucy Lane up to date and Wycliffe summed up, 'It seems clear that the six young people who stayed at the chalet during the weekend Wilder disappeared were in some degree involved in his death and that it was they who buried him with his belongings in the sand.

'But that's a very different matter from framing charges and formulating a case which would stand up in court. The six are now adult, almost certainly advised by a lawyer and fully aware of their rights. So we start with their versions of the story on paper. That means formal statements from five of the six. The doctor's wife is pregnant, so leave her out for the moment.'

Wycliffe massaged the back of his skull and decided to treat himself to a couple of aspirins before seeing Penrose.

'In addition, I think we should know more about the background of those six teenagers, and their school might be the place to start.' He turned to Kersey, 'That's all work for the DCs but I want you to talk to the painter and Lucy can pay a visit to Lisa Bell – after she's been with me to see Penrose. Show her the necklace, Lucy, get her to identify it, and see what else you can get. No pressure until we are more sure of our ground.'

Wycliffe was pleased to have Lucy Lane in his immediate team again. He could not have identified the particular gap which seemed to exist when she wasn't at hand on a case but whatever it was, she filled it. It was the same with Helen when he was at home. Perhaps it was that particular brand of female logic which is more direct, with fewer reservations and conditional clauses than the male brand.

Lucy drove him to St Ives; they left the car in front of the police station and walked down to the Wharf. The sun shone out of a cloudless sky and the tide was spreading over the yellow sand of the harbour where many of the craft now grounded would be afloat within the hour.

Wycliffe pointed out Studio Limbo as they passed, wedged between a café and a gift shop.

'Julian, the painter,' Lucy said, as though responding to a catechism.

A door next to an arcade of small shops carried a worn brass plate: 'Penrose and Son, Solicitors and Commissioners for Oaths', and a small notice beside it read, 'Please ring and walk up'.

At the top of the stairs on a carpeted landing a young blonde sat behind a desk, her fingers pecking away at the keys of a word processor. 'Can I help you?' And then, 'I'll see if he's free.'

Almost at once Penrose came out of one of the offices, hand held out, his features creased in a broad smile. To Wycliffe's surprise he was plump, almost rotund and slightly balding. No Romeo.

'A pleasure to meet you, Chief Superintendent. Of course I hear a lot about you in legal circles . . .'

To which the correct reply would have been, 'Some of it good, I hope!' But Wycliffe didn't speak the language. He introduced Lucy Lane.

'Do come in . . . Do come in!'

The office overlooked the harbour, now seen through slatted blinds.

Seated, Wycliffe said, 'You wanted to talk to me.'

Penrose ran a hand through his dark, thinning curls

then straightened some files on his desk. 'This is difficult.'

'I presume that it has some connection with the discovery of Cochran Wilder's body in the sandhills.'

Penrose smiled an uneasy smile. 'Yes. What absurd names some parents wish on their children! One is inclined to wonder what effect a name like that might have had on the poor boy's future.' A throat clearing. 'Yes, well, you will understand, Mr Wycliffe, that I have no official standing in the matter. It just happens that your inquiries have involved people who are friends of mine and I thought that a little chat might be useful to them and perhaps to you.'

Wycliffe let in a cold draught. 'I assume that your friends are among the six people who, fifteen years ago, during the weekend that Wilder disappeared, were occupying the chalet nearest to where his body was recently found.'

Penrose studied the superintendent for a moment or two before saying, 'I suppose you could put it that way.'

'But you don't represent these people professionally?'

'No.'

'So, presumably you have some information which you think might be helpful?'

Things were not going the way Penrose had hoped; the atmosphere was decidedly chilly. He drummed on the desk-top with his finger tips. 'I should make it clear that I am only anxious to see your inquiry brought to a speedy conclusion so that my friends can get on with their lives without this cloud hanging over them. Although I am naturally concerned for my friends, I have good reason to believe that all six of those involved are in a similar position.'

'So what position is that?'

The telephone rang and irritably Penrose reached for the receiver. 'No calls, Delia!' He turned again to Wycliffe. 'You are not making it easy for me, Mr Wycliffe. However, I intended to be helpful and I shall be.' There was a pause while he studied his chubby hands which looked as soft and tender as a young girl's. 'As you might expect, these people, some of them well known in the district, are embarrassed by your inquiries, and their situation is being aggravated by anonymous communications.'

'What sort of communications? Abusive? Threatening?'

'Judge for yourself.' Penrose took an envelope from a drawer and passed it over. The envelope was unsealed and Wycliffe slipped its contents on to the desk-top – two plain postcards. Both were stamped and franked, and addressed on a typewriter to Miss Gillian Grey, The Health Shop, Bethel Street, St Ives. On the correspondence side of the first card was an outline map of a stretch of coastline with an arrow indicating a certain point, and on the other card was a question, again in type, 'Who killed the Cock?' followed by, 'I shall keep in touch.'

Penrose said, 'I know that four of the others have received similar cards. Julian Angove, the painter, has refused to say one way or the other.'

Wycliffe, still holding the cards, said, 'There appears to be no suggestion of blackmail.'

'How could there be without evidence of guilt? And there can be no such evidence because there is no guilt. I mean, who could believe that these six young people . . .' The plump hands were dismissive. 'It would be too absurd! . . . All the same, Mr Wycliffe, you must agree that communications of this sort, on top of your inquiries, are bound to be very disturbing to people with professional responsibilities in the district.'

Lucy Lane had watched and listened but Wycliffe had refrained from giving her any cue to intervene. Evidently she was there to observe, so observe she did and came to the obvious conclusion that Wycliffe was deliberately pushing the lawyer off balance.

Wycliffe held up the cards. 'I may keep these?' Polite.

'Of course.'

Wycliffe slid them into the envelope and put the envelope in his pocket. He took his time about it and all the while his eyes never left the lawyer's. Finally he said, 'Do you have any idea who might have sent these, Mr Penrose?'

'Certainly not!'

There was an uneasy silence during which they could hear people talking on the Wharf below. Abruptly Wycliffe changed his manner, becoming conversational as though the business of the visit was over. 'The other day I was in that extraordinary shop – opposite where your Miss Grey has her premises. It's run by an elderly man called Badger. Odd sort of chap, eccentric, but obviously very intelligent. Did I hear that he's a relative of yours?'

Penrose did not relax; if anything he seemed troubled by the change of topic. 'Henry Badger is my uncle, my mother's brother. As you say, he's an eccentric.'

'I was impressed by his miniature ship models, and by the architectural model he is building.' Wycliffe sounded chatty.

A forced laugh. 'The IPF computer centre. He hasn't touched it for years and the place is probably built by now. That was his last commission and he never finished it.'

'Obviously a very skilled man.'

'Yes, he trained as an architect, but at heart he was a craftsman and he had considerable talent. Unfortunately he gave up work quite suddenly, almost from one day to the next. I've no idea why.'

Wycliffe said, 'He seems to be something of a recluse; he told me that he rarely goes out by day and that he lives alone with just a woman coming in for an hour or two, mainly to do his shopping.'

Penrose nodded. 'That's quite true and it seems to be as he wants it. But occasionally, for two or three days together, he will lock himself in and see nobody, not even the woman who is supposed to look after him. At least I assume that he locks himself in, but I suppose it's possible that he goes away. But where would he go? Anyway, it can be very awkward. If he is there he doesn't even answer the phone.'

Wycliffe was tentative. 'I believe you've had problems with him writing letters – letters which could have led to legal complications.'

'Letters which did lead to legal complications though I was able to avoid the courts. But I see your drift, Mr Wycliffe; for a moment I was beginning to think that we were just chatting about a difficult relative. I should have known. You are hinting at the possibility that he might be responsible for these cards.'

'Is it a possibility?'

Penrose played with the cord of his telephone. 'I think it's very unlikely. I can't imagine why he should feel animosity towards the people concerned. On the other hand, if there is the slightest chance of such a thing I shall be glad of a little time to look into the matter.'

'Does he own a typewriter?'

'A typewriter? Oh, I see what you mean. I couldn't say for certain but I shouldn't think he'd give such a thing houseroom – he's always prided himself on his calligraphy.'

Wycliffe had not quite finished. 'There is, of course, another difficulty: how could your uncle have got hold of the information that these young people were occupying the chalet at the time Wilder disappeared?'

Penrose nodded, thoughtful. 'That *is* a point, certainly. On the other hand, I have to admit that it may not be an insurmountable one. You see, Julian Angove, one of the six, is a regular visitor at the Modelmakers – almost the only one. I've never understood the nature of the attraction, unless it's a common tendency to make mischief.'

Wycliffe seemed satisfied. 'Very well, Mr Penrose; I think we understand each other.'

As Wycliffe was on the point of leaving he said casually, 'Oh, perhaps I should tell you that there's been a break-in at the chalet – Sunset Cott. I was out there yesterday evening and I found that the door had been forced. I was foolish enough to investigate in the dark and I collected a blow to the back of my head.'

Penrose appeared genuinely shocked, and it was a moment or two before he said, 'I'm very sorry to hear that. Of course there has been a good deal of vandalism and some trouble with dossers out there recently. I hope it's nothing serious?'

'Oh, no. Dr Hart thinks I shall live.'

When they were once more out on the Wharf Lucy said, 'You made a contest of that, sir; but not knowing the rules of the game it was difficult to follow. Was it chess, or snakes and ladders?'

Wycliffe growled, 'I haven't made up my mind myself.'

'Do you think your Modelmaker man is harassing these people, sir?'

Your Modelmaker. For Lucy, and almost certainly for Kersey, Badger had become his private property, a fringe character who happened to have caught his imagination. He passed Lucy's question back. 'Do you?'

Lucy gave up and they ambled along the Wharf with the visitors.

They reached the painter's studio and Wycliffe hesitated.

'Are you going in?'

Another pause then, 'No, I think we'll leave him to Mr Kersey.'

They arrived at the lifeboat station and Wycliffe stopped again. 'Now you can go along to see Lisa Bell. As I said, tackle her about the necklace but don't put her under too much pressure, just get her talking.'

'But the Bells live in Carbis Bay; will you drop me off?'

'No. You take the car and I'll get a patrol car to run me back.'

When Lucy had gone, instead of turning up the hill to the town, Wycliffe followed the footpath past the public toilets along the border of the sea.

Blackened and jagged rocks and a stretch of yellow sand separated the raised walk from the sea. Gulls swooped and planed overhead, apparently for fun, and a few tourists strolled along the path with less obvious pleasure.

Wycliffe told himself, I can't get to grips with this. A young man disappears and fifteen years later his body is found buried in the dunes. During those years only the father talked about possible foul play, and that was because he couldn't accept the implications of suicide. In fifteen years there have been no accusations, yet within a day or two of the discovery of the body, people who could have been involved were being targeted with veiled threats and a photograph was sent to me, obviously with the intention of setting the police on their tails.

Surely whoever was doing all this now must have been in a position to do it at any time?

He passed the back of GG's health shop with the window of her office overlooking the sea, then turned up into Bethel Street where her shop and Badger's faced each other on diagonally opposite corners. He crossed the road and made to enter the Modelmakers but the door was locked. Then he noticed a fly-blown card which read 'Closed'.

Was Badger's involvement anything more than a fanciful idea which had come to him after a chance encounter? The lawyer, while denying its likelihood, had given the idea greater substance. Not only was the old man's niece one of the six but Angove, the painter, was a regular visitor at the model shop.

Wycliffe stood back to take stock of the property. There was a high stone wall reaching some distance up the hill behind the shop, presumably the length of Badger's wilderness garden. Wycliffe walked to the end of it and found an alley which separated the backs of the properties in Bethel Street from those in the street running parallel to it. The alley, carpeted with weeds and grass, was too narrow for a vehicle; it ran between six-foot stone walls, with plank doors into the premises on either side. Wycliffe tried Badger's door and found it secured.

He walked back down the hill with the intention of enquiring after Badger's likely whereabouts at the health shop, but changed his mind and went instead to a newsagent and tobacconist next door.

The owner looked like a retired wrestler. 'Is the old fool gone off again? All I know is that he was there yesterday. Anyway, if he runs to form, he'll be back Monday.'

'You've no idea where he goes?'

The man's face went blank. 'To be honest, Mister, for all I know he might still be in there. He's a pain, always complaining about other people, and look at the state of his place. I mean, it lets down the whole bloody street.'

'Can you remember when you last saw him?'

'Yes. It was the night before last, about eight. He was off on his usual. Every night he goes off somewhere about that time. God knows where . . .'

'You didn't see him last night?'

'No, I didn't, but that don't mean he wasn't around. It means I wasn't.'

Kersey arrived at Studio Limbo, pushed open the glass door, and found himself in the passage-like interior with paintings crowding in on either side. He waited but nobody came so he walked down the shop until he arrived at the stairs and called, 'Anybody home?'

There was a strong smell of frying. A stocky young man came to the top of the stairs and Kersey held up his warrant card. 'Police. Detective Inspector Kersey.'

'Oh, I thought we were overdue for a visit. You'd better come on up.' At the top of the stairs Kersey entered the long narrow room. At the end opposite the window a door was open into a tiny kitchen where a girl wearing an apron manipulated the contents of a wok on a stove. A table was set for a meal by the window; all very cosy and domesticated.

The painter pointed to the long bench. 'Take the weight off your feet.'

Kersey, unprepared for this casual reception, tried to play the heavy. 'I think you know why I'm here.'

Angove sat beside him on the bench. 'I suppose it's about this nonsense over the body they've dug out of the dunes.'

'We don't regard an investigation into violent death as nonsense, Mr Angove.'

The painter was unperturbed. 'Neither do I. It's the fact that some busybody who chooses to send anonymous bits of crap through the post is taken seriously.'

'This busybody of yours is in possession of information which gives substance to his crap as you call it.'

Angove had the mobile features of a clown and he looked at Kersey with amused surprise. 'What information? The fact that fifteen years ago half a dozen adolescents spent a sexy weekend in a beach chalet.'

'It is ready.' The girl, standing in the doorway of the kitchen, spoke with clipped precision. 'I must serve out or it will spoil.' She was slim and dark. South-east Asian? Filipino? As well as an apron she wore a jade green frock, sleeveless and brief.

The painter said, 'This is Elena. Can you stretch it for the inspector?'

'Of course.'

'There you are then, Inspector – diced pork with bean sprouts, onions, mushrooms and noodles.'

The smell was mouth-watering and Kersey was tempted, but declined.

'Then you'll have to watch us eat. It's too good to spoil. If you want to talk at the same time you'd better pull up a chair.'

Kersey pulled up a chair and talked to keep himself in countenance. 'You are taking your own position and that of your friends too lightly, Mr Angove. Wilder was killed in some sort of tussle by a blow on the head. The indications are that he died and was buried on the

Saturday evening of the weekend you spent at the chalet – the nearest, incidentally, to where the body was found.'

Angove and the girl went on with their meal showing as little concern as if Kersey had been talking about the weather. With his mouth full the painter said, 'I don't see what connects all this with our chalet party. The chap had a row with somebody in the dunes which turned into a fight, and presumably he got the worst of it.'

'A pretty violent row it must have been, and only a hundred yards or so from your chalet, but you heard and saw nothing. A bit surprising, don't you think? Of course Wilder was naked when he was found, so perhaps he and his opponent were indulging in some sort of ceremonial combat. His body was wrapped in a nylon bed sheet which they no doubt brought along as part of the ritual, and the concrete fragments embedded in Wilder's cracked skull must surely mean that the *coup de grâce* was administered with a ceremonial concrete block.'

The painter was grinning broadly while the girl continued eating her food with demure precision as though unaware that anything unusual was taking place. Angove said, 'Very funny!'

But Kersey became serious. 'Not so funny, really. Whatever sort of scrap Wilder was involved in took place in one of the chalets. I'm not saying that it was murder, it could have been manslaughter or even self-defence. That will be for the coroner, and perhaps a jury, to decide when we get that far. But however he died, his body was wrapped in that bed sheet and carried to a convenient place for burial in the foredunes.'

Kersey sat back in his chair allowing time for this to sink in, then went on, 'Just add the famous necklace found in Wilder's trouser pocket and it seems to me we're not all that far from identifying the chalet where it all began.'

The painter, wrestling with some reluctant noodles, remained silent and Kersey was forced to continue. 'The position of you and your friends would have been more credible if, when Wilder's body was found or when photographs of the necklace appeared on TV and in the press, you had come forward and told us that you were in the chalet during that weekend instead of waiting for our inquiries to lead us to you.'

Angove gave him a quizzical look. 'Are you married, Inspector? Do you live in a cosy little village or in a suburb where everybody knows you as the police inspector? Would you want the bloody-fool antics of your youth broadcast? It's not the sort of thing to worry me but I'm a professional drop-out.'

Kersey said, 'You should have been a lawyer, Mr Angove. But think over what I've said. For the moment, there's just one other point: I believe that you are on friendly terms with Henry Badger at the Modelmakers, and we know that Mr Badger has something of a reputation as a letter writer . . .'

The painter was amused. 'What naughty thoughts you policemen have! Ingenious, too. But a non-starter. I've got nothing against my former schoolmates and, if I had, I wouldn't involve poor old Badger.'

Kersey stood up, 'Very well, I shall leave you to it. We need a formal statement confirming what we already know plus what more you feel disposed to tell us. So let's say, at the local police station at three. I shall be sending someone along.'

The painter had finished his meal and he came down with Kersey to see him off at the shop door. 'Sure I can't interest you in original work by a local artist – a memento of your visit?'

Kersey grinned despite himself. 'Get stuffed!'

Lucy Lane drove to Carbis Bay. From a street map she discovered that Lelant Crescent was between the main road and the coast. She found it without difficulty, a row of modest semi-detached houses which, because of the steepness of the slope, had a commanding view of the bay. Like most of the others in the crescent, number fifteen had an escallonia hedge and a patch of grass with a couple of wind-blown Cordyline palms to proclaim the balmy south-west. Lucy pulled into the kerb, got out, and climbed the steep path and steps to the front door. The bell-push set off a chime which was answered almost at once.

'Mrs Lisa Bell . . . ? Detective Sergeant Lane.' Lucy showed her warrant card.

Lisa was recognizable from the snap taken fifteen years ago, the blonde hair, the rather long face and the thin, prim lips; but she was pale, her eyes were frightened and she had difficulty in finding her voice.

Lucy was taken into the lounge, a large room with the inevitable view of the bay. Otherwise it was depressingly ordinary and correct with a selection of framed prints and ornaments which could have been ordered along with the carpet and the suite.

'What a wonderful view. My name is Lucy. Do you mind if I call you Lisa?'

'If you like.' But Lisa was not interested in small talk 'Why have you come? Has something happened?'

They sat opposite each other in armchairs on either side of the unlit gas fire. 'I've come to talk to you about the necklace that was found with Cochran Wilder's body. I expect you've seen pictures of it and read the description but it's necessary that you should identify it formally.' From her shoulder bag she brought out the polythene bag containing the necklace and passed it over.

The young woman held the package in the palm of her hand, staring down at it as though it were some strange object.

'You are satisfied that it is your necklace?'

'Yes.' The word was barely audible.

'I'm afraid that it will have to remain in the custody of the police until the investigations are complete and whatever court proceedings there may be are over. Then, of course, it will be returned to you.'

Lisa continued to stare at the necklace but she said

nothing and Lucy went on, 'Although Wilder's body was naked, you probably know that his clothes were buried with him. You may not know, because it has not been mentioned by the media, that the necklace was actually found in his trouser pocket. Obviously we have to try to find out how it got there.'

Abruptly, in an uncontrolled movement, Lisa held out the bag. 'Here, take it! I don't want to see it again.' Her hands free, she thrust them together between her knees and leaned forward in her chair, every muscle tense.

Lucy said, 'How did Wilder get hold of the necklace?'

'I lost it.' She said the words as though they were a complete answer to the question.

'Where did you lose it?'

'In the dunes. I don't know where.'

'Can you tell me when and in what circumstances? I mean, when did you miss it? What had you been doing since you last had it?'

She shifted uncomfortably on the edge of her chair. 'I went for a walk. I know I was wearing it when I left the chalet and I missed it when I came back.'

'Did you walk with someone?'

'Yes, with Julian – Julian Angove, just the two of us.'

'Where did you walk?'

'Just down to the beach and back.'

'This was in the afternoon?'

She hesitated. 'In the evening.'

'Before dark?'

'Oh, yes.'

'When you got back from your walk was Barbara – Mrs Hart, as she is now – in the chalet?'

'Oh, yes. They all were.'

'Did she tell you about the man who had asked her if she had seen his friend?'

She answered quickly, 'I don't know. I mean I can't remember.'

'I suppose, Lisa, the necklace had a great deal of sentimental value for you?'

'Yes. It had been in the family for a long time. My parents died young and I was brought up by my grandmother so it came to me through her. She had my initials engraved on it and gave it to me on my eighteenth birthday.'

Lisa was having difficulty in holding back tears but she went on, 'I was so anxious to show it off . . . Like a fool!'

'So you must have been very upset when you lost it. Did you spend a lot of time looking for it?'

'Oh, yes, we all did.'

'In the dark?'

'Until it was dark . . . And next day.'

'Cochran Wilder must have arrived in your area at about half past eight, what were you doing at about that time?'

She hesitated briefly, then, 'We must have been searching for the necklace.'

'But you saw nothing of any stranger?'

'No.'

'How long did you stay on in the chalet on the Sunday? I mean when did you leave for home?'

The question troubled her. After an interval, she said, 'It was during the morning some time; I can't remember exactly when.'

'Was the weather still good?'

'Oh, yes.'

'But you wanted to get back?'

'Yes.'

'So you spent only the one night in the chalet – Saturday night?'

'Yes.'

'Who did you sleep with?'

She looked up, abruptly. 'Sleep with?'

'Well there were six of you and only three beds. Don't tell me that you shared your bed with a girl.'

'I slept with Paul.'

'With Paul Drew. All night?'

She flushed. 'No, we didn't stay together.' She looked at Lucy, as though in appeal. 'I couldn't stand it. He was . . . Well, it doesn't matter now.'

'So what did you do?'

'I left him and went into the living room . . . I spent the rest of the night on the sofa.'

'And you weren't disturbed? At some time during that late evening and night a man was killed and his naked body was carried through the dunes to be buried in the sand. All this within a hundred yards of the chalet, but you heard and saw nothing. Is that correct?'

Her answer was inaudible, her features creased, tears came and she covered her face with her hand. Whatever the cause she was genuinely distressed and Wycliffe had warned against applying pressure.

Lucy waited until she had recovered sufficiently to wipe her eyes and look up with a blotchy tear-stained face, then changed the subject. She asked gently, 'When did you first hear that Cochran Wilder was missing?'

'I can't remember exactly but it must have been early in the following week. His photograph was in the papers.'

'You recognized him?'

A sharp, hurt, response. 'What? No. Of course I didn't! I'd never seen him before.'

'Was the fact that Wilder went missing while you were in the chalet talked about among your sixth-form group?'

She sobbed. 'Yes, but we decided not to say anything because we shouldn't have been there.'

'Are you prepared to put all this in a statement?'

'Will it be in the papers or on the radio?' Plaintive.

'Not unless it turns out to be relevant.'

She sighed. 'All right; if I must.'

Chapter Six

Friday (continued)

It was well past one o'clock and Wycliffe was thinking about lunch. He felt better and he decided that his pride had suffered more than his skull. Still in Bethel Street, he was attracted to the Bay Wholefood Restaurant. It sounded healthy and non-alcoholic, and looking in he saw ten or a dozen marble-topped tables, most of them occupied, and plain colour-washed walls; none of the plastics and laminates which go so well with soggy chips. What more could he want?

'Just one, sir?' He was given a table for two in the fairway. 'Something to drink, sir? We do a good selection of wines including a very pleasant cottage wine made from elderflower . . .' This from a young waitress in a frilly pinafore. He must rid himself of the lingering notion that vegetarians are invariably teetotal. Many of them don't contemplate their navels either.

'Apple juice, please. And I'll have the ratatouille with garlic bread.'

While he was waiting, he took in the clientele; a mixed bag; some of them were visitors but quite a few were obvious locals – men in suits with newspapers; girls in twos and even foursomes, straight out of their shops and offices, chattering away like sparrows. At a table by the window, he spotted GG's red head and, opposite her, the sparse greying curls of her lawyer cousin. Penrose reporting? Their conversation was serious and intent.

They got up to leave when Wycliffe was halfway through his meal and they had to pass his table to reach the exit. Penrose looked vaguely embarrassed, but GG said, 'Congratulations, Superintendent! I wouldn't have put you down as a vegetarian.'

Wycliffe decided to profit from the encounter. 'I was going to phone you, Mr Penrose. I wondered if you could tell me the name of the woman who looks after your uncle?'

'Why? Is there something wrong?'

'He appears to have shut himself up again, or whatever it is he does, and I'm rather anxious to talk to him.'

Penrose looked concerned. 'I suppose he's about due for another spell, but I'm afraid the woman won't be able to help you.'

'All the same . . .'

'Very well.' Resigned. 'She's called Trewin – Elsie Trewin, I think, and she lives somewhere in Bal Lane, I've no idea of the number. It's off Norway Square.'

'I don't suppose you have access to the place, Mr Penrose?'

Penrose actually laughed. 'The very idea would give the old man a stroke!'

'What about you, Miss Grey?'

'Me?' A grim smile. 'I never go there unless I'm sent for.'

'And that happens?'

'Oh, yes, it happens; I am his niece.'

She turned to her cousin. 'We're blocking the gangway, Arnold.'

When he left the restaurant Wycliffe checked again on the Modelmakers, which was still shut up, then he strolled through the narrow main street, blocked to vehicles by a lorry unloading. There were drifting tourists, mainly pensioners, but the resident population was still in evidence, going about its business in the streets and shops, not yet submerged by the flocks of high-summer migrants.

He found Bal Lane, a double row of cottages with granite steps up to their doors. Some of them had earthenware bowls on the steps, bristling with daffodils, vivid, blatant and beautiful. Occasionally there was a cat as well; drowsily elegant. A woman, cleaning her front window, directed him to number five.

His knock was answered by Elsie herself, middle-aged, lean, dark, going grey and inclined to be waspish.

'Mr Badger? You're going to be unlucky. I couldn't get in this morning to do my work.'

'Has he gone away?'

'That's asking. What you want him for?'

'I called on him yesterday and I wanted to meet him again. Does it often happen like this – I mean that you are unable to get in?'

'Sometimes. Are you from the police? What's he done now? More letters?'

'Perhaps we could talk inside?'

'I suppose so.' Without enthusiasm she led him into the little sitting room, which after the sunlit street seemed almost dark.

Wycliffe said, 'As far as I know Mr Badger has done nothing wrong.'

'Well, that's something.' She straightened a picture over the mantelpiece and became more communicative. 'He's a bit queer. You asked me if he's gone away and the answer is I don't know for sure. I mean, it happens. Things is going on as normal for three or four weeks together then, without a word from him, for two or three days at a time, I find myself locked out. I've got used to it.'

'What happens?'

'I turn up there, usual time, and one fine morning there he is, same as ever. He always says he's been away, but it wouldn't surprise me if he just locked himself in. I mean, where would he go?' Mrs Trewin echoed the words of the lawyer. 'And there's usually some food missing out of the freezer, not much – but some; and people tell me they've seen lights on there at night when he's supposed to be away.

'I asked him once why he couldn't tell me when he

wasn't going to need me, and he said, "Why the hell should I? I pay you just the same." So now I don't bother. I mean, if people don't want you to take an interest . . .' She shrugged. 'Anyway, not to worry! It's Friday today, he'll be about again by Monday, that's for sure.'

Wycliffe said, 'I'm concerned about Mr Badger and I'm asking these questions in his interest. I think you know, or at least suspect, more than you've told me.'

With great care she was rearranging the window curtains to arrive at a gap which met with her approval. 'I don't want to get drawn into something, but I'll tell you this, whether he goes away or locks himself in, he looks like death afterwards. And there's always bottles in the bin-bag in the yard that he thinks I don't notice.'

'Whisky?'

She gave him a quick, appraising look. 'Brandy. But if you say I told you, I shall deny it.'

'Does he have visitors?'

'I'm only there mornings. I see the lawyer now and then, and sometimes there's the health-shop woman.'

Wycliffe returned to the sunshine and rejoined the strollers. He was in St Ives with no transport and he would have to get a lift in a patrol car. He made his way to the nick, thoughtful. So the old grey Badger went in for more or less regular but solitary binges.

So what?

All the same, the more he learned of the old man the more uneasy he became, though he had difficulty in finding any logical reason for his concern. Unless Badger was a real threat to the six, or to any one of them.

There was, as Kersey had said, a smell; something which offended that delicately sensitive organ, the copper's nose. For a fleeting moment he thought he had the glimmerings of an idea, but it faded as he tried to bring it into focus. In any case he was mixing his metaphors.

In practical terms he had to find a cast-iron link

between the dead boy and the six. It was just possible that the chalet might provide it. After all, somebody had thought it worthwhile to break in. But if nothing came out of the chalet he would have to adopt Kersey's tactic and start to turn the screw on one of the six. That, he felt sure, would be a messy business and do nothing to address what he believed to be the broader issue.

At the nick he had to wait while they called in a patrol car to take him back to Hayle and the Incident Room.

Iris Thorn, the new DC, had been given the job of getting some background on the chalet party when they were pupils in the sixth form at John Harvey's Grammar School. But police officers, like middle-aged men in plastic raincoats, tend to be suspect in the vicinity of schools. Iris was told that there was no member of staff available in a position to help. Persistent, she was given the address of a retired teacher, Geoffrey Prowse, who had been head of the sixth form in the seventies.

New to her role as a DC, she experienced a slight trepidation at the prospect of interrogating a school-teacher; it was hardly five years since she had been on the receiving end herself.

She found the Prowses in a former farmhouse off the Zennor road, overlooking the sea. Warrant card in hand, she said, 'I would like a word with Mr Prowse if that is possible.'

Mrs Prowse, plump and good-natured, looked twice, swallowed, and said, 'Oh yes, dear. Of course. The school phoned to say somebody might be coming from the police.'

She found Geoffrey Prowse in his study, seated at his desk, surrounded by books and maps which overflowed on to the floor. He seemed an amiable specimen of the breed and Mrs Prowse spoke of him as she might have done of a large pet dog. 'He spends most of his time in here when he isn't at the county records office or the museum. But he's no trouble.'

There was, of course, the standard view of the bay, a single vast sweep from Clodgy Point to beyond Godrevy.

Prowse removed his spectacles, looked from the girl to his desk then back again. 'I'm having a go at a new county history.' He said it with a mixture of bravado and diffidence. 'Quite an undertaking; there's a lot of excellent work from the past to live up to, but there are always gaps . . .'

It took a few minutes to get him orientated. 'Nineteen seventy-seven . . . That was the year before I retired . . . Give me a name . . .'

Iris had briefed herself. 'Gillian Grey, Alan Hart – there were six of them.'

A quick smile. 'I'm with you – GG and her little coterie. Odd, that was; such an unlikely grouping. Young people are so intriguing, don't you think? So unpredictable! Anyway, what do you want to know?'

It was evident that whatever rumours were circulating Prowse had not heard them. In any case he was more intrigued by his visitor. He kept looking at her and turning away quickly, as though caught out. Iris was used to it.

'This is a confidential inquiry, sir. It might be useful to know whether those six young people achieved what was expected of them in their examinations?'

Prowse, puzzled, became more wary. 'I can't imagine why you should want to know such a thing, but there can be no harm in telling you that to the best of my recollection, they did not.' He hesitated, looking at her again, this time doubtfully. 'I suppose you know about our examination system? . . . A-levels, and all that?'

'I think I have a rough idea.'

The gentle sarcasm was not lost on him. 'Of course! I'm sorry, my dear! You must excuse an old man.' After a pause he went on with a mischievous grin, 'I've accustomed myself to the invasion of this county by the Windmill Hill people, the Beaker folk, the Celts and the Saxons—'

'But the Afro-Caribbeans make one too many.'

They had a good laugh over this and from then on he was eating out of her hand. He got up from his chair, crossed the room to some bookshelves and came back with an exercise book. 'I suppose it's absurd, but I still keep my records of the examination results and final placings of all the sixth formers who passed through my hands while I was tutor.'

He turned the pages of neatly arranged columns. 'Here we are – A-level results for seventy-seven . . . I had forgotten how poorly . . .' He broke off. 'I suppose I ought not to enter into details, although the results of public examinations are public property. Anyway, I will tell you this much, Alan Hart got into medical school, but not the one of his choice, and only by the skin of his teeth. Julian Angove got into his art college, but there the academic requirements were not high. Of the remaining four, three who were expected to go on to university failed to secure places.'

Iris decided to push a little. 'In your opinion, was this due to last-minute nerves? Or had they thrown up the sponge earlier?'

'They certainly hadn't thrown up the sponge. I don't know about nerves but it must have been something which happened late on. I see from this that their results in the February mock examinations were fully up to expectations . . . They seemed to go to pieces in the last two or three weeks before the real thing; there was even a certain amount of absenteeism which is most unusual at such a time . . .' Prowse fiddled with the papers in front of him. 'All I can say is that I and their subject teachers were surprised and disappointed by their results.'

'And this did not apply to the other candidates?'

Prowse was emphatic. 'By no means. Seventy-seven was a good year, a very good year.' He spoke as though discussing a vintage. Then a new aspect seemed to occur to him and he became more schoolmasterish. 'But I must say, young lady, that I am at a loss to understand where all this is leading. You surely can't be investigating something in which they might have been involved all that time ago?'

Iris said something about the possibility that they had been witnesses to an incident.

Abruptly, Prowse put two and two together. 'You are talking about the body in the dunes. Oh, dear! Surely these young people could not possibly . . .' He was as much fascinated as shocked by the notion.

She said, 'To be frank, we are casting about for anybody – anybody who might help us with our investigation. At this stage there is no implication of guilt.'

But Prowse's thoughts were following their own line. He said, reflectively, 'GG – everybody called her that, even the staff – Gillian Grey; she had a good deal of charm, but I'm afraid she was not a good influence on those who became her friends.'

She thanked him and left him to his county history, with good feeling on both sides.

Kersey said, 'Fox seems to think he's struck oil and he wants to know whether to carry on or hand over to Forensic.'

'What's he found?'

Kersey grinned. 'I gather it's a hole in the floor, but you know Fox. "The preliminary indications are that there may be a link between the chalet and the crime. It is too early to speak with certainty . . ." ' Kersey mimicked Fox's precise yet elliptical style. 'I didn't bother with cross-examination on the phone; I've tried it before.'

'Shall we have a look? Take my car; you drive. But before we go, is there anything else?'

Kersey shuffled among the reports. 'There's one item that might amount to something. Potter, on house-to-house in Phillack, came across a young girl. It seems that some couples around here still go for walks instead of straight to bed—'

'Give it a rest, Doug!'

'Yes, well, this girl and her boyfriend went walking on the towans last evening and she says there was a car parked in the clearing and another tucked away in a little alley between two chalets. When they came back the car in the alley was gone, but the other was still there. She doesn't know anything about cars so Potter dug out her boyfriend. He says the remaining car was a grey Rover saloon – an up-market job.'

'Mine.'

'Looks like it, sir.' Kersey was grinning broadly. 'He wasn't sure of the other. Could have been an Escort, and probably red.'

'What time was this?'

'They were both vague about time.'

Lucy Lane had left Wycliffe's car parked by the Incident Room. He disliked motor cars but they were indispensable so he got others to drive him whenever he could.

The sun was still shining but clouds were building up from the west. The forecast, which had promised heavy showers in late afternoon, looked like being right. As he and Kersey left the car and set out for the chalet a strong gust of wind, funnelled by the dunes, rippled the surface of the sand.

When they reached the chalet they could see the sea. The scene was dramatic; blue sky and sparkling sea were being invaded from the west by masses of leaden cloud beneath which the sea was turning almost black with crests of startling whiteness. The door of the chalet was open and, just inside, Fox's photographic gear was stacked in its canvas covers. They could see through the living room into the kitchen and just beyond the spot where Wycliffe had been attacked, Collis, Fox's long-suffering assistant, was on his knees by a gap in the floorboards. He muttered something and Fox's head came round the door.

'It's all right to come in, sir. I've finished in the living room.'

The carpet in the main room had been rolled back, exposing the floorboards. On the big table, clipped to a drawing board, was a plan of the chalet, and clustered in a certain area of the plan were small, numbered crosses. Also on the table were four or five glass specimen tubes, each with a label, and each containing what looked like a quantity of soil.

Fox switched to his lecture mode. 'I've taken detailed photographs of the chalet as I found it and, as you see, sir, I am preparing the usual plan—'

'What's in the specimen tubes?'

'Ah! As you see, the carpet is rolled back. It certainly wasn't here fifteen years ago. The floorboards were treated with a wood stain and it is my belief that at that time they had mats on the bare boards—'

'And the little tubes?'

'I was coming to that. They contain material scraped from the gaps between the floorboards. As you will see, in places the boards have shrunk—'

'You had some idea in mind when you began your scraping?'

'Yes, sir, I did. I had spotted a couple of very tiny fragments of glass so I scraped every gap and collected the material.'

'You found more glass?'

'Yes, several glass fragments and others which look like bits of china. I've plotted where they were found on my plan. You will see that they are concentrated in an area where the table now stands. On the evidence I would say that there could have been some sort of struggle in which a number of glass and china utensils were smashed. Most of it was swept up but those tiny fragments remained lodged between the boards.'

Fox was very good at his job but it was hard to take

him seriously. Quite apart from his pedantic manner, he was physically a cartoon character; abnormally long and thin, his legs in particular suggested that they had been expressly designed for that discriminating stalking practised by flamingos along the margins of African lakes.

Wycliffe said, 'That's a good start. Anything else?'

'Yes, sir, there is the matter of possible bloodstains. In the same general area as I found the particles of glass, I noticed that the boards were discoloured in a way that I associate with very old bloodstains. I lifted one of the boards and found that the discoloration was more pronounced where the wood stain didn't reach.'

'The blood had seeped through?'

'If it is blood, sir. I'm by no means certain.'

'You've done very well. We must get Forensic on to the bloodstains.'

But Fox had not yet finished. 'You may have noticed that this chalet is built into the side of a small but steep dune so that although there are several steps up to the veranda, and one can even walk about under the front part of the chalet, the kitchen, which in my opinion was built on later, is on almost level ground, and its floor is nowhere much more than a foot above the sand.'

It was Kersey's turn to stem the flow. 'So you've found something under the floor in the kitchen. Is that it?'

Fox said, 'No sir, I have not found anything under the floorboards, not yet anyway.' Fox had no love for Kersey and he turned back to Wycliffe. 'The fact is, sir, a small section of the floor in the kitchen had already been lifted when I arrived. I assume that it was done by whoever was on the premises when you were here last night . . . If you will come this way . . . Watch out for the hole.'

The hole, which Collis was still investigating with a torch, had been made by removing three boards.

Fox said, 'I removed two additional boards to make it easier to see whatever might be hidden under the floor but there seems to be nothing there.'

'So?'

Fox became even more pedantic. 'I cannot, of course, speak with any certainty but in my opinion whatever was under the floor was removed by last night's intruder. In fact, I wouldn't be surprised if that was the purpose of his visit.'

Wycliffe had a disquieting vision of the intruder taking off with vital evidence under his very nose. It also occurred to him that if he had taken another step into the kitchen he would probably have had an injured leg to worry about as well as a sore head.

But Fox was still talking. 'I suspect that the object removed from under the boards was soft and compressible, perhaps a blanket or a rolled-up rug which had probably become bloodstained. The intruder, who must have known exactly where to look, had to drag it up through the narrow space, with the result that there are fibres adhering to the edges of the boards.'

It was difficult to congratulate Fox who gave the impression that such were his skills that he could effortlessly repeat these feats anywhere and at any time. Wycliffe did his best but Fox had another trick up his sleeve. From a canvas bag he produced a brace-like tool in a polythene bag. At one end it had a chisel shape and at the other a socket.

'It's a tyre lever and wheel brace, sir. From the tool kit of a car. I found it on the kitchen floor and I suspect that the intruder used it to break in and, later, to attack you. Fortunately there are good identifiable prints. It's a question of matching them against those of possible suspects.'

Kersey said, 'The red Escort.'

They had not noticed the darkening sky and suddenly the rain came, beating on the roof and blowing in through the open door. Fox rushed to close the door to protect his precious equipment. Collis had given up his hole and was hovering in the kitchen doorway.

Collis, whom Wycliffe was convinced grew physically

more like his sergeant day by day, was hesitant. 'I can see glass in the beam of the torch, Sarge, and quite large bits of china. It's some distance in and we shall have to lift other boards to get at it.'

Fox said, 'All right. I'll see to it later.'

'It could have been thrown in there when they swept up before they pushed the rug in.'

'Do you know that it was a rug, Collis? Have you become an expert on fibres?'

'Well no, Sarge, but they looked like they came from—'

'Yes, well, don't let speculation run away with you, Collis.'

Wycliffe said, 'I'll make arrangements with Forensic to examine the timbers. You'd better get your scrapings off to them right away in case they're contaminated with blood; the fibres too. They should be able to tell us what sort of material they came from.'

They scuttled back to the car through the rain. The sand was turning from almost white to pale brown. Once in the car Kersey said, 'How does Collis stick it? He tags around after Fox like a dispirited dog, and Fox treats him like one.'

'I expect he sees Fox as his pack leader.'

Kersey sighed. 'God help him!'

All the same, Fox had done a good job. The argument in favour of a struggle was strong: probable bloodstains, minute fragments of glass and china trapped between the floorboards, and larger pieces apparently hidden under the floor. Add to that a rug (or blanket) which had recently been removed and it all amounted to real evidence – for a change.

Kersey said, 'All the same it would help even more if they found a bloodstained lump of concrete under the floor.'

'True.'

When they arrived back at the Incident Room, they found DC Thorn typing a report. She stood up as they came in with the obvious intention of saying something, but Kersey cut her short.

'Did you see the school people?'

'I talked with the group's sixth-form tutor. He's retired now. He said that the six had unexpectedly poor results in their examinations.'

'I suppose it's in your report? . . . What about the statements?'

'DC Curnow and I divided the interviews between us, sir. He took Dr Hart and Lisa Bell, while I did Gillian Grey and Julian Angove—'

'What did Angove have to say? Where was he last night?'

A flicker of amusement. Iris evidently had memories of the painter. 'He said that he was in all yesterday evening – that he usually found his entertainment at home.'

'And Paul Drew?'

'We weren't able to interview Paul Drew—'

'You mean he refused?'

'No, sir. I telephoned his office and they said that he was unwell and wouldn't be in today.'

'So you went to the house?'

'No, sir. As we were told to avoid marital complications where possible we thought it best to wait for instructions, but—'

'Then we'd better find out about this illness; sounds too convenient to me. Where's DS Lane? Where's Curnow?'

'I'm trying to explain, sir.' Patient.

Wycliffe, on the sidelines, was intrigued. The girl's manner matched her presence. Unhurried and unruffled, she went on, 'Fifteen minutes ago there was a call from Mrs Drew reporting that her husband was missing. It seems that he went off in his car last night and she hasn't seen him since—'

'She took her time! So we notify all stations to look out for him. He probably hasn't gone far. Just panicked.

You've got his reg number? Where's Lucy Lane? Where's Curnow?'

'We don't have his number, sir, Mrs Drew couldn't remember it, but she did say that it was a red Escort. I gather she was very confused on the telephone and DS Lane has gone with DC Curnow to sort it all out.'

Kersey followed Wycliffe into the inner office. 'We shall have to watch that one. Too smart for her own good.' He caught Wycliffe smiling and grinned himself.

Wycliffe said, 'I only hope she hits it off with Lucy Lane.'

'Yes, well . . . Anyway, what do you make of this little lot, sir? The last couple of hours have changed things a bit, don't you think? I knew that Drew would crack one way or another and it's obvious it was he who tapped you on the head.

'Now it's a question of what's happened to him. Has he just cleared out? He can't be such a fool as to imagine he could get away with it. Suicide is more likely in my book for that type. On the other hand, it's just possible that the others saw him as an unacceptable risk.'

Wycliffe sat back in his chair and massaged the back of his skull. 'Don't be daft, Doug. Drew may be on the run, he may even have done away with himself, but as for the others having got rid of him . . . These people are not a bunch of cold-blooded killers. They're scared, perhaps too scared to think rationally, but they're hardly likely to start killing each other.'

Kersey lit a cigarette. 'I've known you a long time, sir, and I think you have a reason for holding back. We are close to being able to show that Wilder died at the chalet in violent circumstances, probably some sort of fight, and that these six were responsible for concealing his death by burying the body. We haven't got the whole story yet but there's enough to screw the rest out of them.'

Wycliffe was silent for a while, then he said, 'I'm holding back because I think that to some extent we are being led by the nose – those bits of nonsense sent through the post, appearing to threaten the six, the attempt to implicate them through a photograph sent to me . . . It's phoney, Doug – stage-managed; and I want to know who did it, and why.'

Kersey tapped ash from his cigarette into a tin lid. 'Does it matter? The pointers were in the right direction.'

Any comment from Wycliffe was rendered unnecessary by the telephone. 'The chief's on the line, sir.'

'Charles?' . . . Wycliffe signalled to Kersey to stay.

'I've been reading the reports. Anything fresh?'

Wycliffe told him.

'Then what are we waiting for, Charles? A video recording?'

Wycliffe was frosty, pushing protocol to its limit. 'I will take action, sir, when I have sufficient evidence to sustain it; in particular when I have the forensic report on material taken from the chalet. That should be early in the coming week.'

The chief capitulated. 'All right, Charles! All right! But you don't fool me; I can't help wondering just what hare you are chasing. It's as well old Wilder seems to have quietened down. With any luck I shan't have him on my back.'

Wycliffe put down the phone. 'At least we've got a stay of execution.'

'But you'll need to be careful, sir.'

'I shall be. Don't worry.'

They spent the next half-hour going through the statements and reports, which filled in gaps but told them nothing really new. It was part of the documentation process which occupies half the man-hours spent on any case, and has become a matter of obsessive concern since the Guildford Four, the Birmingham Six and the Cardiff Three.

Rain beat down on the roof of the little office which was built on to the main building. The windows were steamed over and the atmosphere was claustrophobic. Lucy Lane arrived and joined them. Wycliffe had coffee brought in and the three settled around the table.

'Well?'

Lucy made a gesture of distaste. 'That woman is impossible! I'm not surprised that Drew has cleared out; I only wonder why he waited for this. At any rate I've got the gen on his car: red Ford Escort, reg number F426 AFZ. Curnow is putting it out. As far as I can tell, Drew has taken nothing with him except the clothes he stood up in. She thinks he's got a couple of credit cards in his wallet.'

Wycliffe had rarely seen Lucy so incensed.

'She said with a sort of glee that he'd got no friends or relatives to whom he could go and she showed not the slightest interest in getting him back. She made a point of explaining that she was financially independent and that they have separate bank accounts. Her main concern was about possible publicity.'

'Did she want to know why we were involved?'

'No, she seemed to think that a missing husband was more than enough to bring us in. Incidentally, I've got a fairly recent photograph; do you want it circulated, sir?'

Wycliffe hesitated. 'Give it until morning. Has anybody talked to Drew's partner across the road?'

'Not yet, sir.'

Wycliffe glanced at his watch. 'I might catch him before he shuts up shop for the night.'

The young woman was just putting the cover on her typewriter but she was almost welcoming. 'I know who you are. You want to see Mr Stanton?' And without waiting for an answer she had picked up the telephone.

Stanton, short and stout, neat, brisk and balding, came out to greet him. 'I've been half expecting a call . . . Come through and take a pew!' He sat in his executive chair, elbows on the arms, finger tips together, judicial. 'I take it this is about my young partner. I don't mind telling you I'm worried, Superintendent – very worried. I've tried to talk to his wife but, between you and me, that woman is a fool.'

Wycliffe said, 'You may know that Mr Drew has been of some help to us in connection with the death of Cochran Wilder fifteen years ago. I am not suggesting that he was criminally involved. I understand he did not turn up for work yesterday morning and his wife told you he was unwell.'

'When I telephoned her, yes, but—'

Wycliffe cut in. 'Since then Mrs Drew has reported that she has not seen her husband since last evening when he went off in his car. Have you any idea at all where he might have gone?'

The pale blue eyes looked at him over rimless half-glasses. 'None whatever. I knew nothing of Paul's private life apart from his unfortunate marriage.'

'As a matter of routine I must ask if you suspect any irregularity, any defalcation—'

It was Stanton's turn to interrupt. 'Nothing like that, Superintendent, I've checked; though such a thing would be hardly possible with my system, anyway.' He went on, 'There is, however, one small matter that might interest you; Paul returned to the office at some time during last evening or night.'

'How do you know?'

'I think my niece might be better able to explain that, Mr Wycliffe. In the outer office. It's connected with her machine and Sandra understands it; I don't.'

Wycliffe followed him out.

'Sandra, tell Mr Wycliffe what you found when we opened this morning.'

Sandra whisked the cover off her machine like a conjuror opening her act. 'Well, that's one thing, the cover was on the floor. But he also left the machine switched on. I mean, he sometimes comes in here after hours and uses it but he'd never leave it like that unless he was in a state.'

'Is there any way of telling what he actually used it for? Isn't this a word processor? Wouldn't there be a record on disc?'

She gave him a winning smile. 'I see you know what you're talking about, Mr Wycliffe; but you can use this as an ordinary typewriter and when I came in this morning it was in the typewriting mode.' She picked up the cover to replace it. 'So, unless he used a carbon there's no way of knowing what he did.'

Wycliffe turned to Stanton. 'I suppose it's certain that it was Drew?'

'Unless someone else had his key. There are only two keys; he has one and I have the other.'

Odd. Presumably Drew had used the machine to write to someone. An explanation? A justification? A farewell note? If it had been any one of these it should turn up somewhere.

He thanked Stanton and the girl, and left.

That evening they were all three at the Copperhouse Arms. They ate in the little dining room overlooking the courtyard garden and they had it to themselves. It was still raining; no cat and no tortoise to be seen.

'Rabbit pie tonight,' the landlady said.

'*Rabbit* pie?'

'That's what I said.' She turned to Wycliffe. 'You'll remember what rabbit pie was like before the myxo – better'n any chicken, specially they battery things, an' that's what you'll have tonight. Tommy Burton from up the road do go out shooting an' he brought me in a han'som brace this lunchtime. It'll go down well with a lager or a bottle of medium to dryish white . . . Nothing too heavy – not with rabbit.'

She was right on all counts and the pie seemed to melt in the mouth.

Afterwards they settled comfortably to gossip over their coffee until Wycliffe said, later than usual, 'Time for my walk.'

But he walked only as far as his car, parked by the Incident Room, then he drove to St Ives. The roads were quiet. He left the car behind the Sloop then walked along the Wharf. A light wind blew in from the sea, sweeping curtains of misty rain before it. It was grey overhead and there were heavier clouds out to sea. Dusk was closing in and the harbour lights were on; half tide, with the water darker than the sky.

In the painter's upstairs room the curtains were undrawn, and he could distinguish two forms seated at the table by the window.

The lifeboat house, the public toilets, the footpath by the sea; a gentle surge broke in lilliputian waves against the rocks and across the sand. There was a light in a window of GG's flat and he noticed for the first time that there was a back entrance to the premises. He turned up into Bethel Street; GG's shop and the Badger's faced each other blindly across the junction. There was no-one about and apart from a solitary street lamp, no lights anywhere.

He had no particular objective in mind, but he persuaded himself that he could think more clearly about people when he shared with them the sights, sounds and smells which were the background of their lives. He felt certain Badger was at home. He was not in his shop. Was he in his workshop? In his kitchen? Or sprawled on his bed, drinking himself into a stupor?

The man both intrigued and repelled him. Badger had got under his skin, piercing the flimsy veneer of his self-confidence. It rankled. But had he truly professional reasons for his interest? It was easily possible that the old man had sent the anonymous bits of nonsense to at least five of the established citizens who had once, in their adolescence, been panicked into crime. But he suspected something more than that; something at the same time more adult and more sordid; and he saw Badger as the possible victim rather than the perpetrator.

Wondering about his true reason for being there, Wycliffe walked up the hill beside the high wall of Badger's wilderness garden and came to the alley. With no expectation that it would yield, he tried the latch of the plank door and it opened.

There was a path of sorts through the waist-high growth of weeds and he reached the back door of the house without difficulty. Again he was in luck; the door into the house was not locked. For form's sake he banged on it but there was no response so he let himself in. This time he had brought a pocket torch. He was in the kitchen. He called out, 'Anyone at home?' But his voice echoed in emptiness. He searched for a light switch and brought a forty-watt bulb to life.

Apart from a modern freezer, the kitchen could have been lifted complete out of an issue of *Ideal Home* from the early fifties. But, forty years on, neglect had brought squalor. He went through into the workshop, dimly lit by the street lamp outside, and walked past the skeletal model to the shop door. Nothing seemed to have changed. Back in the kitchen he called up the narrow stairs, again with no response. It was only when he reached the landing that he found Badger.

Badger was sprawled, head down, on the second flight of stairs. His head rested on the landing while his feet were some way up the flight. It looked as though he might have tripped at the top and fallen forwards. The stair carpet was everywhere frayed and in holes.

Wycliffe found a light switch. The old man's head was twisted sideways, his eyes were open and staring, and the hand that Wycliffe felt was cold; the fingers were flaccid. Badger had been dead for some time, long enough for rigor to become established and then to disappear.

Wycliffe looked down at the slight figure, dressed as he had first seen him in the same baggy trousers, the grubby shirt and unbuttoned waistcoat. The thin face was unshaven and his wispy grey hair stood out like a halo.

Wycliffe remembered: '. . . I don't fancy dying as a cover-up for others.' And then, 'All I'm asking is that *if* anything happens to me I shan't be shuffled off to the crematorium with no questions asked.'

There was a telephone in the workshop; he remembered seeing it on his first visit. He went back downstairs and telephoned Kersey at the pub. 'I'm at the model shop. Badger is dead. It could have been an accident, but it could equally have been arranged to look like one. We shall need the whole works.'

Chapter Seven

Friday evening

High-ranking CID officers who know their place do not discover bodies, nor do they get clobbered over the head; they have risen above such diversions. So, when he had telephoned, Wycliffe had to remind himself that this night's work might mean a court appearance with his notebook. He fished it out of his pocket and recorded incident, location and time. It was 22.09. Then he went back upstairs.

Both protocol and the Book dictated that he should now await the arrival of his experts, but if it had been his habit to heed either he would not have been there in the first place.

On the landing, looking up, he saw that the second flight of stairs ended at a door which stood open, presumably to another room. There was no landing up there so it was easy to imagine Badger, preoccupied or drunk, coming out of the room and tumbling down the stairs. In the poor light, Wycliffe could make out nothing of the interior of the room so he climbed the stairs, edging around the body, and went in. He fumbled for and found a light switch. The room was a typical attic, sloping ceiling, exposed rafters, dwarf walls and dormer window. It was large and everywhere there was chaos. Books had been swept off shelves; a filing cabinet had been emptied by the simple expedient of pulling out the drawers and upending them on to the floor; and the drawers of a desk in the dormer had been similarly treated. On the top of a wooden cupboard there was an ancient typewriter; the cupboard doors were open, and three of the shelves were

148

empty, their former contents, a great quantity of magazines, were heaped in a mound on the floor.

On the fourth shelf, the bottom one, there were several
bottles of brandy, unopened. The only other items in the
room, apparently undisturbed, were a series of framed
charcoal cartoons which hung above the bookshelves,
presumably the work of Julian Angove which Badger
had admired. One of them stood out: Badger himself,
instantly recognizable; his skull-like head and skinny
neck were set on a tiny body built of struts and ties like
the model downstairs. The initials J.A. appeared in one
corner.

The old man must have had an objective view of
himself to appreciate that.

And on a grubby piece of cardboard pinned to a rafter
there was a quotation, written in a good bold flowing
script with a felt pen: 'All that is solid melts into air, all
that is holy is profaned – Karl Marx.' No arguing with
that. At least the sage got that one right.

But Wycliffe was trying to take in the message of the
immediate chaos about him. It was blatant: there had
been a search. Too blatant?

Anyway, one thing was clear; if he wanted to know
more of what had made the strange old man at the bottom
of the stairs tick, this was the place to start. He walked
over to the desk. By the desk was a chair and on the
desk-top a bottle of brandy, a goblet with some of the
spirit remaining, and an open book – *Thomas Creevey's
Papers*. It looked as though Badger had been easing
himself into a literary bender.

Wycliffe returned to the typewriter: a pre-war
Remington, almost a museum piece. The anonymous bits
of nonsense which had been sent to five of the six, and
the cut-out photograph sent to the police, had all been
addressed on a vintage typewriter, the type poorly aligned
and much worn. No problem for the experts to decide
whether or not this was the machine.

Those messages, in particular their style, had troubled

149

him; there was something childish about them, reminiscent of the way one kid will sometimes hiss at another 'I know about you!'

For a little while he stood, looking out of the window. Due to the steeply rising ground and the extra storey, he was a good deal higher than any of the properties around. There was an uninterrupted view of the bay. He could see Godrevy light, and away to his left the lights of the town; while below him the narrow streets of the junction were wet and gleaming under the street lamp.

As he watched, a police car slipped into place beside the shop. No flashing lights, no siren. Sensible. Time to go down.

It was Lucy Lane with a uniformed PC. 'Mr Kersey has gone to the Incident Room; the doctor is on his way. Fox too. He and Collis finished late at the chalet so they're staying overnight with some of Fox's relatives in Hayle.'

Odd to be reminded that Fox must have relatives like other people. Wycliffe knew that he had a wife and that they were childless, but of his life away from work no-one had any inkling.

It was Lucy's first visit and she looked about her in the dark workshop with curiosity. Wycliffe was tired and his head was beginning to throb, but she looked as fresh as the girl who's had Vitabran for breakfast. He watched her as she stood looking down at the body of the old man, her expression grave and compassionate.

'So this is Badger . . . I wish I'd met him.' Then she turned to Wycliffe, 'I suppose the question now is, did he fall or was he pushed?'

Wycliffe smiled to himself. That was Lucy.

'If you look at the chaos upstairs it might help you to sort out your ideas.'

The uniformed man had been left outside to direct new arrivals and they heard somebody downstairs. Wycliffe went down. It was the irascible Dr Hocking.

'Oh, so we've got the brass here. What's happened to the old Badger to bring you in?'

'You know him?'

'I should do. He's been my patient for twenty-odd years. I suppose he's dead?' He followed Wycliffe up the first flight of stairs. A brief examination, then, 'Can I disturb him?'

'As little as possible. I want photographs.'

The little doctor shrugged. 'Well, he still stinks of drink and he was almost certainly drunk. I suppose he fell down the stairs.'

'And that killed him?'

Hocking became more cautious. 'Perhaps not, in itself. His heart was dodgy and that probably let him down finally; he's been asking for it for some time, pickling his liver in regular drinking bouts.' He looked at Wycliffe. 'I still don't understand what all the fuss is about.'

Wycliffe said, vaguely, 'It looks as though there was an intruder.'

'In other words it's not my business. All right, what do you want from me?'

'Can you give me any idea how long he's been here?'

'By divination, I suppose. Well, he's been here long enough for rigor to have come and gone, as you must know. Say twenty-four hours, which means he was killed on Thursday night. Are you going to have him shifted?'

'To the mortuary. I want Franks to do the PM.'

'So there is something fishy.'

'As far as you know, did he have any friends?'

'I believe there's a painter chap who comes here . . . Badger was a funny old bugger, a loner. Intelligent, well read . . . And a first-class craftsman . . . But there was a daft streak. Arnold Penrose, the lawyer, is his nephew and I reckon he's had his work cut out, keeping the old man out of trouble . . . Anyway, is that all? If so I'll get home to my bed.'

Wycliffe saw him to his car, and as he was returning to the house Fox arrived with his van.

From the workshop he telephoned Arnold Penrose. A female voice, incisive, non-committal, recited the number.

'Mrs Penrose? . . . This is Chief Superintendent Wycliffe. I would like to speak to your husband if he is available.'

'I'm sorry; he is not. Do you want to leave a message?' Wycliffe did.

Penrose joined them around midnight. He looked from his uncle's body, up the stairs. 'I suppose something of the sort was bound to happen sooner or later. His heart . . .'

'I don't want to involve you in technicalities tonight, but I assume that there is no-one else we need to inform? I mean, you are looking after his affairs?'

'Yes.'

Penrose was not drunk but he had, as the Irish say so precisely, 'drink taken', and he seemed to have difficulty in focusing his ideas. 'Yes . . . Yes, I suppose so. As far as I know, there is nobody else directly concerned with his affairs.'

Fox had photographed the body, according to the Book, 'from every angle', and the mortuary van arrived shortly after Penrose.

Wycliffe said, 'There will have to be a post mortem. I shall ask the coroner to nominate Franks.'

This appeared to shake the lawyer. 'Franks? But the PM is no more than a formality, surely?'

'I would like you to take a look upstairs.'

Penrose stood in the doorway of the attic and surveyed the chaos in silence. Finally, he said, 'He must have done this himself. I mean, why would anyone . . . ?' After a pause he went on, 'Where did that typewriter come from?'

'At least you will understand that there has to be an investigation. Everything will be left as it is until the morning but there will be a constable downstairs.'

Penrose seemed dazed. 'Of course you will do as you

think necessary. I must admit this is beyond me at the moment.'

It was after one when Wycliffe and Lucy Lane returned to their cars, leaving a constable on watch. All the surrounding buildings were in darkness, the peace of the neighbourhood had not been disturbed. The rain had gone, it was a clear night and overhead there were stars.

They joined Kersey in the Incident Room where he had stayed to handle any development that might have arisen. Wycliffe gave him a brief update and all three crossed the road to the Copperhouse Arms, and bed. They had keys, so they let themselves in with as little noise as possible and for once there was no telephone call to Helen.

Wycliffe made up his mind that he would be a long time getting to sleep and he lay there staring at the dim rectangle of the window. His room was at the back of the house, away from the street lamps. Half-awake, half-dreaming, he was thinking of Badger, when the model maker's head seemed to materialize out of the darkness, the thin features, the straggling moustache and wispy beard, but as the image seemed about to come into perfect focus, it faded.

Wycliffe turned over on his side, muttering, 'Badger fell down the stairs.' And a moment later he added, 'All these steps and stairs!' And fell asleep.

Saturday morning, 16 May

Before breakfast he telephoned Helen and confessed to his knock on the head. 'In case some idiot gets it into the papers, believe me it was nothing . . . Yes, I've seen a doctor and he agrees.'

'You'll be home this evening?'

'Yes, but I have to look in at St Germans on the way. I should be home by about half-seven, but I can't say for sure at the moment.' He had to make up his mind whether to put the inquiry on hold over Sunday. Even in a murder case he had to take account of overtime as well as the need to give everybody a break.

They breakfasted in the little dining room of the pub, all three of them feeling like the morning after. Wycliffe and Lucy Lane had fruit juice, toast and coffee; Kersey ventured on a boiled egg.

Wycliffe yawned and felt his bump. 'I shall be leaving this afternoon; I have to be at St Germans by six. I want a house-to-house in the Bethel Street area. Find out if anyone saw or heard anybody or anything during the whole of Thursday evening and night. Obviously we are interested mainly in Badger's place and the health shop – remember, by the way, there's an entrance to her flat from the sea side as well as through the shop. But don't set a limit to their inquiries. Let's hear about anyone seen in the locality whom the residents can put a name to.'

'Do they tackle the lady herself?'

'Why not? Get it organized, Doug. Curnow, with the help of a uniformed man, should be able to manage that. For the rest of us, short of any dramatic developments, we shall pack it in this afternoon until Monday. We haven't had Franks's report on the Badger PM, and I doubt if we shall hear from Forensic on the chalet stuff until early next week. I'll arrange for Division to notify me if anything crops up – in particular if they pick up Drew or his car.'

He turned to Lucy Lane. 'Fox will be starting at Badger's place. For today, let Iris Thorn join the team. It will be experience for her if only in getting used to Fox's little ways.' And then, to Kersey, 'I want you to keep an eye on that set-up, Doug.'

Kersey said, 'What will they be looking for in particular?'

'Obviously, anything which links Badger with the six – anything at all. And you'd better fix for somebody to look at that typewriter and compare the type with the anonymous notes. I've no doubt they'll match, but we need to be sure. It's important that Fox should record any prints which might turn out to be identifiable.'

The rain had moved away overnight and the morning was warm and sunny. On their way to the Incident Room, Kersey, as usual, bought the *Morning News*. And on the front page, with a two-column spread near the bottom, was a report under twin headlines:

Police Chief in Mysterious Attack

Link with Wilder Tragedy?

It has just become known that on Thursday evening Detective Chief Superintendent Wycliffe was assaulted while investigating a break-in at a holiday chalet on the towans at Hayle. Mr Wycliffe, who was alone at the time, was not seriously hurt, but there has been no explanation of how a senior officer came to be involved in such an apparently trivial incident.

It is known that the police were showing considerable interest in the chalet before the attack, probably because of its proximity to the duncs in which the body of Cochran Wilder was uncovered on Monday. At present officers of the Area Crime Squad are engaged in a detailed examination of the chalet and we understand that certain objects have been removed for forensic examination . . .

Wycliffe muttered under his breath and pushed the paper aside. Kersey growled, 'And now they've got a dead Badger.'

Wycliffe was in a curious mood. Perhaps because he was tired, he felt oddly detached and yet responsible. He seemed to be watching a play in which he had no part and over which he had no control. He was trying to discover a plot which eluded him, and he felt guilty.

Badger had called him off the street to say, 'I want you to know that my life may be in danger.' Admittedly the old man had refused help and warned against interference. 'I shall resent any attempt you make to pry into my affairs.' All the same . . .

Kersey was saying to Lucy Lane, 'As I see it Badger's death at this time is the kind of coincidence that a hungry shark wouldn't swallow. Apart from anything else, are we to believe that he created all the havoc we saw last night himself?'

Lucy agreed. 'On the other hand, if somebody killed him and searched the place, what were they looking for? In the chaos they created I would have thought they were unlikely to find much.'

Kersey said, 'Panic. My money is on the estate agent, Drew. It was obvious when I talked to him that he was teetering on the edge. He decided to remove evidence from the chalet, got trapped, and landed himself in a bigger mess by clobbering the chief. Then, frantic, he turns on Badger in the belief that the old man was the other source of danger. He broke in when Badger was out for his evening walk, searched the place, and was caught in the act.'

The exchange was for Wycliffe's benefit and Kersey was coat-trailing as usual, this time with Lucy Lane aiding and abetting. But Wycliffe would not be drawn. All he said was, 'So, for one reason or another we've got to find Drew, and I don't imagine that's going to be too difficult. When we hear what Franks has to say about Badger's death and what Fox and Co find in the model shop, I hope we shall be in a better position to make up our minds.'

Restless, he decided to look in at the Modelmakers again. From the first he had been uneasy about the nature of any link Badger may have had with the dead boy or, for that matter, with the six, and he had been inclined to minimize their importance. But now Badger was dead and as Kersey said, that was a coincidence too many.

*   *   *

Saturday. No school, but Lisa and Martin had breakfast at the usual time. Martin had eaten his toast and was drinking his second cup of coffee. The eight o'clock news was on the radio and Lisa listened, tense in the fear that each item as it came might tell of a fresh development, a new threat. But the Wilder case was not mentioned.

She felt that she was nearing the end of her tether. In the bathroom mirror she had seen the face of an older woman, haggard; and when Martin came downstairs to breakfast he had remarked, uniquely, 'You look peaky. Don't you feel well?'

'Now the local news. A report has just come in of the death of a well-known figure in St Ives. Mr Henry Badger of the model shop on the corner of Bethel Street, who for many years has lived alone in the rooms above his shop, was found dead last night at the bottom of a flight of stairs leading to an attic. It seems likely that his death was due to falling down the stairs but the police are unable at the moment to exclude entirely the possibility of foul play. An investigation of the circumstances is under way.'

Lisa, her hands clenched beneath the table, whispered, 'Oh, God!' But she controlled herself.

Martin said, 'He was asking for it, an old man living alone like that.' He added after a pause, 'Funny old boy . . . He's been there ever since I can remember and he doesn't seem to have changed much.'

It was unusual for Martin to be so reflective.

Lisa plucked up courage. 'I don't know what you intend to do today but I saw Barbara Hart yesterday in town. She's pregnant again and I promised I would look in for a chat some time this morning. It would probably mean staying to lunch.'

Lisa was lying, and she was not very good at it, but Martin seemed not to notice. 'I thought you'd cut yourself off from your schoolfriends. You've said so often enough.'

'I know, but she was very pleasant and anxious for a bit of gossip so I didn't like to be awkward. If you could get yourself something for lunch – there's plenty of stuff in the freezer.'

'I expect I'll manage. It might even cheer you up.'

GG was in her office behind the shop. She had no client with her and she was staring out of the big window without seeing the familiar scene. People passed along the footwalk from time to time but she did not see them either. Arnold had telephoned her at two in the morning, his manner almost professional. He had offered no consolation or reassurance and he was non-committal. 'We shall have to see where this leads.'

GG told herself, 'He's washing his hands, the bastard!'

She had listened to the eight o'clock news with its hint of foul play, and their parting shot, 'An investigation of the circumstances is under way.' What circumstances? Arnold had told her no details.

Adding to her concern she had in front of her the *Morning News*, 'Police Chief in Mysterious Attack'. She looked at the telephone, she had to talk to someone. Julian was no use. Alan Hart would be in the middle of his morning surgery . . .

One of the shop girls tapped on the door and came in. 'A Mrs Bell wants to see you.'

She was about to ask who Mrs Bell was when she saw Lisa standing in the doorway. 'Lisa! I can never think of you as Mrs Bell.'

GG's welcome was unexpectedly warm; the two women had exchanged no more than a passing greeting in years.

'My dear! You look all in. Let's have some tea. I'll get one of the girls to . . .' She went through to the shop. A very different GG.

They were sitting opposite each other with their tea cups on the desk . . . Lisa was still nervous. 'I hesitated about coming. I thought you might have clients . . .'

'No clients on Saturday. Saturday is my day off.' She reached into a drawer and brought out a packet of cigarettes. 'It's the only time I can smoke in here, too. You mustn't let them smell it, and they've got noses like bloodhounds. Have one?'

'I don't, thanks.'

GG had lit up and was taking that first luxurious drag. 'It's all that keeps me sane, but most days I have to sneak upstairs.' She broke off. 'You don't have to tell me why you're here. I can guess.'

GG pushed back her mop of red hair.

Lisa said, 'I don't think I can take much more. Nothing could be worse than just sitting back and waiting for the next thing.'

GG was looking at her through a cloud of tobacco smoke. 'Keep your voice down. Those two in the shop have ears like microphones.' She pushed over the *Morning News* and pointed. 'Have you seen this?'

Lisa read the report through to the end and when she had finished she looked up. 'You think that was Paul?'

'Who else? He's crazy. He's never been normal – you, if anybody, should know that. And then he goes and marries that ghastly woman. After all, who was it who started all this?'

Lisa was shaken by the matter of fact, almost casual way in which GG referred to events of which she could not bear to think, let alone speak. And yet, the fact that it was possible to talk brought with it a feeling of release.

In a timid voice scarcely above a whisper, she asked, 'And the old man? Do you think Paul . . . ?'

GG didn't bother to answer directly. 'It's always the weak ones who turn to violence. Alan did his best to get some sense into him before it was too late but he was over the top and now he's cleared out.'

Lisa shivered. 'That night . . .'

'Don't think about it.'

'But when they catch him . . .'

'*If* they catch him.'

159

Lisa raised herself to the sticking point. 'You really think Badger sent us those . . . those notes?'

GG tapped ash from her cigarette. 'Arnold thinks so; although he denies it to the police. It's the kind of trick the old man's been up to lately.'

'But how did he get to know about us?'

GG frowned. 'That's a question; but we don't know what tongues have been wagging over the years. In any case, Julian has been a regular visitor across the road.'

'Julian? You can't believe that he would want to cause trouble for us.' Lisa was gathering her courage. 'And then there's the photograph – somebody cut me out of the photo Barbara took and sent it to the police. That's how they found out about the necklace.'

GG looked at her, eyes narrowed. 'I suppose Julian had a copy of the photo like the rest of us. I wonder if he's got it now.'

'But why would he want to stir up all this? It could only do him harm.'

GG stubbed out her cigarette. 'I think we should get together, all of us, and talk this out.'

Wycliffe drove to St Ives, parked his car, and walked along the Wharf. It had become almost a routine, but today the sun was shining and there was a taste of summer in the air. The little shops in Bethel Street selling paintings and books were emerging from hibernation, their windows gleamed, there were fresh pictures on show and some of the doors were open. But the Model-makers had not changed. Wycliffe went up the hill and entered by the back way. A constable in the kitchen said, 'They're upstairs, sir.'

Lucy Lane was in the sitting room on the first floor. The furniture was quality stuff from the fifties but there was a pervasive smell of damp and disuse. A bloom of mould on the arms of the leather chairs, and on the tops of little tables; peeling wallpaper, and a large damp patch on the chimney breast told their tale of neglect.

Lucy said, 'The others are up in the attic. I thought I'd take a more general look around.'

Although there was such chaos in the attic, nothing seemed to have been disturbed elsewhere. Did this mean that the searcher had found what he was looking for upstairs?

Lucy went on, 'This room sheds a different light on Badger's past.'

It did. Along with some quite acceptable landscapes on the walls there was a single framed photograph, a wedding photograph. The lean Badger, beardless, but with a good head of brown hair, middle-thirties, a figure of dignity in a well-cut suit, stood close to his bride. The bride, an attractive young woman in pale blue with a broad-brimmed hat, carried a bouquet of carnations, and the groom wore a buttonhole.

'Harry and Lydia 2 September 1951' was inscribed at the bottom.

Wycliffe protested, 'Coombes told me Badger married a widow. That girl is younger than he is.'

Lucy said, 'I suppose there are widows under thirty. But look at these.' She opened an album that was lying on an occasional table and turned the pages. 'This was in the lacquered cupboard by the window.' More photographs of the couple, mostly in climbing gear, roped together or alone on some precipitous slope, abseiling down a vertical face or clinging to invisible finger and toe holds. There were cryptic labels: 'In the Fells', 'Chamonix', 'At the Climbing School', 'Snowdonia' . . . The dates were spread over five years and the photographs covered eight or ten pages of the album; the rest was empty.

'You carry on snooping, I'll take a look upstairs.'

The attic had been tidied; Iris Thorn had piled the magazines (all architectural publications) in heaps, and was stacking them in the cupboard from which they had come. Collis was working through the books still on their shelves, examining them one at a time. Fox was still sorting the litter of folders, letters and pamphlets which had come from the filing cabinet.

He turned to Wycliffe. 'No luck, sir; nothing so far, anyway. Nothing that could connect Badger with the chalet lot.'

'The typewriter?'

'Oh, that's a different matter. I got a chap over from Redruth who knows about typewriters and he's prepared to give evidence in court if necessary. He's in no doubt that the anonymous communications were addressed on the Remington machine in the attic. He says the type itself is unusual, it's also out of alignment in distinctive ways, and at least eight of the letters have defects which identify them.'

Fox stroked his long nose. 'If you ask me, sir, whoever searched the place went off with the evidence we are looking for, evidence that would have incriminated him and his friends.'

Wycliffe was watching Collis working through his books, unhurried but never stopping: pick one up, flip through it, put it on the shelf, pick up another . . . Given the job, Collis would have worked through the Bodleian at Oxford with the same equanimity.

Wycliffe said, 'You've seen a lot of searches conducted by amateurs in your time, Fox. Did you ever see one which created the kind of senseless havoc you found here?'

'Panic, sir.'

'You think so? You don't think the whole thing was a fake? People who fabricate evidence usually over-do it.'

'I can't see the point, sir.'

'What about prints?'

'The old man's everywhere, apart from that just two strangers, a man and a woman – several specimens of the man's, only two of the woman's.'

'The keys of the typewriter?'

'Wiped clean, and that takes a bit of doing.'

'Compare those you've got with Penrose, Angove and the Grey woman.'

'Yes, sir. And still on the matter of prints, I've checked those on the wheel brace with the ones on the photograph Drew gave Mr Kersey. They match. It was Drew who clobbered you, sir. No doubt about that.'

For the first time Wycliffe took a look at the other framed charcoal drawings above the bookshelves. Badger was probably right, Julian Angove was wasting his talent on pot-boilers. Here was a series of contemporary political figures in the guise of *Alice* characters: John Major as the White Rabbit with the Maastricht Treaty under his arm, John Smith as Old Father William, balancing an eel labelled 'Middle Class' on the end of his nose . . . Lord Tebbit as the March Hare . . . Wycliffe chuckled, and earned a strange look from Fox.

Wycliffe said, 'Good! Carry on here for the rest of the day, then pack it in. Come back on Monday and work through the rest of the house.'

Wycliffe had lunch at the café in Bethel Street. Neither Penrose nor GG was there. So it was Drew who had clobbered him with the wheel brace. No surprise about that. But had he then gone on to the Modelmakers to devastate the attic and assault Badger?

After his meal Wycliffe drove back to Hayle and spent an hour with Kersey in the Incident Room. Shortly before he left, the telephone rang and he answered it. 'Put her through.'

It was Molly Bissett, sounding unusually disturbed. She spoke in a low voice. 'I wanted to make sure that you will be here this evening . . . Earlier if you can make it . . . Something has cropped up . . .' She finished hurriedly, 'I can't talk now.'

Father playing up? Trouble at the funeral? Wycliffe was puzzled. Molly Bissett was not the sort to become flustered.

He turned to Kersey. 'I'll be off then; see you on

Monday. Make the most of the weekend.' He collected his bag from the pub and set out for St Germans.

He arrived there shortly after five. The sun was shining and the street was deserted except for a car parked here and there and a dog asleep outside the pub. The white gate of Franklin's stood open. He left his car and walked up the drive between the sombre laurels. Two cars were parked in the open space before the house. Molly answered his ring almost at once. 'I'm so glad you've come.' She lowered her voice. 'He's had a very disturbing letter and it's upset him.' Then, speaking normally, she added, 'We're in the drawing room.'

This was the room he had been in before. Two men stood up as he entered. Wilder was instantly recognizable from his TV exposure, heavily built, short necked, loose jowled and florid. The other was Molly's naval-officer husband, tall, slim, greying and dignified, looking vaguely uncomfortable in civvies.

On a low table in front of the fireplace there was a decanter of whisky and glasses. Molly's introductions were perfunctory. 'You've spoken to father on the phone, now here he is in the flesh; and this is my husband, Tony; I've told you about him. He's supposed to be in Gibraltar but he flew home for the funeral.'

They were all three on edge. Wilder said, 'Drink, Wycliffe?'

'Thanks, but I still have to drive home.'

That seemed to put the damper on any thaw there might have been.

'Anyway, let's sit down.'

Molly said, 'Tony and I will leave you to it. I'll make some tea; I'm sure we can all do with a cup.'

When they had gone Wilder mumbled, 'Good of you to come, Wycliffe, in view of what's gone before . . . Anyway, I'm asking a favour.' He fished in an inside pocket and produced a folded piece of paper. 'Here, read this! It came this morning but I said nothing until after the funeral. Of course you've got to see it, but I'd give a lot to keep it out of the hands of the media.'

Wycliffe unfolded the paper, obviously a piece from which a printed heading had been roughly cut away. It was typewritten and unaddressed, a statement rather than a letter. Wycliffe noted that the type itself was modern and faultless but the text was telegraphic and disjointed. The spacing was uneven and the punctuation erratic. A man at the end of his tether trying desperately to seize upon a few salient facts from the tumult of his mind and commit them to paper.

'It was an accident nobody wanted your son to die He was being turned out for what he had done to a girl he was naked and we were going to throw his clothes and his belongings after him he was standing at the top of the steps calling us names when somebody gave him a push he overbalanced and fell and hit his head on the concrete He was dead It was an accident and we were scared we were terrified. What we did after that has never been out of my mind We did not want to hurt your son it was an accident We did not . . .' And there the statement ended.

Wycliffe took time to read it and when he had finished he said, 'Very strange.'

'Is that all you can find to say?' Wilder, instantly aggressive, calmed down almost at once. 'I apologize! I'm on edge.' He looked at Wycliffe, his eyes moist and his voice barely under control. 'Do you think that's what happened? Do you think this man, whoever he is, is telling the truth?'

'I think that your son's death was accidental in the sense that it was unintentional. This is only one person's version of the circumstances, but I have no doubt that, broadly speaking, it is true.'

Wilder beat out a tattoo with his fingers on the arm of his chair. 'No, neither have I. It's got the stamp of truth. And all this happened in the chalet place they've mentioned in the papers?'

'I'm waiting for forensic confirmation but that seems to be the case.'

Wilder muttered to himself, 'A fight over a girl.'

Wycliffe said nothing. The black marble clock on the mantelpiece chimed the half-hour and abruptly Wilder leaned forward and reached for the decanter. 'Let's have a drink!' He poured whisky into two glasses. 'A small one won't push you over the limit for God's sake!'

Wycliffe would have been glad of that cup of tea but Molly was keeping away.

Wilder pointed to the typewritten sheet which now lay on the table between them. 'You know who wrote this, don't you?'

'I suspect; I don't know.'

Wilder said nothing and the silence lengthened. He sipped his drink. Once or twice he seemed to be on the point of speaking but did not. In the end it came. 'This group in the chalet on whom my son is supposed to have forced his company; how many, and how old?'

'There were six of them, all aged seventeen or eighteen; three boys and three girls. They were all at school preparing for A-levels.'

'I suppose you've talked to them. What do they say?'

'Up until now they've denied having seen your son.'

'They must be in their thirties now . . . My boy would have been thirty-six.' Wilder shifted violently in his chair. 'God, what a mess . . . This necklace all the fuss has been about – how do they account for that?'

'The girl it belonged to says she lost it in the dunes and that your son must have picked it up.'

'Do you believe that?'

It was Wycliffe's turn to remain silent.

'He was ill, Wycliffe; mentally ill. Do you think I don't blame myself for sending him off like that? . . . I thought he was cured; he was so plausible . . . The hospital . . . Bloody doctors!'

It was clear that Wilder was screwing himself up to a commitment. It came at last in the form of a question, but put so casually that it might have had no significance at all, 'Could the whole thing be dropped . . . ? If there was an open verdict from the coroner . . .'

'You know very well, sir, that it would not be up to me; it would be a matter for the Crown Prosecution Service.'

'But your private view?'

'I think that wounds should be given a chance to heal.'

Wilder looked at him. 'You're a good chap, Wycliffe.' He got up and crossed to the door which he opened, and bellowed down the corridor. 'What happened about that tea, Molly?'

Wycliffe arrived home at a little after seven. The two women were in the kitchen preparing a meal and he had a warm welcome. Even Macavity consented to purr when scratched behind the ear. Wycliffe kissed his wife and daughter and thought that Ruth looked better, less strained.

'How goes it?'

She smiled. 'Sometimes I feel as though I've never been away. Of course I miss him.'

The ritual sherry.

Helen said, 'Let me feel your head.' She did. 'Yes, well, it doesn't seem too bad but you're too old to be getting up to tricks like that. Now, by the time you've had your shower this will be ready.'

The ritual cleansing. He hoped that it might wash away a clinging sense of guilt. Badger had been put into cold storage – and that was more than a metaphor. Paul Drew was on the loose somewhere, and there were at least five other people on tenterhooks, wondering where it would all end; and that did not include Wilder. But everything stops for tea.

After their meal they walked down the garden to the water and along the tideline to St Juliot, their nearest village. Across the estuary the lights of the city flared in the night. It brought back memories of night walks along the shore when the twins were young. He felt nostalgic, sentimental, but he could not get the Wilders out of his mind.

Abruptly, he said, 'Ruth, do you remember when you were in the Sixth at school?'

'Of course I do, why?'

'I don't mean the things you did, but how you felt about certain things when you were in your late teens.'

Helen said, 'You'll have to be more specific, Charles.'

'I was afraid of that. I'll try again. Looking back, do you think that in certain circumstances, along with your friends, and out of anger or fear or even loyalty to those friends, you might, conceivably, have committed or connived in a serious criminal act?'

He thought how easy it was to make a sensible question sound like ponderous nonsense.

Ruth was silent while they crunched over the sandy gravel for another fifty yards or so, then she said, 'You sound like a policeman, Dad – or worse, like a lawyer, and I've just realized what you're getting at. It's the Wilder case, isn't it? Why not come out with it? Through listening to the news and hearing you talk I've got a pretty good idea of what's in your mind. You don't think he was deliberately killed, do you? . . . I suppose it was a fight where tempers got out of hand.'

'Not even that. As far as I can see it was no more than a quarrel which led to a scuffle in which Wilder got pushed down a flight of steps. And I've no doubt they were shocked and horrified by it. But what troubles me is their planned, cold-blooded cover-up. To take Wilder's body, wrapped in a sheet, and carry it through the dunes to a suitable spot and to bury it along with his belongings . . . To me, that seems inexplicable behaviour for a group of average sixth-formers . . . Can you understand it?'

They were passing the backs of little houses, outposts of the village, and there were lights in some of the windows. Boats were drawn up on the shingle, others were moored off, and ahead they could see the shadowy outline of the disused jetty.

Wycliffe had given up expecting a reply and when it came he was surprised by Ruth's grave, reflective manner. 'Yes. I can understand it. At that age, and in a group, I think something like it could have happened to me. With my schooldays coming to an end and my whole future suddenly under threat, I might easily have panicked and at least have followed somebody else's lead in a cover-up.'

Wycliffe would have liked to probe further but Ruth had taken his question to heart, so he said, 'I see.' And after a pause, he added, 'Interesting.'

They climbed the steps to the jetty and picked their way over its uneven surface to the road. Wycliffe was aware that by his question he had created an inexplicable tension.

Again it was Ruth who broke the silence. 'I think there's something else which could have had something to do with how your teenagers reacted. It wouldn't have been wholly out of fear for the future. Part of it might have been that they couldn't face the recriminations, especially the silent ones, from family and teachers. I don't think that parents in particular realize the burden of responsibility they put upon their children merely by being proud of them.'

She broke off with a self-conscious little laugh, then added, 'Now can we change the subject?'

They were passing the pub and Wycliffe, embarrassed by the confidences he had provoked, said, 'Why don't we go in for a drink?'

Helen, who had not spoken for some time, said, 'Yes, let's do that.'

There were three or four customers on stools by the bar and a couple playing pool, but the tables were empty and they took their drinks to a corner – two gin and tonics, and a lager.

*   *   *

Although he was tired Wycliffe lay awake. The moon had risen and despite the curtains the room was almost like day. He was thinking about the strange communication Wilder had received that morning. From Drew of course. Drew had visited the estate agent's office at some time during Thursday night in order to type it; after the fracas in the chalet, the final straw. By that time he had given up all hope, and yet he still had a compelling need to, as he saw it, put the record straight. Was that it? If so, does a man with nothing to lose always tell the truth?

'He was standing at the top of the steps . . . Somebody gave him a push . . . He overbalanced and fell . . . He hit his head on the concrete . . .'

Franks had argued that because the injury was to the vertex of the skull it was unlikely to have been caused by a fall. But a fall occasioned by a push down a flight of steps on to concrete?

There was concrete dust in the head wound. But what concrete? Wycliffe turned over heavily and Helen murmured, 'Can't you sleep?'

He wished that he had in front of him two photographs, one taken by Barbara Hart (as she now was) fifteen years ago, and one of many taken by Fox on Friday morning.

And then he thought of Drew and the declaration which he had sent to Wilder. Unsigned but unmistakably coming from him. Wycliffe's respect for the man was increasing, and his last thought before he gave up and finally drifted into sleep was, 'Poor devil!'

Sunday, another pleasant day, a late breakfast and another walk to St Juliot, this time for the papers. The church bells of St Juliot were pealing, sending their dying ripples of sound chasing each other across the estuary and the countryside. Wycliffe was aware of the Sabbath atmosphere, that sense of calm which, in the countryside at least, seems to have survived Sunday opening, Sunday sport and the Sunday supplements.

Before lunch there was a telephone call from David,

Ruth's twin, who, married with a child, was living and working in Kenya.

Jonathan piped, 'Hullo Granny!' on the telephone and, 'Thank you for your birthday present.' And afterwards Ruth talked with her brother in that cryptospeak which is only intelligible between twins.

The women spent much of the day gardening and Wycliffe was allowed to sit on the terrace, reading and dozing with Macavity for company. He spent some of the time thinking, in a drowsy sort of way – brooding was the better word. There was Helen, the girl he had met by chance more than thirty years ago. Now, like himself, she was on the wrong side of middle age, yet still he could not bear the thought of any separation. And there, working beside her mother was Ruth, their daughter, a grown woman. A little while ago he had spoken on the telephone to their son, to their son's wife, and to their grandson . . .

They were an ordinary family, and yet so very strange.

Last night it had been brought home to him how strange families are.

They had a scratch lunch, and jointly prepared their evening meal which was not entirely spoiled by too many cooks.

Chapter Eight

Monday morning, 18 May

By previous arrangement with his deputy, John Scales, and Diane, Wycliffe was early at the office and by nine o'clock they had dealt with items which had proved too tricky for the telephone. John Scales's forte was administration, and that was lucky for Wycliffe who regarded an office chair as having all the appeal of a straight jacket.

At the door, on his way out, Wycliffe said, 'Just one more thing, John, see what you can pick up in our legal department about Penrose and Son, Solicitors. They're an old-established firm and they must be known in the fraternity.'

Wycliffe escaped, and was driving out of the car park as the chief was driving in. Just in time; another minute would have cost him at least an hour.

The morning was bright and brassy, that false start which weather watchers know only too well, and by the time Wycliffe reached the moors mist was closing in. In Hayle there was a fine drizzle, insidiously wet.

He arrived there well before eleven and outside the Incident Room he had to run the gauntlet of the press, the largest contingent so far, three men and two women.

'How did Badger die, Mr Wycliffe?'

'I don't know. He was found at the bottom of a flight of stairs with injuries consistent with a fall. I haven't yet had the report of the pathologist.'

'Is it true that his place was ransacked?'

'No. One room – an attic, was turned over.'

'Somebody looking for something?'

'It's possible, but if they were I don't know what.'

'Any connection with the Wilder affair?'

'I don't think that Mr Badger was in any way concerned in Cochran Wilder's death.'

'What about Paul Drew?'

'What about him? We are anxious to contact him and so far we have been unable to do so.'

'How is your head?'

'I think I shall live.'

They let him through. Kersey had driven down straight from home and was already well settled in. 'I couldn't get rid of them, they knew or guessed that you were on your way here. Anyway, Franks has been on the line and wants you to ring him back. Lucy is at the Modelmakers with Fox . . .'

'Any news of Paul Drew?'

'Yes. Curnow's house-to-house turned up two people who claim to have seen him on Thursday evening at about eleven. He was walking along Bethel Street in the direction of the Modelmakers.'

'All right! Say it. You knew that Drew was our man.'

Kersey grinned. 'No comment, sir. It's safer.'

'Any of the others seen in the neighbourhood?'

'The lawyer, Penrose. He was seen in Bethel Street around ten, apparently on his way to GG's place, and about an hour later he was seen again . . . Everybody in the neighbourhood knows the drill. He parks his car, by arrangement, in a yard close by and sometimes it's there all night. Incidentally, Curnow spoke to GG and she said she hadn't seen anybody on Thursday evening because she didn't go out.'

'It seems Penrose wasn't with her for long – under the hour according to your witnesses. Has anything come in since?'

'Nothing significant, sir. Nothing more on Drew or his car since those sightings on Thursday evening. It's odd. I could understand it if he was an old hand but the man's an innocent, he hardly knows his way in out of the wet.'

'And his wife is no help?'

'Lucy had a good go but if the woman knows or suspects anything she's keeping it to herself. But Lucy's impression was that she doesn't care a damn what's happened to him. The house is in her name and she's got money of her own. So what? Can you imagine being married to such a woman?'

'Take a look at that.' Wycliffe handed over the statement which had been sent to Wilder.

Kersey read and reread the typewritten sheet. 'Drew?'

'Who else?'

Kersey nodded. 'I could see that he couldn't hold out for much longer; he had to get it off his chest. I wonder which of the girls . . . ?'

'Didn't Lisa Bell tell Lucy that she walked out on Drew in the middle of the night? Where could she go except into the living room?'

'Where Wilder must have been dossing down on the sofa or the floor. It adds up. Are you going to tackle the girl?'

'I would like to find Drew first. In the meantime I want to get some early background on Badger: who he married, how she came to be a widow at such an early age, where her money came from and how she died. She must have been still short of forty then . . . I think I'll pay a visit to Mrs Penrose.'

'The lawyer's wife?'

'His mother. After all she's Badger's sister and it's time we talked to someone who was around when it was all happening.'

Kersey looked doubtful. 'I know you've got an idea, sir, but I can't for the life of me see where Badger's early life comes into it.'

Wycliffe ignored the implied question. 'Of course what I get from Mrs Penrose is sure to be prejudiced, but if there's anything that seems worth following up we can get Coombes to turn up an outsider who knows about the family.'

He was going through his case file. 'Before I ring Franks I want to look at a couple of photographs.' He selected the two which interested him, studied them for a moment, then passed them to Kersey. 'In the first one, the famous photograph of the six, you can see in the background the lower steps of the flight leading up to the chalet as they were fifteen years ago. In the second, taken by Fox, you can see the whole flight of steps as it is today.'

Kersey said, 'Those steps have been replaced.'

'And?'

'There used to be a concrete kerb at the bottom that isn't there now.'

'And it was on that kerb that Wilder hit his head.'

'You're not suggesting that the steps were renewed because—'

'Of course not, but it's something we should have noticed.' He reached for the telephone. 'We'll see what Franks thinks.'

Franks got in first. 'I've had a look at your Badger offering, Charles. Not much of him was there? Not in bulk anyway. So he fell head-first down the stairs; that would square well enough with his various contusions, the fracture of his right ulna and the dislocation of his right shoulder.'

'But the question is, did he fall or was he pushed?'

'I don't know, I wasn't there, but the nature of his injuries makes it clear that he went down head first and that suggests that he might have been pushed.'

'What did he die of?'

'Not as a direct result of the fall. He must have been in a pretty bad way when he reached the bottom, and with his dicky heart he wouldn't have survived for long, but somebody finished him off with a blow to the back of the neck at the base of the skull. I missed it at first but there is no doubt about it; that's what finished him off. It was not a very powerful blow but, unusually, it displaced the atlas vertebra and damaged the cord.'

'Any idea of the weapon?'

'Would you believe a blunt instrument? A stout metal rod for instance, half an inch or more in thickness, would be my guess.'

'Presumably, whoever did it needed to make sure he was dead.'

'That sounds reasonable but they needn't have bothered, the Badger wouldn't have kept them waiting long.'

Wycliffe told him about the steps at the chalet. 'Steps and stairs are a recurring theme in this case. Anyway, it seems likely that Wilder was standing at the top of those steps, being thrown out, naked, when one of the party pushed him and he went headlong down the steps, striking his head on a concrete kerb. Does that sound half-way credible to you?'

Franks hesitated. 'You can't expect a firm quotable opinion off the cuff but, between ourselves, yes, it does. The Badger affair sounds like a repeat performance but without the concrete kerb.'

'Good! That's what I wanted to hear. Thanks.'

Franks was impressed. 'What have I said to earn such effusive gratitude? I'm not used to it.'

The truth was that Wycliffe was beginning to feel on firmer ground; the pattern which he had suspected was defining itself. He turned to Kersey. 'Whether Badger was pushed or not is academic, but he was murdered by a blow to the back of the head. The weapon, according to Franks, could have been a stout metal bar of some sort. I want Fox back at the Modelmakers looking for it. There's a whole armoury of tools in the old man's workshop.'

'There is also the small matter of laying our hands on Drew, sir.'

Wycliffe was almost dismissive. 'Drew will turn up. Meanwhile, I'm going to talk to the dowager Mrs Penrose.'

Kersey said, as though it were an accusation, 'You sound positively cheerful.'

*　*　*

The Penroses lived in a pleasant house in a large garden high above St Ives; overlooking the bay, of course, but now all was shrouded in mist.

Wycliffe's ring was answered by a pretty girl with a mass of chestnut hair to her shoulders; three children in the three to six age range, trailed behind her in the hall, two girls and a boy.

'May I help you, please?' Perfect English – too perfect, the words were handled as though with chopsticks. A French *au pair*?

'Superintendent Wycliffe.' He showed his warrant card.

'Police? You wish to see Mr Penrose? I am sorry—'

'No, I would like a word with Mrs Penrose – his mother.'

'Ah, I will see . . . Be good, children!'

A very attractive girl; jeans and a T-shirt do more for some than the wiles of fashion. She flitted along a corridor and in a couple of minutes she was back. 'If you will come this way, please . . .'

He was taken to a room with a window facing towards the sea. A thin, bony, vigorous woman, waited to greet him. Her white straight hair was cut in an uncompromising 'bob' and she wore a plain grey frock, severely cut. She could have been the retired headmistress of an old-style girls' school.

'Chief Superintendent Wycliffe.'

'Clarice Penrose. I suppose it really is me that you wish to see, Mr Wycliffe?'

Wycliffe assured her.

'Well, that's something these days. Do make yourself comfortable.'

It was a comfortable room: a couple of not-too-easy chairs, a *chaise-longue*, a table and a writing desk, a workbox on casters, a television and plenty of books and magazines.

'This is my room. I come here whenever I am in people's way, or they are in mine.'

Involuntarily Wycliffe was comparing the room with Badger's attic. He expressed sympathy at the death of her brother and she thanked him. 'It is sad, even in old age, to lose someone who shared one's memories of childhood and youth. Henry was only a little older than I . . . Of course he shouldn't have been living alone, but that was his choice.'

Wycliffe avoided the mistake of speaking too soon, before he had heard all he was likely to hear, and he was rewarded.

She seemed to make up her mind to qualify what she had said by speaking plainly. 'All the same, it's no use me pretending that there was deep feeling between us. Although we both lived in the same small town we rarely saw each other.'

It made Wycliffe's task easier. 'I have to tell you that your brother's death was not an accident.'

She was disturbed. 'But he fell downstairs.'

'I don't want to distress you, Mrs Penrose, but it seems that very shortly after he fell he received a blow which was certainly not accidental, and that blow was the immediate cause of death. It raises a question as to whether the fall itself was accidental.'

'You think that he was murdered?'

'I think that is established.'

'Have you discussed this with my son?'

'No, I've come straight to you on the assumption that you and your sister in Shropshire are Mr Badger's next of kin.'

'Yes, and I've already spoken to Jennifer on the telephone.' She hesitated. 'Perhaps I ought to say that my sister and Henry were not on good terms; I doubt if she has had any contact since before they moved up north about five years ago. Of course it was only right that she should be told of his death. I told her that it was an accident because that is what I believed.'

Wycliffe said, 'You must forgive me if I probe, but I have no idea what may or may not be important. Do you know the reason for this rift between your brother and sister?'

She hesitated only briefly. 'I suppose there can be no harm in telling you; it was common gossip at the time. My brother-in-law had a small engineering works in Camborne into which Henry put some money and then, after a year or two, withdrew it for no obvious reason and almost without warning. The works had to close.'

'I see.'

The woman sat, entirely composed, with her long bony hands resting in her lap. Suddenly a fresh idea seemed to strike her. 'I hope you are not connecting my brother's death with the discovery of that young man's body . . . ? My son has told me of your suspicion that Henry might have sent certain rather childish anonymous communications, but it would be absurd to suppose that even if it were true . . .' She broke off.

'I have to look at every possibility.'

'But there must be some other explanation.'

Wycliffe was soothing. 'That is what I have to find out, and I hope that you may be able to help me. I would like to know a little more about your brother's background, his marriage, his circumstances . . .'

She was an intelligent woman and she was trying to match his words against his likely purpose, but she continued to speak with engaging frankness. 'There were no secrets in my brother's life as far as I know, Mr Wycliffe. He qualified as an architect and worked for a London firm where he seemed to do quite well. He became keen on climbing and it was at a climbing school in Scotland that he met Lydia, his wife to be. Lydia was a young widow, very well off, and within a month or two they were married.'

Wycliffe sat back in his chair looking bland and receptive. He rarely asked questions until it seemed that the other party would have no more to say.

'To everyone's surprise they decided to settle in his native St Ives. He was disillusioned with architecture, at heart he was a craftsman, and between them they started the Modelmakers. Henry used his London contacts to secure commissions for architectural models and, at the same time, they developed a profitable business in model boats – precise copies of the originals. Lydia had a flair for sales and they were soon getting orders and commissions from all over the place.'

'So the marriage was successful?'

'In business terms, certainly. I know nothing of the domestic side.' The disclaimer was tart.

There was a perfunctory tap at the door and it opened. 'Oh, I had no idea that you had someone with you . . .'

A woman in her late thirties, very fair; a good figure, well-cut skirt, silk blouse, and patterned waistcoat. A sculptured hair-do which must have presented a problem at night.

The elder Mrs Penrose was not taken in by the surprise act. Her manner was distant. 'My daughter-in-law, Mrs Catherine Penrose; Detective Chief Superintendent Wycliffe.' There was a certain emphasis on the official title. 'Mr Wycliffe has been telling me about Henry.'

Catherine Penrose looked from one to the other. 'Wouldn't it be less distressing for you, dear, to leave all this to Arnold?'

A slight gesture. 'My dear Catherine, I am not in the least distressed. We were having a most interesting conversation.'

There was an awkward pause while Catherine conceded defeat and went out, closing the door behind her.

'Where were we?'

Wycliffe said, 'I was about to ask you when, and how, did Lydia die?'

She stopped to think. 'It must have been in fifty-six. It was an accident. They were on holiday, climbing somewhere in North Wales. I don't know exactly what happened, but she fell and was dead on arrival at hospital.

There was an inquest of course, and a verdict of accidental death.'

'Your brother took it badly?'

Wycliffe was aware of her penetrating gaze. Now each question was being examined and assessed before it was answered. 'At first he seemed to carry on as before, but slowly, over many years, there was a process of what I can only call disintegration.' She made a slight gesture with her hands. 'You have seen for yourself where it led.'

Wycliffe was appreciative. 'You are being most frank and very helpful, Mrs Penrose. I have just one more question. Can you suggest any reason at all why someone might hate or fear your brother sufficiently to contrive his death?'

She pursed her lips which were lightly made up. 'No, I most certainly cannot. He rubbed a lot of people up the wrong way by writing foolish letters and by his general behaviour, but I find it very difficult to believe that anyone took him seriously.'

They parted amicably, pleased with each other. Wycliffe felt that his visit had not been wasted though there remained questions which he could only put to the lawyer.

Wycliffe had no sooner returned to his car than there was a call from the Incident Room. It was Kersey. 'I've just had word from the local nick, sir. I think we've found Drew's car. A woman who lives on the Lelant Saltings, not far from the railway halt, has reported a car parked over the weekend in the drive of an empty house next door to hers.

'She says she saw it first on Saturday morning but she didn't think much about it because it looked like the estate agent's car which, as the house is for sale, has been around several times lately. She did notice that the driver's door was wide open. Because of the trees, she can only see the drive from her attic window and she didn't happen to look again until this morning, when she saw that it was still there, looking exactly the same.

'Out of curiosity she went to take a closer look and found the driver's seat and the interior of the car on that side very wet where the rain had blown in through the open door. It was then that she rang the nick. She had the good sense to take the number. It's Drew's all right.'

'I'll join you out there.'

Wycliffe studied the map. He had to drive back through Carbis Bay to Lelant village, then turn off towards the church. Lelant Church and its churchyard, despite the ghostly mists, looked serene and peaceful enough with its weathered headstones and holm oaks, but more than once in its history it has been all but overwhelmed by sand. The road beside the Saltings is narrow, and a single-track railway separates it from the shore. On the landward side there are houses, screened by trees, and in a lay-by outside one of these Wycliffe pulled in behind a police car. There was a 'For Sale' notice secured to a tree: 'Sole Agents: Stanton and Drew, Hayle'.

The car was not visible until he had passed through the screen of trees; then, there it was, a red Escort, parked on the gravelled drive in front of a substantial Edwardian house. Kersey turned up from somewhere in the shrubbery. 'I thought I'd better wait. Once I'd made sure that we'd got it right, I sent for Fox. He's on his way.'

There was not much they could do. As the woman had said, rain had blown in through the open door soaking the upholstery. Kersey pointed out, 'He's left his keys in the ignition. I suppose as the agent he would have had a house key and he might have kipped down in there, but his car has been here since Saturday at least, perhaps earlier.'

'Let's take a look in the boot.'

With the keys from the ignition Kersey unlocked the boot. It was empty except for a rolled-up pile rug.

Kersey said, 'We know where that came from.'

Wycliffe was restless. 'You hold on here. I'll take a look around.'

A quiet and secluded neighbourhood, the brochure would say. Very. The house was attractive, steep roofs and tall chimneys; 1910 vintage. The front door was set back under a deep porch. Wycliffe tried the door but it was locked, so he went around to the back. The back door was not only unlocked, but open, and Wycliffe had a feeling of *déjà vu*. The door led into a tiled hall with the kitchen off; there was a passage through to the front of the house, and stairs to the next floor – back stairs. There would be a more impressive flight from the front hall.

Wycliffe muttered, 'They still had servants when this was built.' He called out, just in case, then he searched the ground floor: dining room, drawing room, breakfast room, and two others of indeterminate use, all as empty as the removals men could contrive. And it was the same with the first floor. He was left with a narrow flight of stairs leading to the attics.

There were four, and in these odd items of furniture remained. It was in the second of the two at the front of the house that he found Drew. The estate agent was sprawled on the floor by the window in a mess of blood, his thin, pallid features contorted in an agonized grimace, his right arm outstretched, his hand clutching a blood-stained Stanley knife. There were flies, and a smell of putrefaction.

Drew's throat was cut.

'Poor devil!' Wycliffe found himself saying it of Drew for the second time in a couple of days.

Near the body a wicker chair had been overturned. It looked as though Drew had been seated facing the window when the shock of the self-inflicted wound induced a convulsive reflex which tumbled him on to the floor.

Wycliffe looked around the bare attic. On the floor, not far from the body, there was an empty lager can lying on its side and a plastic bag about half-full of potato crisps.

'Why here?'

The situation had been chosen, everything pointed to it. Sitting in that chair Drew could look out over the trees, across the green and ochreous sandbanks and converging channels of the saltings towards Hayle, though now the town was hidden by the mist.

Suicide. It troubled Wycliffe almost more than murder. He was at a loss to understand how (except in a terminal illness) a man or woman finds the courage to choose death rather than life. But he had to be quite certain that this was suicide.

From time to time he had tried to acquaint himself with the elements of forensic pathology, mainly to keep his end up with Franks. His source was an old copy of *Taylor* and he remembered a section on incised throat wounds in which there was a gruesome table setting out the differences between the homicidal and the suicidal. For the suicide the wound or wounds tend to be at the front of the throat, not at the sides; there are often tentative preliminary cuts, and the main cut curves across the throat, deepening, and shallowing. The weapon is usually retained in the hand, firmly gripped . . .

On all counts it seemed that Drew had taken his own life.

Dr Hocking agreed with him but Wycliffe none the less went through the same ritual as he would have done in a case of suspected murder. Fox and Collis were engaged in their double act. Photographs had been taken, measurements made and prints were being sought. Franks was brought in, by which time it was mid-afternoon. Kersey, joined by the rabbit-featured DI Gross, had made the routine arrangements and Drew's car was taken for examination to the garage at Division. The rug from the boot was sent to the area lab.

Franks was puzzled. 'I don't know what you expect me to say, Charles. As you've pointed out, this has all the marks of a classic suicide.'

Wycliffe mumbled, 'All right! I needed to be sure . . . This man's death could be convenient for someone.' Taciturn since the discovery of the body, he had that dogged almost sullen look, which was characteristic of him when he had made up his mind to a course of action that was certain to arouse opposition.

The two men were joined by Kersey on the attic landing where they awaited the arrival of the van from the mortuary service.

Franks said, 'I suppose you want to know how long he's been dead?' And when there was no answer he went on, 'All right, I'll tell you. From the general condition of the body and the state of the extravasated blood, I'd say he's been dead about three days. This is Monday, so that would make it some time on Friday. Of course I might have to think again after I've had a real look at him.'

Wycliffe was unappreciative. 'If it really was suicide, then all this is largely academic and we can leave it to Gross.' He turned to Kersey, 'Tell him to make sure that the widow is informed. I shall want you with me so that we can get on with the real business.'

Lucy Lane and Iris Thorn, deserted by the experts, were left at the Modelmakers to sort out the contents of the filing cabinet which, along with everything else in the attic, had been tumbled on to the floor in a heap. The object was not so much to tidy the mess as to find anything which might shed a chink of light on the enigmatic Badger and his relationships.

'This stuff is all of it fifteen to twenty years old.' Iris slipped another wad of papers into a file and slapped it into the cabinet.

They were dealing with outdated correspondence with firms and individuals, customers and suppliers; and though the pile on the floor was getting smaller, they had so far found nothing remotely personal.

Lucy said, 'This man is supposed to have been

well-off, with property and investments. I mean, even if his lawyer-nephew handled his affairs you would expect some correspondence and regular statements.'

In the end they found the statements, almost the last item in the heap; a neat bundle, held together by tape. They covered more than thirty tax years and they were up to date. The form of the statement had varied little and in each case the accompanying letter carried the same florid, embossed heading. The last four had been signed by Arnold Penrose, all the others, by his father.

Lucy said, 'I know nothing about accountancy but he seems to have been very well fixed. We've still found nothing really personal; surely he must have had a private bank account with a cheque book, and bank statements . . . There must have been domestic bills which he paid . . .'

Iris Thorn brushed herself off and perched on a handy stool. 'His money doesn't seem to have done him much good. Do you get many jobs like this? All this work with hardly anything to show for it?'

Lucy found a chair. 'It happens. Taking it altogether, probably more than two-thirds of our time goes in chasing rainbows and writing reports about it . . . But we have our moments.'

The two women were getting to know each other and liking what they found. Iris had a fund of anecdotes about her grandfather's early encounters in London as an immigrant bus conductor and several times Lucy had been heard to giggle, a previously all but unknown phenomenon.

Iris said, 'Feel like a coffee – or tea? There must be something down in that murky old kitchen.'

Lucy got up. 'Let's see what we can find.'

On the next landing Badger's bedroom door stood open and Iris looked in at the unmade bed with its soiled sheets and pillows. 'My dad is a jobbing plumber and he's got a little office where he does his accounts and all that, but his "papers" as he calls them, more personal things, he keeps in a tin box under the bed. It makes a bump in the mattress – very inconvenient sometimes, mum says . . . I just wondered . . .'

'It's worth a look.'

Iris got down on her knees. 'Nothing but spiders.'

But Lucy had opened the little bedside cupboard. On its single shelf there was a bulky A4 envelope, a scratch pad, a ball-point, and a few paper clips. 'Looks as though he did his office work in bed.'

The envelope carried the Penrose imprint in one corner and was labelled, 'Mitchell's Loft and 17 Bethel Street'. The envelope was sealed. Lucy hesitated, 'I suppose we should bring the lawyer in on this, but I think we'll chance it and take it with us.'

Iris Thorn said, 'Let's get that coffee.'

Chapter Nine

Monday afternoon

Instead of returning to the Incident Room as Kersey expected, Wycliffe told him to drive into St Ives. 'We are going to talk to the lawyer, so park behind the Sloop if you can.'

Kersey said, 'Did you really think Drew might have been murdered?'

'No, but I wanted there to be no possible doubt about it.'

'Surely the picture is pretty clear now: Drew does for the old man and then for himself.'

'In this panic you keep talking about.'

'Well, yes. You don't agree?'

'No.'

And that was as far as Kersey could get.

The lawyer was with a client but they had not long to wait. Immediately his client left Penrose came out. He looked a worried man. Gone was the beaming smile and the stock of small chat which had marked Wycliffe's first visit. He acknowledged Kersey, then, 'I tried to contact you over the weekend but they told me you weren't available and I had the same answer from your Incident Room this morning.'

When they were seated in the office Penrose went on, 'I'm afraid I left you with a rather bad impression on Friday night, but it was quite a shock, seeing the old man lying there. And when you seemed unwilling to agree that it was an accident, I was at a loss what to think. As well as being a relative, I look after his affairs, and it will fall to me to administer his estate. I'm naturally concerned to know the post mortem findings. Was it an accident?'

His manner was nervous and plaintive rather than aggressive.

Wycliffe said, 'It is possible that your uncle fell down the stairs accidentally but it seems more likely that he was pushed. In any case, after the fall he received a blow to the back of his head and that was the immediate cause of death according to the pathologist. In other words, he was murdered.'

Penrose shook his head. 'It's hard to believe.' He fiddled with the papers on his desk. 'Is there any news of Drew?'

'He is the reason I wasn't in touch with you earlier today.'

A quick look. 'You've got him?'

'I'm afraid Paul Drew is dead and the indications are that he committed suicide.'

'Good God! How? When?'

'This morning his car was found in the drive of an empty house on the Lelant Saltings. His body was in one of the attics of the house.'

'Bosavern.'

'I beg your pardon?'

'The name of the house – I think it's Cornish for "the house by the river". Anyway, it's where he was born and spent his childhood. The Drews were quite well off at one time. Paul's father was chairman of a small finance company that went bust in the early seventies. A few weeks after the crash the man shot himself. His widow had to get out of the house, salvaging what she could.'

Wycliffe said, 'So that is why he chose to end things there. Childhood memories.'

'It looks that way.'

Penrose ran his fingers through his sparse curls. 'God, what a mess!'

'Presumably you have your uncle's will?'

'His will? Yes, I have a will.'

'I may ask you for a copy later, but for the moment perhaps you will tell me its main provisions.'

Penrose seemed taken aback by the request as well as by the abrupt change of subject. 'Is that relevant?'

Wycliffe was emphatic. 'Mr Penrose, your uncle was murdered and it's my job to find out who was responsible.'

The lawyer looked at Wycliffe with tired eyes. 'But surely we know who was responsible.'

'Do we? Late Thursday evening your uncle was in his attic, three storeys up, with a book open in front of him and a glass of brandy at his elbow. He was not deaf, but his hearing was impaired. How much noise would a visitor have had to make in order to attract his attention and fetch him downstairs to open either the shop or the back door? There is no bell fitted to either – not even a knocker. But even assuming that the visitor was heard and admitted, without attracting the attention of the neighbourhood, which of his possible visitors would he have taken upstairs to the attic?'

Penrose was silent, staring down at his desk-top. When he spoke his voice and manner were subdued. 'I don't accept the conclusion you seem to draw from all this but I can see that you need to satisfy yourself on matters of fact. You asked for details of the will in my possession. It's not complicated. He leaves ten thousand pounds to Julian Angove; the residue to be divided equally between my mother and her sister, Mrs Jennifer Grey – Gillian's mother.'

'What will the residue amount to – very roughly?'

Penrose frowned. 'I can't give you a meaningful answer to that question until valuations have been made.'

'A substantial sum?'

'Yes.' Penrose was becoming more restive. 'You must understand, Mr Wycliffe, that my uncle was a very strange man, deliberately unpredictable – mischievous.'

'So?'

'It wouldn't surprise me if another will turned up,

more recent than the one I hold. For all I know it could be in the hands of another solicitor. He often reminded me that the will I held might not be his final word, or even his current intention . . . He delighted in mystifying people . . .'

Kersey had been listening, saying nothing because he felt out of his depth; now he seemed to touch bottom. 'Perhaps he thought he had good reason.'

Penrose bristled. 'I think you should explain that remark!'

Kersey looked across at Wycliffe for the green light and got it. 'Mr Badger confided to the police that he believed his life might be in danger. He refused categorically to enlarge on that and denied that he was asking for any sort of assistance. What he did want was an assurance that if any suspicion should attach to his death when it came, it would be thoroughly investigated.'

Penrose nodded. 'That's Badger! It doesn't really surprise me.' He turned to Wycliffe, 'Don't you see? He was always play-acting – it was all a sort of game to him.'

Wycliffe said, 'And a dangerous one apparently. Your uncle *is* dead, and he *was* murdered.'

Penrose looked at him and said, with great gravity, 'And I am confident that the man who killed him is also dead.'

Wycliffe seemed prepared to leave it at that. He stood up. 'Thank you for your time, Mr Penrose.'

Penrose followed them out to the top of the stairs, obviously taken aback by the abruptness of the leave taking. 'I hope that our conversation . . .' But Wycliffe was halfway down the stairs.

They were turning up the slope to the car park before Kersey spoke. 'We seem to be a long way from Cochran Wilder and the six youngsters in that chalet fifteen years ago.'

Wycliffe made a curious sound between a grunt and a growl. 'As far as Badger is concerned, this case was never about Wilder; that nonsense with the photograph and the cryptic messages was no more than an opportunist attempt at providing a cover. Badger's death is about money.'

'Anyway, I thought Penrose stood up to it very well.'

'He's a lawyer.'

Kersey said, 'Where to?' They were sitting in the car in the car park.

'It's gone four and we haven't had any lunch.'

Kersey said, 'I noticed.'

'Do you think a glass of beer and a sandwich?'

So they got out again and went into the Sloop. Wycliffe was subdued, almost morose. He held so many pieces. He knew why and how young Wilder had met his death; he understood why the discovery of Wilder's body had led to the anonymous communications, including the mutilated photograph which had arrived on his own desk. He thought he knew why Badger had to die. What he did not know and could not make up his mind about was who of the possible suspects had contrived his death.

He said, aloud, 'Somebody prepared to take a hell of a risk.'

They were sitting at a corner table in one of the bars; there were pictures by local painters on the walls, predecessors of Julian Angove but of greater distinction.

Kersey said, 'Penny for them.'

'You'd be robbed. I was wondering what sort of person is most likely to stake all on a real gamble. Is it always someone with nothing much to lose?'

They drove back to the Incident Room. Hayle, in the late afternoon, under a continuous drizzle, exactly suited Wycliffe's mood. In the big room, beneath the lurid print of Armageddon, Lucy Lane was concocting her report.

Laid out on a trestle table there was a collection of polythene evidence-bags of various sizes, all tagged.

'What's this?' But he knew: Paul Drew's clothes and

the contents of his pockets. There was a typed schedule and he glanced through it. 'What's this pocket tape recorder?'

Lucy Lane joined him by the table. 'Fox brought this stuff in a short time ago, sir.' She picked up a small pack containing the recorder. 'I suppose Drew carried one of these in his work. I believe a lot of estate agents do, to record details of properties instead of making notes.'

'Has anybody played this thing back?'

'Not to my knowledge, sir, but we can do it on one of ours.'

'Then we'd better do it. Take it into the little office and get somebody to bring coffee for three.'

Wycliffe sat in his chair with Lucy and Kersey opposite. When the coffee arrived he said, 'All right, Lucy; let's hear it.'

The tape began to play, there was a certain amount of mush, but the voice was clear enough.

Kersey said, 'That's Drew all right, I'd know that voice anywhere.'

The voice was subdued and the words came slowly, there were hesitations and pauses. 'I am sitting here in this attic room which was mine as a child, and it is here that I shall put an end to it all. For many years I have been conscious of people looking at me in a way that they do not look at others . . . They look at me and they say to themselves, "There goes Paul Drew, the estate agent, the man who . . ." And they smile, a horrid little inward smile. And I ask myself, "The man who what?" . . . And all the time I feel exposed as though television cameras were trained on me from every direction . . .

'Is it the way I walk? The way I look? The way I behave? Is it my marriage? Is it because they know, as my wife reminds me, that in the firm of Stanton and Drew I count for less than the girl in the office? Or is it because all those years ago my father went bankrupt and shot himself?'

There was a break, but the three who were listening

193

did not take their eyes off the little black box which now emitted only a faint whirring sound.

Then, abruptly, the voice resumed, more husky now, less distinct. 'I ask myself, if it is like that now, what will it be when they *know*? Not only the police, but the newspapers, Stanton, the girl, – my wife . . . I shall be, "The man who helped to bury the body . . . The man who attacked the policeman . . ." '

There was another break before the voice resumed with unexpected firmness. 'I was a fool! I tried, as they say, to put the genie back in the bottle. I went to the chalet . . . It was a futile attempt and it ended in another act of violence . . .

'From then on I behaved like a madman. I think I *was* mad . . . At one stage I drove home . . . I was going to tell everything to my wife . . . Of course I did not, and the next thing I remember is being in St Ives and telephoning Alan Hart from a box near his surgery . . . He said he would meet me there but I don't think he did . . . I know that I went into a pub and bought a can of lager and a bag of crisps . . . I think it was then that I telephoned GG . . . there was no answer but I decided to go anyway . . . I left the car and started walking . . . I walked along by the sea and when I reached the back of GG's place I could see a light in her flat . . . I rang the bell but there was no reply on her entry phone . . . I kept on ringing but it was no good. I thought she must be with Penrose . . . There was hardly anybody in the streets and I just wandered about . . . Then I saw Penrose; he was in a hurry and he passed me without seeing me . . . I thought he must have just left GG so I went back and tried again, but she still did not answer . . .'

The break this time was longer and he seemed to have finished, but after a while the voice took up the story once more.

'I walked back to the Wharf and sat in the car . . . It was then that I decided. The keys of Bosavern were in the glove compartment with two or three small tools I always keep there – *including* a Stanley knife . . . It was as though providence, or whoever looks after these things, was saying to me, "This is the way!" . . . And suddenly I was calm; I knew exactly what I must do, and I felt a tremendous sense of *relief*.

'I went to the office and typed the statement which I intended to send to Wilder's father so that he would know the truth. I put that in the post . . . and I came here.'

Lucy Lane was the first to break the silence. 'Poor man!'

It was a moment or two before anyone moved, then Lucy switched off the tape and Wycliffe, as though in a reflex response, sipped his coffee. It was cold.

Kersey said, 'That puts GG and Penrose in the frame; both or either could have been helping Badger on his way out.'

Wycliffe was staring at the recorder as though at a living witness who might be persuaded to tell more. 'Yes. The chances are that Drew was there in Bethel Street when Badger was killed . . . We must get that into type, and we shall also want certified copies of the tape. You'd better get Shaw on that.' He broke off, but it was obvious there was more to come.

'If we use this properly we can put an end to the charade we've been playing over the Wilder affair and go some way with the other.' He turned to Kersey. 'I want you to arrange for the five remaining members of the chalet party and Penrose to attend here at, say, two o'clock tomorrow afternoon. Contact them in person. They can make it under their own steam or we will fetch them, but I want them here. I don't think any of them will refuse.' He glanced at his watch. 'It's nearly six . . . We've had about enough for today . . . Nothing else, is there?'

Lucy Lane said, 'There is something which might be worth following up. When we finished in Badger's attic, Iris Thorn suggested that we should take a look around in odd places where Badger could have kept some of his more personal papers. In fact all we found was a large envelope in his bedside cupboard. Obviously he'd been looking through the papers in bed but the envelope had been resealed. It carried the lawyer's imprint, and it was labelled, Mitchell's Loft and seventeen Bethel Street.'

'So?'

'Well, I checked. Gillian Grey's health shop is seventeen Bethel Street, and Mitchell's Loft is the old name for that odd little building where Julian Angove has his studio.'

'You brought the stuff in?'

'Yes, sir. I know I should have checked with the lawyer but if it's of any importance I thought it would be safer here.'

'All right. Let's compound the offence and take a look.'

Lucy fetched the package and Wycliffe examined it. The envelope had been opened, presumably by Badger, and resealed with sticky tape. Wycliffe slit through the tape with a paper knife and tipped out the contents. There were two leases and a covering letter from Penrose. The letter was dated 8 May and headed with the addresses of the two properties and the names of the lessees. The text was simple and brief:

In accordance with our standard practice I enclose two leases which expire at Michaelmas 1992 and I shall be glad to receive your instructions concerning them so that any changes may be notified in good time to comply with the terms of the lease.

Across the bottom of the letter Badger had written two lines in his admirable script:

Mitchell's Loft. Renew. Terms as before.
17 Bethel Street. Lease to be terminated. I intend to repossess.

Wycliffe pushed the letter over to Kersey who read it and passed it to Lucy Lane.

Kersey said, 'Things are looking black for Ginger. If we can show that she had the news before dear uncle was helped over the threshold . . .'

Lucy said, 'The date is interesting – four days before the discovery of Wilder's body.'

Wycliffe was enigmatic. 'We shall have to see. Now, put that in the safe, Lucy, and let's get out of here.'

'It's spare ribs of beef tonight in my own marinade. If you don't like garlic you'd better settle for cold meat, but you'll be missing something if you do.'

They decided that they liked garlic.

'Then you're going to want a glass or two of a nice red to go with it.'

The landlady was not at all bothered by the arcane lore of the gourmet or the wine buff; she knew what she liked and her customers had better like it too. So far there were no complaints from the police contingent.

Kersey was in his element. 'That woman can cook.'

When, over coffee, they had reached the reflective stage, Wycliffe said, 'Well, Doug, do you still think Drew tried to kill the Badger?'

'No. I think he told the truth as he saw it on that tape. We are left without much choice in the way of suspects but, with what wc've heard and seen in the last hour I don't suppose we need a choice. Will you tackle her in the morning?'

Wycliffe took time to think. 'No, I shall wait until we have them all together tomorrow afternoon, then let the tape do it.'

Kersey, with a wary eye on Lucy Lane, lit a cigarette. 'But the anonymous threats or whatever they were, and presumably the snapshot, did appear to come from Badger himself.'

'Only because the typing was done on his machine.'

'All right, let's assume it was GG who did it, sneaking

in when the old man was out on his evening walk. But she, after all, was one of the chalet party and by drawing attention to them she incriminates herself.'

Wycliffe agreed. 'That's a point I want to make. I realized that if we looked for Badger's killer among the chalet party it would have to be one who was prepared to have his part in the Wilder affair known, as the price of any gain from Badger's death. If Wilder had been murdered that price would be high, but if his death was accidental the only charges against the group would have to centre upon conspiracy to conceal a death.'

The landlady came over, all smiles. 'I can see you enjoyed that. Like some more coffee?'

When she had gone, Kersey, thoughtful, said, 'I suppose that after fifteen years, bearing in mind that these people were juveniles at the time with no subsequent criminal record, any court would take a lenient view.'

Wycliffe agreed. 'But there would be penalties apart from the law, the publicity and the nine-day scandal. That would bear unequally on the different individuals. The doctor and his wife would probably suffer most. They might have to move, and there could be disciplinary proceedings by his professional body. Then there is Drew, we already know how he panicked at the mere possibility of exposure.'

Lucy Lane cut in, 'And from what I saw of Lisa Bell, she isn't far from panic either.'

Kersey waved smoke away. 'Which leaves GG and Angove. I doubt if exposure would trouble either of them much. With ten grand in his pocket Angove wouldn't even notice it.'

Wycliffe said, 'But it's GG who is in the frame. All the same, a chat with the painter might not come amiss.' He turned to Lucy Lane. 'You haven't met him and neither have I. How would you feel about putting that right this evening?'

'I would like to.'

'Nothing planned?'

Lucy grinned. 'Is it likely?'

'All right, we'll meet him together.'

It was unprecedented. Wycliffe's solitary evening walks were part of an established tradition.

Kersey said, 'You'd better phone and say you're coming, otherwise he probably won't answer the door.'

The skies had cleared, as on this coast they often do in the evening of a thoroughly wet day. Lights were coming on in the streets and houses. They parked behind the Sloop and walked along the Wharf to the painter's studio. There was no breath of wind and the moored craft were dimly reflected in the still waters of the harbour. A few couples strolled along, stopping now and then to look at this or that, and Wycliffe was conscious of the fact that he and Lucy could have been just such another pair.

There was a light in the painter's upstairs room. Wycliffe rang the bell and a moment or two later the shop lit up and Angove came trundling towards them between the double row of his pictures. The door opened and he stood there, stocky and powerful as a young bull, but his manner was bantering rather than aggressive.

'I thought you lot were not supposed to disturb respectable citizens after sunset.'

'You must be thinking of search warrants, Mr Angove, and we haven't got there yet. I am Detective Chief Superintendent Wycliffe, and this is Detective Sergeant Lane.' Wycliffe showed his warrant card.

'All right. I must say I prefer the female of the species, but come on up both of you.'

They followed him through the shop and up the stairs into the long narrow room which had once been a fisherman's loft. Angove drew a heavy curtain across the top of the stairs. 'The draught comes up there like a chimney.'

A bottled-gas stove stood near the window giving out a cosy glow, and three old basket-work chairs were drawn up to it. It seemed that Angove was prepared to be hospitable.

'Elena – my girlfriend – has gone off to bed. She soon gets bored and anyway she needs her sleep.'

They sat down, and when the symphony of creaks had subsided Wycliffe said, 'A lot has happened, Mr Angove, since Inspector Kersey talked to you on Friday. I suppose you've heard that Henry Badger and Paul Drew are both dead?'

Angove contented himself with a simple 'Yes.'

'We believe that Drew took his own life but Badger's death was premeditated murder.'

'I know. Penrose told me.'

'Did he also tell you that he was in possession of Badger's will?'

'No, but I suppose he would be.'

'If no later will is found, you stand to inherit ten thousand pounds.'

It seemed that Angove was taken totally by surprise. His look of astonishment was almost comical. Then he laughed. 'The old bastard!'

Lucy Lane said, 'An odd reaction, Mr Angove.'

He turned towards her. 'I suppose it is, but I can't get over it. Three or four years back I couldn't pay my rent and Penrose was turning the screw so I took a chance and went to see the Badger. For some reason we clicked, we had the same perverted sense of humour. Anyway he told me to forget the rent and we became friends – real friends I like to think. I go to see him – went to see him – often, and he used to say, "As long as you keep me alive, boy, you can swan along doing bugger all as usual, but when I'm gone Penrose will move in with the bailiffs." '

'It seems he liked your cartoons.'

A broad grin. 'Yes, but he would also say to me, "You're the worst bloody painter in this town, and that's saying something. Why don't you sell picture postcards? At least you wouldn't be swindling the punters." '

'Did he talk much about death?' Lucy again.

The painter had been looking her over with approval ever since he had set eyes on her. 'Yes, in a cheerful, cynical sort of way. He pretended to think that there were those anxious to help him out of the world. I suppose he could have believed it, but I never took him seriously.'

'And now?'

'Well, it makes you think.'

'What does it make you think?'

Wycliffe's manner was no longer conversational and for the first time Angove became cautious. 'I'm not in the business of pointing the finger.'

Wycliffe leaned forward in his chair so that it creaked abominably. 'That finger may well point at you, Mr Angove. Think it over. Now, one or two questions: You admit to being a frequent visitor at the house, was there anyone else to your knowledge on the same footing?'

'I don't know about the same footing, whatever that was, but Penrose was there quite often. I mean, it was only natural; Badger rarely went out except for his evening walks, and Penrose, apart from being his nephew, looked after his business affairs. He was always bringing along this and that for signature.'

'Anyone else?'

'Well, GG would be called in now and then for a few minutes, just to satisfy himself that he was in control. After all she's only across the street and she was his niece.'

'You say "called in". What does that mean?'

'It means she wouldn't go there unless he asked her to. And neither would I. Unsolicited visits were not appreciated.'

'Does she have a key?'

'I've got one, so I suppose she has. If he was upstairs he didn't like having to come down to let you in.'

'It all sounds highly autocratic.'

'You could say that, but I enjoyed his company and I suppose we each had practical reasons for letting him call the tune. He must have been very profitable to Penrose, and GG and I were both in hock for our rent – for different reasons. I haven't got it and GG doesn't like spending it.'

'Did he get on with his niece?'

Angove contorted his mobile features into a grimace. 'The plain answer to that is – No! He used to bait her and she couldn't take it. He always called her "Maggie" after the Iron Lady, and that annoyed her. The two of them were like oil and water . . . Badger had a cruel streak, he liked to rile people and GG was an easy target.'

'I see. Now I have just one more question: Had you any reason to think that your lease might not be renewed in September?'

Angove looked surprised. 'No, but I hadn't given it much thought. I know GG was getting a bit edgy; she rang me up to ask if I'd heard anything. She said both our leases ran out on the same date.'

'When did she telephone?'

'A week or ten days ago, I suppose. I can't say exactly.'

Wycliffe stood up. 'Mr Angove, I want you to come to our Incident Room in Hayle at two o'clock tomorrow afternoon. In the meantime please don't discuss our conversation this evening with anyone. You understand?'

'If you say so.'

Wycliffe was making for the stairs and the painter followed, seeing them off the premises.

They were on their way back to Hayle, driving around the Causeway. Lights showed dimly from houses on the Saltings and there were odd reflections in the waters. Overhead there were stars.

Wycliffe spoke first. 'I can understand why Badger took to him.'

Lucy did not answer at once, then she said, 'A man's man.'

Wycliffe was surprised. 'You think so? He seems to have no trouble in getting female sleeping partners.'

'That's a different matter.'

Wycliffe said, 'No doubt you're right. I'm going to have a small whisky, ring home, then go to bed.'

Chapter Ten

Tuesday morning, 19 May

The sun was shining, it was half past eight, and Wycliffe walked along Commercial Road on his way to the Incident Room. Kersey had stopped at a little shop to buy his newspaper and cigarettes; Lucy Lane had gone ahead of them both. It was a routine which had been repeated many times over the years in all sorts of locations over the two counties.

Wycliffe was confident now that he was dealing with two quite separate cases. Early in the Wilder investigation he had realized that he was sorting out the erratic behaviour of a bunch of teenagers, their messy emotions, unpredictable loyalties and obstinate lies. And it was strange to see them, fifteen years later, still reacting as teenagers to that traumatic episode in their lives.

But the case of Henry Badger was different; here was no hot-headed quarrel followed by a clumsy accident and cover-up, but an adult crime, premeditated, over-elaborate in its planning and carried out in cold blood. The only link between the two was a deviously contrived attempt to use the one in order to confuse the other.

There was circumstantial evidence which could point to Gillian Grey or to Penrose. Both had the opportunity, means presented no problem, and both stood to gain directly or indirectly from the old man's death. Finding the weapon and identifying it with one of them could be crucial.

Kersey said, 'I'll look in on Fox. See what's happening.'

Wycliffe was marking time and when John Scales rang

it was a relief from boredom. 'I've made a few enquiries about the Penrose firm but you know what lawyers are, even our own are cagey about discussing their kind. However, old Simmonds loosened up. It seems he started his career under Arnold's father. The word is that Arnold tends to sit on his backside and wait for business to drop into his lap, but it no longer works that way. The firm is using up accumulated fat and Arnold has acquired a taste for the good life. No crisis; but cause for concern.'

'In other words a fresh injection of capital would be more than welcome.'

'That's the message, sir.'

The morning passed. Wycliffe talked to the chief, Lucy filed reports, they drank coffee, and at half past twelve they crossed over to the pub for a snack lunch. Kersey was still at the Modelmakers.

When they got back Wycliffe asked the duty officer, 'Anything from Sergeant Fox?'

'Nothing, sir.'

Tuesday afternoon

Wycliffe waited in his little office with the door sufficiently ajar to give him a view of most of the big room. He was counting on progress but the gathering had no official status and any developments would have to be formalized through individual interviews and statements.

The first to arrive was Lisa Bell. Wycliffe had never met her but recognized her from the photograph. Lucy brought her to the table and pulled out a chair. She sat down, taut and withdrawn, handbag in lap, caught up in the dentist's waiting-room syndrome.

Julian Angove came next, looking about him in bored appraisal until he caught sight of Lisa and took the chair beside her. In no time at all they were deep in conversation that was almost animated.

At one fifty-eight by Wycliffe's watch the Harts arrived, the doctor, grave and suspicious, clearly doubting whether he should be there at all. His wife, Barbara, another whom Wycliffe had not yet met, came as a surprise; she was plump, pink and fair, inclined to be fluffy; whereas he had imagined her as a type specimen of the young matron. Her pregnancy scarcely showed.

The doctor staked out his position to Lucy. 'I hope this won't take long, it's come at a most inconvenient time.'

The Harts sat opposite the other two and there was obvious constraint. Angove's casual 'Hi, you two!' was coldly received.

Arnold Penrose and Gillian Grey came in together, both were flushed and flustered as though interrupted in mid-quarrel. Absent-mindedly they took the seats Lucy offered and fended off subdued greetings from the others.

Wycliffe gave the gathering a minute or two before taking his seat at the head of the table. When he did, he had Alan Hart on his right and GG on his left.

'Thank you for coming.' His manner was dry and distant. 'This is an unofficial gathering but it will be recorded to ensure that your rights are not infringed.'

He looked up from the notes he had in front of him. 'My investigation began with the discovery of the body of Cochran Wilder. Since then two of the people who seemed to be linked with the discovery have died. There is evidence to show that Henry Badger was murdered and that Paul Drew took his own life.'

Wycliffe had not raised his voice above a conversational level but there was no need. Whenever he stopped speaking the silence in the room was only broken by the muffled sound of passing traffic.

A brief pause and he went on, 'DS Lane will give each of you a photocopy of a statement sent by Paul Drew, shortly before his death, to the dead boy's father. You

206

will see that the statement is disjointed and reflects great distress of mind.'

The papers were distributed and read. There were audible sighs and murmurs and an appreciable time went by before anyone looked up from the few lines of type. Lisa Bell said in a whisper, 'Oh, my God!'

When eventually they had done, Wycliffe said, 'You see that Paul Drew has indicated in outline his version of what happened on that May night in 1977. Later, I shall ask for your individual recollections. I am aware that so far none of you has admitted to having seen Wilder either then or at any other time but that fiction can no longer be taken seriously.'

Lucy Lane, listening and watching, hardly recognized Wycliffe in the remote, sombre personage that now appeared. By his matter-of-fact delivery and his economy in words, he had already cut himself off totally from the emotions of his audience, so that she was beginning to feel, as they must, in a limbo of isolation.

He was speaking again. 'Staying with Paul Drew, I want you to listen to his voice on a pocket recorder which he used in his business. The tape was found on his body.'

Lucy Lane placed the little machine for the play-back in the middle of the table, switched it on, and withdrew.

If there was tension before, now it was almost tangible. It was a grey day and the lighting in the cavernous room was poor. Lucy was hearing the tape for the third time, but in these circumstances she was more than ever moved by the pathos of this man who, failing to find a human confidant, finally strips himself bare to a coil of magnetic tape.

Lucy watched the group around the table as they listened to the voice of the dead man. Each of them looked steadily at the table-top as though fearful of catching another's eye.

'. . . I shall be, "The man who helped to bury the body

. . . The man who attacked the policeman . . ." From then on I behaved like a madman . . .'

They heard about the keys of Bosavern, about the tools in the glove compartment of his car and about the Stanley knife.

'. . . And suddenly I was calm; I knew exactly what I must do, and I felt a tremendous sense of relief . . .'

When the tape had run its course there was a wave of uneasiness. Lisa Bell fumbled in her bag for a handkerchief and dabbed her eyes. GG and the lawyer looked at each other, a curious exchange. Alan Hart was the first to speak and his voice was uncertain though intended to be firm. 'I am sorry, but my wife has had enough of this and I must take her home. It was a mistake to bring her.'

Barbara flushed. 'You did not *bring* me, Alan! I insisted on coming, and I shall stay. This thing has blighted all our lives for too long and I am determined that it shall be somehow . . . somehow settled, before our child is born.'

Gillian Grey said in a harsh voice, 'I want to know what this is about.'

There was no other comment and Wycliffe resumed in the same dry, uninflected tone as before. 'The two statements from Paul Drew happen to coincide with two aspects of the investigation. The written statement sent to Wilder senior concerns what happened on that night fifteen years ago, while the recording relates to what has happened since the recovery of young Wilder's body. I want to deal with the two separately.

'You each have a copy of Paul Drew's written statement and now I want you to fill in the gaps.'

Arnold Penrose performed a metaphorical handwashing. 'I'm not sure why I am here unless it's as a lawyer. In which case I must point out that what you contribute is up to each of you. There is no legal obligation for anyone to say anything at all.'

Wycliffe sounded like the crustiest of judges

instructing a jury. 'What Mr Penrose has said about your right to remain silent is of course quite correct. In any case it has been explained to you that your attendance here is voluntary.'

He turned to speak directly to the lawyer. 'About your own status, Mr Penrose, you are not here in connection with the death of Cochran Wilder, but the murder of Henry Badger. You were closely involved with his affairs, you were a frequent visitor at his premises and you were twice seen in the locality on the night that he was murdered. I hope that you will feel able to make a statement about your movements that night.'

Penrose flushed and was about to reply but thought better of it. As Wycliffe turned back to the others he caught the ghost of a smile on GG's lips.

When it seemed that no-one would speak it was Lisa Bell who found her courage. At first she was barely audible but her voice gathered strength. 'I was on the veranda that evening when Cochran Wilder came across the dunes from Gwithian. He seemed to be worn out and he asked for a glass of water . . .'

As Lucy listened to the schoolgirlish voice, faltering at first, but growing firmer and more articulate, that May evening in the chalet on the dunes seemed to come alive. She could see the engaging stranger, worming his way into the chalet party, sharing their meal, showing off his sophistication, his conjuring tricks and his pot-smoking and ending up with a bed on the sofa . . .

Lisa said, 'I was supposed to share with Paul, but it didn't work . . . So, early in the night, I left him. I took a pillow and a blanket and tried to settle in an armchair in the living room where Wilder was. He seemed to be asleep, and eventually I dozed off.

'I woke with Wilder's hand pressed on my mouth. He was standing over me, naked, and he whispered something, but I struggled and the chair I was in turned over on us both. I think I grabbed the tablecloth; glasses and things got pulled to the floor . . .' Lisa broke off, flushed, with tears running down her cheeks.

It was not difficult to imagine the darkened room, the two figures struggling on the floor, the naked man and the girl, the girl's hand clutching at the tablecloth, the littered glasses and china, some of it broken.

Wycliffe said nothing and once more the silence waited. It was Julian Angove who finally made up his mind to speak.

He sounded quite different; subdued, with no trace of banter or cynicism. 'It woke everybody. Lisa was almost hysterical, Wilder was aggressive, and there was chaos for a bit until Alan and I bundled Wilder out of the door, naked as he was, and locked it. While Paul was collecting Wilder's clothes and belongings the two girls took Lisa into one of the bedrooms and stayed with her . . . All the time Wilder was banging on the door, and shouting . . .

'When we had his clothes and his backpack we opened the door and tried to give them to him but he struggled to get back in and one of us, perhaps both, gave him a shove . . .' Angove made an expressive gesture. 'He overbalanced . . . He overbalanced, and went head-first down the steps . . .'

The painter stopped, and Lucy realized with a sense of mild shock that the imperturbable Julian was deeply disturbed. After a moment or two he added in a cracked voice, 'It's your turn, Alan.'

The doctor passed a hand over his eyes and began to speak. 'I shall never forget that thud when his head hit the kerb at the bottom . . . We went down to him but it was impossible to see how badly he was hurt. In any case none of us had even an elementary knowledge of first aid . . . I do remember that his awful breathing scared me . . .'

They were not the words of an experienced doctor but of a frightened boy.

'We knew that we had to bring him indoors and,

somehow, we got him up the steps and into the room, where we laid him on the floor and covered him with blankets . . . He was bleeding from a wound in his head . . .

'We had to get help, and Paul was going after a telephone but as he was leaving Wilder made a sort of snorting noise and his breathing stopped . . . We knew enough to check his heart beat and pulse but there was neither . . . He was dead.'

After a longish interval Hart took the story to its conclusion. 'I can't describe our panic and I have no memory of the stages by which we reached the decision to do what we did . . . All I can say is that what we did has affected us all ever since . . . I have a recurring nightmare, endlessly trudging through the dunes in the darkness, clutching at a corner of that awful sheet . . . Then there was the digging and the running sand . . .'

It was a strange scene; the group sitting around the table seemed frozen into immobility, each still avoiding another's eyes.

Only Wycliffe appeared wholly detached, uninvolved. He looked across at GG. 'Have you anything to add, Miss Grey?'

GG swept back her hair with that practised hand. She was flushed. 'I don't know what all this is about. For fifteen years our lives have been blighted by the memory of that wretched boy and now we are assembled to listen to harrowing reminders and to the recorded meanderings of Paul Drew who broke under the strain when the body was discovered. All I can say is that if he was responsible for the death of my uncle I want that established.'

Wycliffe made no direct response. He said, 'I have arranged for your statements to be taken at the St Ives police station during the rest of today. They will be recorded and you will be asked to sign the transcripts.'

It was Barbara Hart who asked, 'And after that?'

Wycliffe shuffled together the few notes he had in front of him and stood up. 'After that, Mrs Hart, the papers concerning the Wilder affair will be passed to the Crown Prosecution Service and it will be up to them to decide what charges if any should be brought.'

It seemed almost an anti-climax, and for a while nobody moved. It was only when Lucy Lane busied herself recovering her photocopies, that the group, still almost silent, began to break up.

Wycliffe returned to his office where Kersey was waiting for him. The air was blue with cigarette smoke.

'Did it come off?'

Wycliffe shrugged. 'I think we've laid the Wilder ghost. As to the other . . . Any news from Fox?'

Kersey grimaced. 'Fox is an old woman; he's been poncing about everywhere except in the bloody workshop where we want him, but I've got him down there at last. Whether he'll find anything is another matter.' Kersey ground out a stub in the ashtray. 'Where do we go from here, sir?'

'Obviously we need to talk to Gillian Grey and Penrose again. My impression is that there's trouble between those two. They arrived together this afternoon but very flustered. They'll be making statements along with the others now so let them simmer until the morning, then we'll see.'

The telephone rang. 'Mr Penrose has come back, sir, he would like a word.'

'Show Mr Penrose in.' Wycliffe spoke to Kersey. 'He's worried.'

The lawyer looked weary, his manner of good-humoured self-satisfaction had taken a battering since their first encounter and he could hardly wait to sit down before he began to speak. 'I feel that I have put myself in an invidious position.'

Wycliffe waited, and he went on, 'In trying to protect

the interests of others, I have come under suspicion myself and I want to clear the air. About the night Badger was killed—'

Wycliffe interrupted, 'If you wish to clear the air, Mr Penrose, let's start further back. Let's start with the anonymous postcards which were addressed on the machine in Badger's attic. At our first meeting you told me you did not think he owned a typewriter. Later, on the night his body was discovered and you were confronted with the machine, you expressed surprise. Did you or did you not know of its existence?'

Penrose studied his hands. 'I did know that there had once been an old machine about the place but I hadn't seen it for years.' He looked up, meeting Wycliffe's gaze. 'I didn't want him accused of stirring up trouble over the Wilder business.'

'So despite your denials to me you believed that your uncle might be responsible for those cards?'

'It seemed possible, the sort of mischievous thing he could do.'

'The keys on that machine were wiped clean. What would have been the point in him doing that? In any case, where did he get his information? Whoever sent those cards knew at least the broad facts about young Wilder's death and must have had a copy of the photograph from which a cut-out was sent to me. Did you imagine that one of the six had confided in him?'

Penrose shook his head. 'Put like that it seems unlikely.'

Kersey spoke for the first time. 'Did *you* know the facts about Wilder's disappearance?'

Penrose stiffened. 'Certainly not! How could I possibly have known?'

'Pillow talk?'

Penrose flushed. 'I resent that—'

Wycliffe cut in, 'Don't bother to get excited, Mr Penrose. It was you who came here to clear the air. In my opinion Badger's killer is someone who benefits directly or indirectly from his death, someone who had access to his premises when he was out on one of his evening walks, and someone who was *either* a member of the chalet party or intimate with one of them.'

Wycliffe waited for some response but none came and he went on, 'That person saw, in the discovery of Wilder's body, the chance to kill Badger and make it appear that his death was a consequence of the anonymous cards he was supposed to have sent to five of the six members of the party. He or she underlined the connection by contriving that Badger's death looked like a repetition of Wilder's. The ransacking of the attic was, of course, an over-done attempt to suggest a frantic search for the mythical evidence in Badger's possession.'

Penrose looked up; he was clearly distressed, little beads of sweat had gathered about his eyes and he dabbed them with a handkerchief. 'I came here in good faith and at some risk to my reputation if this ever comes out in court, to tell you exactly what I did last Thursday, the night Badger died. My reception is more in the nature of an attack.'

Wycliffe was unmoved. 'No-one is attacking you, Mr Penrose. You wanted to clear the air and you know now exactly where we stand. As to what you did on that Thursday night, you were seen in Bethel Street at about ten o'clock and again at around eleven.'

Penrose nodded. 'That is correct. I arrived at Miss Grey's flat at shortly after ten and left just before eleven. I reached home shortly afterwards.'

Kersey said, 'A brief visit.'

'Yes.' He broke off, and shifted uncomfortably in his chair. 'What I came back to tell you is that she wasn't there. I didn't want it to come to this but in view of what happened here this afternoon I felt that I couldn't—'

Wycliffe was leaning forward in his chair. 'You are

saying that when you arrived at the flat around ten o'clock she didn't answer your ring?'

Penrose avoided his eyes and spoke in a lowered voice. 'I am saying that she wasn't there. I have a key and I let myself in. I waited for about an hour, then I left.'

'Had she been expecting you?'

'No, I didn't think I would be able to get away, but I do sometimes drop in like that.'

'What did you think?'

'I thought that she must have had some other engagement; we don't live in each other's pockets.'

'You've spoken about this to her since?'

'Not directly – no. She likes to maintain the idea that we have our separate lives, that we don't question each other.'

'You are willing to put this into your statement?'

'Do I have a choice?'

That evening the three of them had their last meal together in the Copperhouse Arms. Wycliffe was subdued.

Kersey said, 'What's the programme tomorrow, sir?'

'We talk to the woman.' It seemed significant that GG had become 'the woman'.

'You believe the lawyer's tale?'

Wycliffe smiled. 'You sound quite literary, Doug.'

Afterwards he went for his evening walk, along Commercial Street, across the Back Bridge and through Phillack to the dunes. On his way back he stopped at the Bucket of Blood for a drink and collected a leaflet which recorded the gruesome story of the name. He felt detached and uneasy, as though for the past few days he had been living in a book or a play, and that now he was about to return to reality.

Before going to bed he telephoned Helen. 'With any luck I shall be home by the weekend.'

Wycliffe was at the Incident Room by half past eight. There was a pearly mist over the estuary but the sky was bright with the promise of a fine day. On his desk were the transcripts of yesterday's statements; somebody had been working overtime. In the main they were no more than grist for the lawyers' mill. He glanced through them, spending time on only two. Penrose had stuck to his story, and GG to hers.

He said to Kersey, 'I'm going to talk to her on her own ground. There's a risk, but I don't think bringing her in for questioning is the way forward at the moment.'

'You want me?'

'No, there must be a woman. It will have to be Lucy.'

And at a little before ten, Wycliffe and Lucy Lane drove to St Ives. They parked in front of the police station and walked along the Wharf. The sun was out, the sea sparkled and gulls planed, swooped and screeched overhead. In Bethel Street a couple of cafés and boards outside advertising morning coffee and the Modelmakers looked more decrepit than ever.

'Do we call on Fox?'

'No, he'll let us know if he finds anything. He's slow but he gets there.'

There were no customers in the health shop. It was Lucy's first visit and she looked about her with interest. One of the assistants recognized Wycliffe. 'I'll tell Miss Grey.' She seemed pleased at the prospect.

GG came out, self-possessed as ever. 'You'd better come into the office.' She wore a jade-green frock under her white overall, and an antique silver necklace with a Celtic cross. In her office the curtains were drawn back and Lucy received the full impact of that framed, dazzling prospect of sea and rocks and sky.

'Please sit down.' She was assessing Lucy with a critical eye. 'I've made my statement. I don't know what more you want.'

Wycliffe said, 'On the evening your uncle died you say you were in your flat. As you heard yesterday, Drew rang your bell on two occasions but could get no reply.' She was about to interrupt but Wycliffe pressed on. 'We know that Arnold Penrose entered your flat at ten and remained there until eleven. You were not there. Where were you?'

She performed that reflex gesture, sweeping back her hair, and revealed her face, flushed and angry. 'He told you that?'

'Where were you, Miss Grey?'

A momentary hesitation, then, challenging, 'I was across the road at my uncle's.'

'Perhaps you would prefer to be questioned formally in the presence of a solicitor.'

'I can take care of myself.'

'Even so I must tell you that you do not have to answer my questions—'

'Just get on with it.'

'What were you doing at your uncle's?'

'I wanted to talk to him about my lease. I've no doubt Arnold has told you, along with everything else, that my uncle was refusing to renew it.' Her tone was bitter.

'And did you talk to him?'

'No, I did not. He was already dead.' The statement came, bald and dramatic.

Lucy could not help being impressed. It was as though a chess player had recklessly sacrificed his queen in the hope of strategic advantage.

After a pause GG continued, 'I went in by the garden door. It was unlocked and so was the back door of the house. I knew he must be in because there was a light in the attic. I called up the stairs, but there was no answer so I went up and I found him, sprawled at the bottom of the attic stairs.'

Even Wycliffe was momentarily silenced. But when a couple passed by, not far from the window, strolling along the footwalk by the sea, Wycliffe saw that she followed them with her eyes. Despite her apparent confidence, was she already beginning to feel cut off from the rest of the world?

Lucy Lane said, 'What did you do?'

'Do? My first thought was to get help, but something made me go up the stairs to the attic and I saw the chaos there. I admit I was scared. It was obvious that this was something more than an accident. I thought of Drew, and I remembered Wilder, and how he died . . .'

In the silence they could hear the vague murmur of voices from the shop, then the ringing of the telephone startled them, all three.

GG picked up the phone, muttered something, and passed it over. 'It's for you.'

The two women watched him and listened to his cryptic responses.

'Wycliffe . . . Good! . . . In the garden . . . Have you checked it over? . . . You'll get the lab to enhance . . . Yes, I agree . . .'

Once or twice during the conversation he had looked briefly, but significantly at GG. It went through Lucy's mind to wonder whether the occasion had been rehearsed although she knew that it had not.

Wycliffe replaced the telephone. 'That was the Scenes-of-Crime officer who is searching your uncle's premises. In the long grass of the garden he has found a steel bar, a case-opener, which could have been the murder weapon. It seems that there are white hairs adhering to it.' He broke off as though a fresh idea had occurred to him. 'Did you wear gloves when you visited your uncle, Miss Grey?'

'Of course not!'

'No. There are traces of prints on the weapon. It has been wiped, but not, apparently, with complete success.'

GG said nothing. Wycliffe allowed the silence to continue until it was clear that she would not speak then, at a sign from him, Lucy Lane stood up.

'Gillian Grey, you are being detained for questioning in connection with the murder of Henry Badger on or about the evening of Thursday the fourteenth of May. You do not have to say anything . . .'

For the first time GG was disorientated, but she recovered. She looked directly and steadily at Wycliffe. 'You've got a fight on your hands.'

It was Saturday before Wycliffe got home. GG had been charged, and she had made her appearance in the Magistrates' Court to be remanded in custody.

The legal processes, more ponderous than the mills of God, were trundling into action. In six or seven months' time GG would stand in the dock and barristers would display their cleverness, strutting like peacocks under the eyes of judge and jury. It would have little to do with the health shop or the Modelmakers, still less with the chalet in the dunes which had steps leading up to a veranda.

Ruth said, 'What do you think will happen about the Wilder business?'

'The CPS will decide that charges would not be in the public interest and I agree with that.'

The Wycliffes were in their living room. Outside the light was fading, the curtains were undrawn and in the garden shapes and shadows merged in the melancholy twilight. It suited Wycliffe's mood. As often before when an investigation culminated in an arrest, he was experiencing a feeling of anti-climax, even of futility. And this was especially true of the present case.

Ruth said, 'You're very quiet, Dad. Surely you feel relieved if nothing else?'

He did not answer, but spoke to Helen. 'Do you remember old Messinger?'

'He was not the sort you easily forget.'

Wycliffe turned back to Ruth. 'He was my governor at one time and he had a notice over his desk, "No situation is so bad that a policeman can't make it worse".'

Ruth said nothing, and he went on, 'Just think: if we hadn't established the link between young Wilder and the chalet crowd Paul Drew would still be alive, and it might never have occurred to GG to murder her uncle.'

Helen said, 'You're being morbid, Charles. What is it to be – St Juliot for a walk and a quiet drink, or the film on TV?'

THE END

WYCLIFFE AND THE PEA-GREEN BOAT
by W. J. Burley

Tragedy seemed to stalk the Tremain family. Sidney Tremain had hanged himself for no obvious reason. His son, Morley, had had the misfortune to fall in love with a girl who slept around – and get convicted of killing her. And now Cedric Tremain was charged with murdering his wealthy father by blowing up his boat.

Chief Superintendent Wycliffe knew something was wrong, knew that the apparently cut and dried case wasn't what it appeared to be. Carefully he cast his bait – and waited for the real killer to surface

0 552 12804 X

WYCLIFFE AND THE LAST RITES
by W. J. Burley

Michael Jordan, vicar of Moresk, felt a tremor of disquiet even before he opened the door of his sixteenth-century church. There was the noise – a sustained chord of jarring notes from the organ – and the fact that the padlock was missing from the doors. Inside was a hideous violation of the chancel – the body of Jessica Dobell, partially unclothed and with her skull smashed in.

At first the village thought it must be the work of a Satanist cult, but when Superintendent Wycliffe arrived he didn't agree. There was an air of violent hatred prevalent in the village, and not all of it was directed towards the dead woman.

When the second murder occurred, Wycliffe knew that he had to act quickly – but even though he thought he knew who the killer was, how could he prove it?

0 552 14004 X

WYCLIFFE AND HOW TO KILL A CAT
by W. J. Burley

The girl was slim and young, with auburn hair splayed out on the pillow. Wycliffe almost believed her asleep rather than dead – until he saw her face. Although death was by strangulation, someone had smashed her face in *after* she was dead. She lay in a sordid room in a seedy hotel down by the docks, but her luggage, her clothes, and her make-up all indicated she was more expensive and classier than her surroundings.

Superintendent Wycliffe was officially on holiday, but the case fascinated him and he had to find out who she was, why she was lying naked in a shabby hotel room, why she had a thousand pounds hidden under some clothing, and above all, why she had been 'murdered' twice.

As he began to investigate, he found there was too much of everything about the case – too many suspects, too many motives, and too many lies.

0 552 14117 8

WYCLIFFE AND THE GUILT EDGED ALIBI
by W. J. Burley

Caroline Bryce came from the top of the social register in the tranquil town of Treen. So it was quite a scandal when her body was dragged from the bottom of the river. Who would want to kill the beautiful Mrs Bryce? Was it a lover's quarrel? A family feud? A long-smouldering resentment that exploded in a moment of madness?

Superintendent Wycliffe has to unravel the intricate cross currents of love and hate to find a psychotic killer who feels no guilt . . . and will not hesitate to strike again.

'Tense and eventful family whodunit in Cornish port'
Observer

0 552 14115 1

WYCLIFFE AND THE WINSOR BLUE
by W. J. Burley

When Edwin Garland died of a heart attack, no-one outside the expectant circle of his relatives was concerned. But when, on the evening of his funeral, his son was shot dead, the situation changed dramatically and Superintendent Wycliffe was called in to investigate the seemingly motiveless murder.

The disappearance of another relative and a further death occur before Wycliffe manages to unravel a story that had begun several years before, with the death of a famous Cornish artist. Only then is he able to identify the killer.

0 552 13436 8

WYCLIFFE IN PAUL'S COURT
by W. J. Burley

Paul's Court was an oasis of peace set in the heart of the city – until the night when two of its inhabitants met violent deaths. Old Willy Goppel, a German emigré, was found hanging from a beam in his home, and fifteen-year-old Yvette Cole was strangled and her body thrown over the churchyard hedge.

It looked, at first, as though it might be a simple case – Willy Goppel had murdered the girl, then killed himself. But as Chief Superintendent Wycliffe began to question the residents of Paul's Court, a sinister and complex network of antagonism was uncovered, leading to a double crime of unexpected malevolence.

0 552 13433 3

A SELECTED LIST OF CRIME NOVELS
AVAILABLE FROM CORGI BOOKS

THE PRICES SHOWN BELOW WERE CORRECT AT THE TIME OF GOING
TO PRESS. HOWEVER TRANSWORLD PUBLISHERS RESERVE THE RIGHT
TO SHOW NEW RETAIL PRICES ON COVERS WHICH MAY DIFFER FROM
THOSE PREVIOUSLY ADVERTISED IN THE TEXT OR ELSEWHERE.

All Corgi/Bantam Books are available at your bookshop or newsagent, or can be
ordered from the following address:
Transworld Publishers Ltd, Cash Sales Department,
P.O. Box 11, Falmouth, Cornwall TR10 9EN

Please send a cheque or postal order (no currency) and allow £1.00 for postage
and packing for the first book plus 30p for each subsequent book ordered to a
maximum charge of £3.00 if ordering seven or more books.

Overseas customers, including Eire, please allow £2.00 for postage and packing
for the first book, £1.00 for the second book, and an additional 50p for each
subsequent title ordered.

NAME (Block Letters)...

ADDRESS ....

....